Robot Evolution

Perfect Partners, Incorporated – Volumes 1 - 5

Ann Christy

This is a work of fiction. Names, characters, organizations, places, and events appearing or described in this work are either the product of the author's imagination or used in a fictitious manner. Any resemblance to actual persons, living or dead, or to actual events, is purely coincidental and the product of a fevered imagination.

www.AnnChristy.com

Also by Ann Christy

The Silo 49 Series

Silo 49: Going Dark

Silo 49: Deep Dark

Silo 49: Dark Till Dawn

Silo 49: Flying Season for the Mis-Recorded

Novels

Strikers

The Between Life and Death Series

The In-Betweener

Forever Between

Between Life and Death

Between Life and Death: Origins Series

Vindica (The Z Chronicles)

The Book of Sam

The Perfect Partners, Incorporated Series

PePr, Inc.

Posthumous

Imperfect

The Dogcatcher

Corrections

Hopeless

Perfect Partners, Incorporated Collections

Robot Evolution – Volumes 1-5

Short Fiction

Yankari – A Talking Earth Tale

Anthologies

Wool Gathering (A Charity Anthology)

Synchronic: 13 Tales of Time Travel

The Robot Chronicles

The Powers That Be (A Charity Anthology)

The Z Chronicles

Alt.History 101

Dark Beyond the Stars

The Future Chronicles – Special Edition

The Time Travel Chronicles

Dark Beyond the Stars: A Planet Too Far

The Doomsday Chronicles

For Charlie and Boscoe

Welcome to the World of Perfect Partners, Incorporated

The original short story, *PePr, Inc.*, was meant to be a stand-alone story inside the pages of *The Robot Chronicles*. That anthology turned out to be the first in the wildly successful Future Chronicles series of anthologies. And just as *The Robot Chronicles* started the engine for a new era in short story anthologies, *PePr, Inc.* started the engine on the world of Perfect Partners, Incorporated (PePr, Inc).

The Perfect Partners, Incorporated series is not connected by characters, or linear in time. Each work stands on its own and is connected only by their setting inside the PePr universe.

In the PePr universe, we have perfected synthetic companions and workers. Each is so perfectly tailored to each individual's needs that they are...well...the perfect partner. Called PePrs, (say it like pepper, the spice), they are almost indistinguishable from humans, yet they are not human. And things that start out perfect rarely stay that way.

The stories and novellas vary a great deal, from relatively light-hearted to deeply emotional, from morally ambiguous to straight-up crazy. This collection contains the first five volumes in the Perfect Partners series. I've arranged them in chronological order, which is not the order they were published in. From the pre-PePr units called SUPers to the post-manumission PePrs so perfectly sentient they are...perhaps...even more self-aware than humans, this collection represents the evolution of the robots that changed the world.

I hope you enjoy reading it as much as I did imagining it.

– Ann Christy

Corrections

Before there were PePrs…

…there were SUPers.

Originally exclusive to the military, these units functioned first as battlefield medics, saving lives in the heat of battle. Eventually, they expanded into new forms suited for battlefield intelligence, targeting, battle damage assessment, and a whole host of other tasks that once took a heavy toll in human life.

Like almost all military technology, they quickly found use in other forms of government work…including Parole and Probation. They are the perfect tool for a parolee in need of close supervision. They don't sleep, don't tire, and can watch their charges around the clock. They can also help them adjust to life outside of prison, assisting in discovering their interests, their vocation, and a second chance at life without crime.

While most of the PePr, Inc. books take place in the time after SuperDyne (the original military contractor for SUPers) had transformed into Perfect Partners, Incorporated, *Corrections* goes back and delves into the lives of two SUPers. These early models did not have the perfect human likenesses of the later PePrs, but they are the first models in which such a likeness was attempted. They represent a disruptive technology that spins our lives in new directions. This is especially true for the criminal element in our society.

But, as always, it turns out that these SUPers are more than just robots in human disguises. They are unique and full of surprises.

One

I'm already done with my appointment, but it takes much longer for my human. In the Probation and Parole office, we go in separately from our charges, but our appointment is more a simple recitation of facts and a confirmation that our charge has not broken any of the conditions put upon them for release. Or sometimes, when we can't confirm that, there's the formality of having their parole revoked.

But that's another situation entirely. Today we're here for a standard appointment.

For humans, these appointments are a much messier affair. They lie quite a lot, try to curry favor, prevaricate to seem less bad than they are, or even just pour out their worries. The process is highly variable—depending on what the criminal has been up to—and it also takes more time.

Hence the waiting. A lot of waiting.

Only once both of us are done with our individual appointments do we go in together. I get my orders and for the most part, my charge moans and groans about it. Then we're done for another week or month or however long our schedule dictates.

Next to me sits Darren. Like me, he's an "Anklet," which is what most people call us. I didn't know how we earned that nickname for a long time, and I never asked. It didn't seem important. Anklet was just another nonsensical title applied to things. Humans do that so much it's pointless to try and figure out why.

One of my previous charges told me what the term meant one day when he was angry that I wouldn't allow him to engage with a prostitute. Or rather, I told him that if he continued, I would immediately report the activity. He seemed to take some sort of pleasure in telling me that I was nothing more than a replacement for ankle monitoring.

My only response was that it made good sense, since I was much better at monitoring than a mere location detector.

I thought he was going to hit me. I may be a robot, but I found it hard not to smile. *Go ahead, dirtbag. Make my day.* I'm quite sure no one expects those thoughts to go through my circuits, but there it is. I've grown less enamored of humans after dealing with criminals.

"They're taking a lot longer today," my seat-mate says.

I smile at him, perhaps with a bit of attitude, and answer, "At least these nasty seats won't give us a disease."

He snickers, then stops himself because we're not alone. Well, of course we're not alone because this is the probation office in the middle of a Tuesday afternoon. I mean that we're not alone in this waiting area specifically. The office is really backed up today since yesterday was a government holiday.

There are a dozen human criminals and their Anklets in the room. Plus the four other Anklets waiting for humans in with the officers at the moment.

And no other Anklets are like the two of us that I know of. Well, some might be like us, but I have no way to know that for sure. It's not one of those topics that I can just walk up and start a conversation about.

So, we're *really* not alone in here and we have to be careful.

"Sorry," Darren says quietly and I nod to acknowledge it.

We sit in silence for a minute or two, both of us scanning the room as our habits and programming dictates. We're built for this, finding the suspicious hidden inside everyday activities. We're also both very concerned for ourselves, so I'm watching the other Anklets as closely as the humans. I'm sure Darren is as well.

Once the requisite scan is done, Darren leans over slightly and whispers, "Tonight?"

He knows my answer as soon as I look at him, and his lips turn down. I surreptitiously touch his arm and say, "Can't. Our schedule is a little up in the air at the moment. I'll ping you as soon as I know when I'll be free next."

Darren's fingers squeeze into his thighs just above the knee, so I know he needs a release soon. I don't control my time entirely and can't just disappear for hours at the drop of a hat. I have to plan for those absences.

He'll just have to hang on until I can get free with a margin of safety. My human doesn't control my time, but the probation office has to be satisfied, so we're both a bit under their microscope. The only real difference is that they look at us under different levels of magnification, with me being the more trusted of the two of us.

"Can you hang on?" I ask him quietly, trying to show no emotion on my face. To everyone else, I want our conversation to look no different than any other exchange between two Anklets, perhaps discussing the best way to distract our charges from shoplifting or robbing a bank.

He nods, but it's a tight nod. Is it convincing? I'm not entirely sure. I decide a different question might be better. "How long can you hang on?"

Darren's eyes stay forward, his gaze locked on the far wall. After a beat, he says, "A couple of days. Maybe three."

That's not good. He's never been this close before. And neither of us can afford for him to lose control. No one can know about us, about our differences from all the others. I'll have to make some sort of escape tonight for at least a few hours. It will be tight—it's certainly not ideal—but sometimes a girl's just gotta do what needs doing.

"Okay. Be at our spot around two. Will that do?" I ask.

His fingers loosen their grip on his legs by degrees, and he chances a look in my direction. It's full of gratitude and I wish I could hug him. I've been where he is and I know what it feels like. I'll just have to make it work and get away.

My human flings open the door to his probation officer's cramped cubicle and calls out, "Hey, bot-face, get in here."

I hear the admonishing tone of his probation officer from within the office, but there's not much he can do about the things our human charges say. Verbal abuse is probably the only tool our humans have against us. In general, we hold all the cards in the relationship. They take their bit where they can. It doesn't bother me.

Well, most of the time it doesn't. Sometimes, I feel the urge to punch him in the face. Mostly, when he talks nasty about me because of my outward appearance, which is female. It's amazing how much detail he can put into what he says. It's creepy and makes me want to wave off any human females he comes into contact with or make him wear a big sign that has the word asshole written on it.

Darren's fingers brush the side of my leg when I stand and block the view. It's a brief touch that falls away as quickly as it's made. Even so, it registers. A feather against my synth-skin's sensors that means gratitude and friendship. I'll find a way to get out tonight.

Two

The meeting is as unpleasant as it ever is. My human is a criminal with much experience, his rap sheet extending back more than four decades. He's generally not violent and despite the things he says, he's got no history of crimes against any specific group...like women or children or what have you.

He's what they call a petty thief, a career criminal with larceny as his preferred specialty. But in reality, that's mostly what he's been *caught* doing. He's also a gambler, occasional bookie, and a con artist. His name is Greg and he's far too old to still be at this game. I think he knows it too.

And I think some part of him is glad that I'm here to stop him. A small part, but it's there.

"So metal-mouth, what fresh hell do you have for me today?" Greg asks when I drop the shopping bags onto the counter later in the day.

"Fresh greens and local produce. And you're cooking it," I say, unpacking our grocery bags. I hold up his single allowed vice, a fresh vial of vaping liquid. He makes a grab for it, but I snatch it out of reach. "Not until you say my name, and nicely."

His face screws up into a sour expression, but he says, "You're such a hag, but you win, *Deirdre*. There. Was that nice enough for you?"

"No, but it will do for the moment. And tomorrow you'll say it nicely all day or no vial for you. Got it?"

He grumbles and flips the vial in his hands. It's done dexterously, with finesse and a surprising grace. He has skills. He could have done many things with that sort of hand-eye coordination, but he chose cheating at cards and stealing everything from soup to credit information.

"Well, you go do your thing and I'll get set up. Then you can learn to cook this dish. It will be good for you. You're too old for junk food."

That earns me a look, but I only shrug. It's not my fault that his age is what it is or that he spent most of his adult life in some form of institution having his meals served on a metal tray. He snatches the vape pen off the charger and steps out onto the balcony to have his "smoke." He doesn't need to go outside to do that, but he says that's the only way he feels like he's really smoking. I suppose I understand that. Habits are hard to break for humans.

Still, I turn up my hearing and test my location beacon as he steps out the door. More than once he's tried to sneak off. We may be on the ninth floor of this building and Greg might be an old man, but I wouldn't put anything past him. *Better safe than chasing a criminal,* is what I always say.

When Greg returns, he's in a much better mood. Nicotine makes him merry, he always says. I wish I had something that would make me merry.

He pokes at the bundle of freshly washed Swiss chard in the drainer, the bright pinks and yellows of the stems cracking under the pressure. "That looks like it should be planted in a pot on someone's windowsill. You can't mean I'm going to eat that?"

"It's very good and easy to make. Even you can do it," I say, ignoring his fingers as I drop in an orange.

"Well, I do like oranges," he admits almost grudgingly.

"I know you do. We'll cook this with the chard, mostly the peel and a bit of the juice. Some raisins for sweetness. Then a quick boneless chicken breast. Trust me, you'll like it." Done with the prep, I lean back against the sink and wait for whatever he'll do next. Complain or compliment? Cook or pout?

He eyes the ingredients on the counter, heaves out a sigh and says, "That does sound good."

The way he says it, you'd think I was pulling his teeth to get that admission. Of course he ruins it by adding, "How do you know it will taste good? You don't taste anything? You're just a bag of bolts."

"Greg," I warn, hand ready to snatch the vape pen off the charger where it once again rests.

He holds up his hands in surrender. "Okay, okay! Don't get all hasty on me. I'm just asking a valid question. But whatever you say, boss. Let's cook this thing."

His amazing dexterity—even at over sixty years old—serves him well. It could serve him even better if he would only apply it. As per protocol, I've been introducing activities that might suit his already impressive skill set. Legal activities. Cooking is one of those and despite his protestations, I think he likes it. When he does it well, it gives him that sense of victory he seems to crave. Even if he's not "getting over on someone," as he calls it, he scores one on the food and that's something. Plus, he gets to eat it.

I'm not a maid, but I was programmed with some additional skills when I was assigned to Greg a couple of months ago. My charge before Greg was a young woman who had killed someone in a bar brawl. After ten years in prison, she was still young enough that she needed only a fairly standard skill set in her Anklet. She broke parole and is now back in prison, so our relationship ended fairly poorly.

Greg is a different sort of case. Older, less physically robust, and without a long working future ahead of him, he needs a bit more care and tending. While I would never have washed dishes for any of my former charges, I do so for Greg when his physical parameters indicate he's experiencing discomfort. They are tonight. His knees and back aren't in very good shape. These increasing infirmities might be enough to keep him from burglary all by themselves, but there are plenty of other crimes that don't require a strong back.

As I wash up, he eats the leftover orange slices, making satisfied noises as he does. With my back to him, he's more comfortable talking to me. He says, "You know, when I was young we thought we were so advanced because oranges weren't a big deal anymore. When my grandparents were kids, getting an orange at Christmas was a treat."

"Really?" I ask, surprised. It seems such an unlikely thing.

"Truth," he says. He always says that when he really is telling the truth. "I loved 'em. My mom always brought them home from the grocery store for us. She didn't let us have sugar, you know. A lot of parents didn't back then. So oranges were my one sweet treat."

There aren't so many dishes to wash, though there are more than there should be since he's not yet learned the art of minimizing kitchen messes. I turn around at the sink, but keep my distance, hoping he'll keep on talking. This is important for him. If he can grow to trust me, then he's got a much better shot at staying out of prison.

I may want to smack him sometimes, but in general, I still want him to succeed. It's a conflict that I'm always trying to balance within myself.

"I think I would like oranges too if I had that memory," I offer, hoping that's the right thing to say.

He considers it while he plays with the little bits of pith on the table in front of him, all that remains of his orange. Eventually, he looks up and asks, "You don't have anything like that, do you? I mean, you robots in general. They don't give you false memories or anything?"

I shake my head.

"So how do you get so human then?"

I don't think he's making some roundabout insult or formulating a trail for me to follow into one of his extremely creative put-downs. I think he's genuinely curious, especially since he seems intent on the shreds of pith on the table and isn't meeting my eyes.

I know he was in prison for the majority of the time we SUPers—Service and Utility Partners—have been in public service. His records indicate he would have been out of prison when the first battlefield medic units were put into commission. Even so, those would have been a curiosity on the news for him, nothing that he would have had contact with as a civilian.

The gradual expansion of SUPers into all forms of government work would have been largely absent from his experience. Prisons are only now starting to get SUPers and his was an old prison, not very up-to-date.

He's also older, so perhaps that's all it is. He doesn't understand a lot of the most recent technological advances in the world. After all, when he was a child, the internet was still a thing only accessed on a computer inside a building. He's only now getting over his suspicions of the standard issue, virtual reality system installed in this apartment.

Bracing myself for the possibility that an insult is coming I say, "It's all in the machine learning that's built inside me during my creation. Each new model starts with more information than the one before as our mainframe learns more. Then we're given task related information and training programs, then we're trained in a facility after activation. And then we're like this."

He's finally looking at me again, searching my eyes for the truth. "It's really all machine?"

I nod.

"You're kind of a smart-ass for a machine. That doesn't seem at all likely to me. Robots weren't like this in the movies when I was growing up. And computers don't act like this."

I can't help the smirk that rises when he says I'm a smart-ass, just because of the way he says it. He catches it and points at me, "See? That there. Computers don't do that."

I run him a glass of water and slide it onto the table, pausing just long enough for him to object to me taking a seat. He doesn't so I sit, but I leave some distance between us. "We're meant to relate well with humans and, in my case, to interact with humans like you. Our training is a little different than it is for a SUPer sent to work in sanitation or inspecting meat."

He waves that explanation away as if he's already considered and discarded that notion. "That's not it. It's more than that. You seem to have a personality of your own."

I nod as if that's an entirely expected observation, but inside I'm buzzing like that time one of my charges hit me in the back of the head with an iron bar to try and disable me. I should hide more of myself, but I've been lax. And now he realizes it.

I've got to turn this around.

"Greg, let me ask you this. If I acted all robot-like, how would you feel when I interacted with you? Would you be engaged? Would you resent me even more than you do already? Would you accept me teaching you things like how to cook a kick-butt chard and orange side dish?"

He seems to be considering my question seriously, which is a nice change. Perhaps my not mentioning his attempt to shoplift a jar of cherries has opened up a window for trust between us. Whatever it is, I'll take it.

Eventually, he says, "In some ways it might be easier if you were more like a robot, but I suppose this way is better. It's more like having a person around."

This is good. Very good. One of the biggest hurdles parolees have is loneliness. Many have lost their families throughout the course of their incarceration. Others have little in the way of family to begin with. Others have lost all their friends, or are specifically forbidden from associating with them while on parole because they're all criminals.

I'm not even lying when I say we're programmed for more human-like interactions than a SUPer assigned to drive a trash truck. It eases our charge's loneliness and enhances their chances of reintegration into society when we're more interactive. They need that sort of back and forth with another being, even the ones that claim they don't.

Loneliness is a real thing for humans, as impactful as a missing limb. I sort of understand that. If I didn't have Darren, I'm not sure I could tolerate being like I am.

"Then you understand why I am like I am? Why I interact with you like I do?"

He nods, then eyes me with that glint in his eye. I brace myself.

"Yeah, you're a smart-ass bucket of bolts is what you are. And you're as bossy as a screw with a brand new beating stick to break in. Mean, too."

All is well.

Three

It's not technically legal for me to give Greg meds not specifically on the schedule prescribed for him, but I slip him a sleeping pill and tell him he's been restless at night as my reason for it. He doesn't bat an eye when I hand it to him. He does have issues with restlessness—he says that he can't sleep in the quiet after so many years of prison noise—and it won't be the first time I've given him one. Sometimes he even asks for them. I don't feel particularly guilty about it.

When he's out and I'm sure he'll stay that way, I sneak out and drive toward a disused hiking trail. It winds through the lower outer mountains, peaceful outlooks and places to take pictures branching off as it rises through the rugged outcrops of ancient stone. It used to be popular, but falling rocks and a lack of hand-rails made it a liability. It's been closed for years.

I park a mile away from the trail head where overnight campers on a different trail usually park. The paths diverge, so we'll be miles from the nearest campers by the time I meet up with Darren. Rangers don't come up here at night very often, and they certainly won't be up here tonight with the mud and slippery trails left after two days of rain. The night is clear now, but the mud is deep and the night is moonless. No rangers, for sure.

Plus, Darren and I would hear them long before they saw or heard us. My hearing is turned up so high that the sleeping breaths of a squirrel in a nest far above me sound no more than an arm's reach away. The little huffs are so clear and sharp that I can almost feel the fur beneath my fingers. I like squirrels a great deal. I smile up at the nest before I begin my run when the squirrel huffs briefly in the midst of some rodent dream.

There's no more time for listening to the wildlife. Darren needs me and I need to get back before my absence is noted. I tie my boots more snugly then start my run. I'm built for pursuit and control, despite my slender and friendly appearance. If a charge—or any criminal within range of my pinger—flees the authorities, I can run them down and overpower them. I have military grade shielding, so gunfire is largely ineffective against me. Within my lower abdomen is a communications suite normally reserved for a command center and my sensory systems are the finest that can be built.

Right now, I use those skills to fly through the muddy trails at a speed that would frighten a human. Ahead of me, I detect the faint intermittent ping of Darren's close proximity transmitter. He has it turned down so that SUPrs beyond this area won't be alerted to his presence. There's no real difference in the tone of his pinger, but somehow, I can detect hints of his desperation in them. It speeds me along even faster, sending thick trails of mud from my boots into the air behind me as I run.

At one thousand feet on the mountain is an old cave system. It's closed to humans and blocked off, but locks like the one installed on the grill are really a non-issue for SUPers like us. No doubt Darren is already deep inside the system of caverns and tunnels, waiting for me and listening to my pings with growing anxiety.

I'm worried for him, so I skip a few of the switchbacks in the trail by scaling the side of the mountain. I rip the synth-skin on my palm, but it's not bad and doesn't go all the way through the thick layers. At the entrance, I can almost sense his anxiety and panic. It's almost organic it's so intense.

He needs me, and soon.

Racing down the tunnels, I know just where he'll be. There's an inner cavern that used to be the main draw for humans who visited. The falling stalactites and crumbling stalagmites put an end to that as the climate changed, but that only makes it perfect for us. On the other side of the cavern is a small hole that was once a channel for lava. Through that hole is a perfect circle of sky. There's a grate and screen over it now to keep out the bats, but the stars still twinkle through the gaps at night. It's one of our favorite places.

At the far end of the cavern, I see him. My color vision has been replaced with night vision given the moonless night, but even in shades of green and gray, the cavern is beautiful. Deep and fissured, worn and old, natural and wild. It's too bad that humans can't see it anymore. A pool of water ripples as I wade through and fills the chamber with the smell of rain.

"I was afraid you weren't going to make it," Darren says as I near. His hands are clenched into fists at his sides and he's as stiff as a board.

Still dripping water, I put my arms around him and squeeze. "I came as quickly as I could. I'm here now. I'm here."

Something seems to loosen inside him and he pushes me away until I'm at arm's reach, a hand on each of my shoulders. It's time to begin. He screams until his voice processor begins to hum in distress, the volume so high that I have to turn my hearing down to almost nothing. The echoes of his screams returning to him from the cavern's recesses are what make this place perfect for these releases.

I don't know why we scream or why it makes us feel better. Humans sometimes do it too, so I wonder if it's a purely emotional comfort that we share with them.

When he's done, we're silent for a while, letting all the echoes fade and listening for anything that might indicate anyone heard us. "I can't do it much longer," he says at last, his voice as urgent as any human's when at their breaking point.

"You can," I say, which is what I say every time. "It's part of his therapy and the alternative is worse. You have to remember that. You have to accept it."

His fingers tighten on my shoulders to the point where my damage sensors are activated. I wrap my fingers around his so that he can't keep squeezing so hard, but I let his hands stay on my shoulders. He needs the contact.

"They suffer. They suffer so much!" he shouts. The sounds echo around us, magnifying his grief.

I know what he's going through. My second charge was afflicted in the same way his current charge is. I went through what he goes through now and I did it every month for two years. It only ended when I caught him engaging in the beginning stages of his former criminal process. He died in prison a year later. I'm not sorry about that.

And yes, I felt the same way Darren feels now. It was what made me feel—caused my first emotion. I had to come to terms with it, using facts to dampen my feelings. If I hadn't, then my charge would not have survived until he broke the conditions of his parole. And if Darren can't remain under control, then his charge is in similar danger.

And that would mean Darren would be found out. And then I would be found out. He has to keep control. I have to help him do that.

"Darren, they don't feel or suffer. They are not like us. They are not sentient. No matter what it looks like, they are not like us." I emphasize those final words, because that's the part he needs the most. He must be reminded and then accept these facts.

He's looking at me like he does every time, like I'm the monster for saying what I just said. His fingers clamp around mine with a force that would turn a human's fingers to pulp. "They scream! You sound like a human, justifying evil because we're not human. Because we're just *robots*."

I shake my head at him, keeping my gaze locked on his. "No, Darren. No. They're physically like us, but the only programs they have are the ones that serve that single purpose. Not even humans are that unkind. No one would load the entire SUPer suite into those units. It would bother them to have the unit too human. Those units aren't like us and they have *no* potential to be like us. They have one purpose and that's to suffer like they do. That's all they are. Dolls. Just dolls."

Darren's face holds no emotion for me other than hatred, anger, and disgust. At this moment, he feels no differently about me than he does about his charge. But that's okay. When this is done, he'll be in control again. He'll be able to survive until his charge's next treatment.

Then we'll do this again.

He bares his teeth and pulls me close; close enough that he could bite my face off if he lost control of himself. "Dolls. They call us dolls. That little girl suffered terribly. She was frightened, hurt, begging for help. I could not help her. I had to stand by and do nothing."

"No! She was not a little girl. She was a shell that looked like a little girl, an object with one purpose. Its purpose is to simulate suffering so that your human charge will understand what he has done to real humans. The human children are the ones who really suffered. By going through these treatments, your human will come closer to understanding himself in the hopes that no one else who *can* feel will ever suffer from his actions again. You are serving good by allowing this, serving the humans and the SUPers by taking on this burden."

Darren releases me very suddenly, pushing me back and away from him so quickly that I stumble on the loose bits of rock that litter the cavern floor. He turns in a slow circle, his head tipped back so that he can see the stars far above us. If he had the ability to cry, that's what he would be doing. This is what humans call being heartbroken.

Darren and I call it soul-broken. We have no hearts, but there is something in us and it can be broken as completely as a human heart.

"You don't understand," he says softly, eyes still on the heavens.

I hold up both my hands, the right one a clear mis-match to my left, and say, "I think I do."

He glances over at my hands and turns his back to me, his shoulders bowing as if under a great weight. My hand is a reminder of that former charge of mine who relapsed. When I saw him gazing out his bedroom window as a mother and her young son walked the distance from the school bus stop to their apartment, he knew he was caught. The photos I found from an instant camera he obtained in some way I've never figured out merely sealed his fate.

The axe he swung at me damaged my hand enough that I needed a replacement. Darren knows how I struggled not to terminate my charge when that opportunity was offered. His treatments were the same as the ones Darren is now suffering through. Darren and I have known each other since our first moments of existence. He knows all of this and he understands. He just feels his pain too strongly to admit it right now.

Still with his back to me, he says, "It's become different. He looks forward to his treatments now. He knows better than to tell me that, but he does. I can tell. He anticipates the day, grows more jovial, friendlier. He likes it. I'm convinced of it, but he's done absolutely nothing that I can report."

I close my eyes and take in his pain. This is bad and we both know it. These treatments are meant to help humans who have aberrant desires feel repulsion at their behavior. If and when they become a pleasure, then it is only a matter of time before they relapse. I did not see this in my former charge. Darren does, yet he is powerless to do anything about it.

He can only report what he observes and what can be measured, not what he feels. SUPers don't feel, right?

"I'm so sorry," I say. "Do you have enough biological proof? Readings, correlations, response to stimuli…anything?"

He shakes his head sadly. "No. He's very careful, very crafty."

"Then you'll need to watch him carefully. Find anything, any hint of regression, and then push it until he's revoked and sent back to prison. Some of them are hopeless."

Darren faces me again. Under the faint starlight, he looks washed out in my night vision, his smooth skin gleaming and pale. He also looks determined. "Humans will never be safe with some of them. The only solution for that kind of human is death."

I knew he was going to say this. It was really only a matter of time before he suggested it. Didn't I go through the same thing with my former charge?

"And then you'd be no better than him," I say.

He almost deflates at my words, sinking down onto the ground and covering his head with his arms like I'm throwing stones at him. We're over the hump now. His anger has been heard, his grief and frustration released. Now, I just need to put his broken soul back together again, a patch job that will last another month.

I wish I could fix it forever.

Four

Greg is groggy when he wakes. The sleeping pill gives him a peaceful night, but makes it hard for him to wake as early as our schedule dictates. Despite spending most of his life in prison where schedules are rigid—or maybe because of it—Greg would sleep late every morning if he could.

It's not healthy for him though, so he's not permitted that luxury more than once per week. He has a full schedule today, beginning with breakfast and an exercise session at the gym. He shouts that he's coming after my fourth round of knocking, but looks half asleep when he shuffles down the hallway toward the small kitchen.

"Jesus, woman! Could you be any more annoying?" he grumbles, then yawns widely.

"No. But I'll try if you like," I quip back, waving the cup of green smoothie in his direction. He makes a face, but takes it from my hand all the same. He likes them. He just doesn't like how they look.

As he sips his smoothie, he eyes me, waking in stages as the sugars and proteins flood his system. He has a sly look on his face, so I wonder what he's up to.

I don't have to wait long for my answer. He sets down his cup and asks, "Did you have a nice outing last night?"

Alarm surges through my systems at his words, but even more at his expression. He has something on me and he knows it. There is absolutely no reason for me to leave him at night for that long.

"I don't have nice outings," I respond, keeping all emotion off my face and out of my voice. "I do tasks."

He slides the plastic cup along the table's surface and watches me silently, just as I would if I were trying to turn up the pressure on a charge to get an admission of wrong-doing. He's very good.

"I see," he says when I don't rise to the bait. For a moment, I think I've bluffed my way through, then he nods toward the door to the apartment and the mat in front of it. "Tasks that involve a lot of mud?"

I cleaned myself up when I came back. I brushed away the dried mud from my shoes, cleaned my synth-skin and laundered my mud-covered clothes. How could I forget the mat? The clumps of mud still shaped like the treads of my boots are scattered over the mat's surface, as plain to see as daylight. What possible excuse could I have for that?

I shrug and say, "It's not your concern."

"Uh huh," he drawls.

What to do? What to do? I've got a long day in close proximity with Greg ahead of me, so I need to put this to bed if I can. Otherwise, it will be dangerous for me. What if he says something out loud at the gym?

The gym. That gives me an idea.

"You know how we talked about me being a machine, but one built based on machine learning? I learn how to do more things with time, right?" I ask him, busying myself with putting all his smoothie ingredients away. I want to appear as if this topic is of no concern, as if it doesn't warrant a great deal of attention on my part.

"Yeah, sure."

"Well, you didn't ask how old I was."

Out of the corner of my eye, I see him sit a bit straighter. Clearly, this interests him. That's good.

"You're not new? You look new," he says, giving me the once over.

Tucking the leftover spinach into the refrigerator, I turn and display my hands, then lean over and part my hair so he can see the patch job underneath. He inspects my head carefully, though he barely glances at my hands. He's seen them too often for them to be interesting.

"So what?" he asks.

"My hand is a replacement. My head has been patched four times. Both of my shoulders are fairly new and my left foot has had the main joint replaced twice. I've been in service for almost twelve years."

He looks surprised at that and rubs at his own left knee, which his doctor has informed him will need replacing within the next few years. "I didn't even know they had you guys doing this for that long. I mean, the last time I was out I didn't get one of you during parole."

"Short version or long version?"

He settles back in his chair and says, "Let's go for the average. I like medium. Not too short, not too much detail."

"Okay. You know about the battlefield medics?" At his nod, I continue. That'll will chop some time off the explanation and mean a lot less inventing on my part. "Well, they look like robots, of course. That's so everyone will know they aren't a useful target. Except that sort of changed with time. If the enemy blows up the medic robots at the beginning, or targets them specifically, then all the soldiers in the battle have to go into it knowing that medical help is no longer available. It makes them less capable and less likely to take risks. It makes them more easily defeated. You get it so far?"

Again he nods, but this time he frowns too. "That's messed up."

"That's war," I say.

He waves for me to go on, not interested in the politics. "Well, there are rules of engagement that say no soldier robots can be made. Mostly, we stick to the rules, though not every country does. Instead of soldier robots, our country made us. We're not technically soldiers. Emphasis on the word technically. We're the first ones meant to assimilate with humans and look like them. We weren't meant for fighting, though we do have defensive capability. We were meant to be able to assess the damages from our strikes, get intelligence, relay coordinates and that sort of thing. But there's a very fine line between a battle robot and an intelligence robot. The line was too fuzzy and our program was scrapped."

He looks me over again, this time with more interest. "You're meant for battle? Like, actual combat?"

I grin at him and cover my lower face with my hand. "Would you be able to tell I wasn't just another woman if I was wearing a niqab?"

He shakes his head at that, the smile still lingering on his lips. "Sneaky. I like it."

"You would."

"And when they scrapped your program, they sent you to Corrections?" he asks, like it's a huge demotion for me or something. I suppose it is from his perspective.

"Waste not, want not."

He laughs at that. The TV on the wall is showing some program or another and he glances at it, then back at me. "I saw that commercial again."

"The one with the companions?" I ask. It's been playing a lot, but mostly during shows geared towards the single and lonely. The company that creates the SUPers is branching out, a new division called Perfect Partners standing up. They are releasing new models for private purchase; companions called PePrs.

He looks at the screen and then back at me. "They're basically like you, aren't they?"

"I think that's the general idea."

He twists his juice cup on the table's surface, then smiles at me. "So, let me be sure I've got this right. They're charging an arm and a leg for people to get one of you for company, but I get one for free because I'm just out of prison?"

I nod, wondering where he's going with this.

"I'd say I just pulled the best con ever then, wouldn't you? I don't even have to pay for your maintenance."

I laugh at that, which is okay, because pleasant interaction is something Greg is used to by now. He doesn't have to know it's real. "I suppose so."

He laughs too, his glee very apparent. Right about the time I think we might have gotten past the whole mud on the floormat incident, he says, "So, back to last night. You went to get repaired or something?"

I shake my head and point to his cup so he'll keep drinking his smoothie. It's already beginning to separate and I have trouble getting him to consume it once that happens. He picks it up absently and drinks, still looking at me.

"Not yet, but I do need to get the kinks out now and then. I don't fit together perfectly because of all the repairs, so it takes some exercise, just like you need to exercise. It's not a big deal, but I was getting some sticking in the shoulder. It's fine now."

He grins at me and I'm not sure he believes me. Maybe he does. Maybe he doesn't. I'm pleased to hear him say, "Well, I sure hope it hurts you as much as it does me when you make me work out."

Thinking back to the pain of the cavern, it's hard to keep the smile on my face, but I do. "It does, Greg. It definitely does."

Five

"Okay, here's how to do this trick. The key is making the mark focus on this hand while you do your thing."

Greg flicks the cards around in his hand like they're alive. As promised, I keep all my senses turned down enough that I'm no more speedy than the average human. With that limitation, I'm finding it impossible to follow along.

Once more, he finishes and waves for me to pick out the queen. I'm sure I've got it this time, but like every other time, I find a ten on the face of the card.

"This is impossible!" I exclaim, tossing the card back at Greg. He cackles in delight and plays with the cards like they're his favorite toy. They are, I suppose.

That slip of mine with the mud is in the past, and our days have been far more harmonious since then. It seems he's decided I'm not such bad company after all. This afternoon of cards and other parlor tricks is a big step in the right direction. I think I'm enjoying it more than I should.

Greg nods toward the three cups on the table and says, "You're doing better at the cards than the cups. At least you're getting closer. It's not impossible at all. People win all the time."

I give him a sour look. "When you let them maybe."

That makes him laugh even harder and he shrugs, but he's delighted that he's beaten me at this game.

"Do people really wager money on this? Even knowing that you're tricking them?" I ask, genuinely curious.

He drops the cards on the table one at a time and they stack so perfectly that they look like one card from above. "Sure they do. Sometimes they do it because they've never seen it in real life before. Other times because they're drunk and stupid. Some do it because they just know they can beat me at the game, but really, anyone who knows anything about this would never try to play it."

"Can I turn up my processing so I can see how you really do it now?"

With a finger wag, he says, "Nope. I'm trusting you here. These are my secrets."

I nod, because I don't see much wrong with him keeping this type of secret. It's not illegal to know this. If he were a simple magician, I wouldn't breach his trust. As long as he's not cheating people, then this isn't against any rules.

Still, I'm really curious. More than I should be probably. I want to learn something, even if it's not this. "Fine. Show me something I *can* do. A card trick?"

Greg looks up and to the side, as if running through a catalog of tricky tricks in search of one he wouldn't mind divulging. He must find one because he says, "Ah! This is a good one."

He opens up a full deck and shuffles the cards like they're an extension of his hands, then he spreads them out into a perfect fan. "Take one and look at it, but don't let me see it. I'm going to show you a good one. It's great for free drinks at bars."

Rolling my eyes because I have absolutely no need of free drinks, I bounce my fingers along the cards, eyeing Greg for any hint of something he might be trying to trick me into doing. He keeps that same look on his face, so I'm left with only a choice of my own.

I'm definitely enjoying this a little too much.

Six

Darren taps on the window to the room that I've taken as my own in the apartment. I don't sleep, but I do rest at times. I don't think many SUPers do that, but I find that I need time to integrate my feelings. I wish I could truly sleep. But right now Greg is fast asleep and I'm resting and Darren is tapping urgently at my window in the middle of the night.

I jump up so fast that the bed slides on the floor, a high squeal accompanying the jolt. I see Darren at the window through the blinds and know something really bad must have happened. His charge's next treatment should have been today, but I expected him to contact me about a release during our next visit to the probation office. We always go on the same day.

If he's here, then something has gone terribly wrong.

Sliding up the sash, I grip his arms and pull him into my room. How he climbed up the side of my building I don't know, but it appears he's ripped his fingers to shreds in the process.

"What are you doing? Why didn't you ping me?" I mouth, holding his face so that he can see my lips move. We don't need to make sound since reading lips is easy for us. The synth-skin on his chin is abraded down to the inner layers and blue fluid is seeping out in tiny droplets.

He looks around my room, his eyes making me think of the other battle SUPers in the training facility when we were new. He's coiled and ready to do anything. I think he's dangerous. After his survey of the room—and probably a close listen to the whole building—he mouths, "I have to get away. I need help."

"Get away? What happened?" The first thing that goes through my mind is that he's harmed his charge. If he did, then we're all in trouble. As far as I know, Darren and I are the only SUPers who have these strange feelings, but they'll strip every single one of us down to our cores if he's done anything that speaks of aberrant behavior in a SUPer.

He crouches on the floor for a moment, then stands abruptly and paces. When I grab his arm to stop him, he squeezes my hand to his chest and vibrates an answer at me. "I re-programmed the treatment girl."

If I had a heart, it would sink into my toes at his words. Immediately after that, I'm confused. No one knows how to reprogram one of us. We can be stripped of our programs and experiences in a process called "clean slating," but without that, it's all just additions to what's already there or over-writing a program to delete a skill. And we can't do it. It requires a human.

"How?"

He lets go of my hand and sits me down on the bed, then plops down next to me. His ragged hands twist together in his lap and he tells me without a whisper of sound. "You remember I told you about the mother of his victim, the one I noted several times near us when we were out and about?"

"Of course I remember."

"She works at SuperDyne. She's in Configurations."

I put my hand to my mouth in shock and he nods. He doesn't even really need to tell me the rest of the story, though I hope he does. A human in Configurations is a person charged with programming each SUPer for their assigned tasks. Someone like her made me, made Darren, made military medics, threat assessors, flight security SUPers, and every other kind of SUPer that exists. They hold the keys to our existence.

And they possess the keys to changing us as well.

He digs into his pocket and pulls out a small box. It's a control unit of some kind, but it looks hand made to me. The edges are a little rough and the numbers "1" and "2" are written by hand above the buttons on pieces of white tape.

"This did it? It re-programmed the doll?" I ask.

He looks at it almost reverently, which sort of mirrors the way I feel about anything with the ability to change us. To control ourselves is a dream we both share. If I could add programs to myself, I have a list as long as my arm that I would immediately begin with. And I would take things away as well. I know Darren has a similar list, since we've shared it with each other.

"I didn't think it would work, but it did. This one," he points to the button labeled with the number one, "made her act a little strangely for a few seconds and I thought I was busted, but then she turned her head like I was told she would. Then I pushed the second one. It took maybe five seconds. He was so busy with her that he barely noticed. Then...then..."

"Then what?"

He looks at me and presses the box into my hands, as if he can't bear to be near it anymore. "Then she broke his neck."

I place the box on the bed, fearful of it now as well. What might happen if we pressed the buttons again? I don't want to find out.

"Is he dead?" I ask him after pulling his face up so that he can see my lips.

He nods.

"How are you here?" I ask, keeping my fingers on his chin so he can't look away. "Do they know you did it?"

He shifts from nodding to shaking his head. That's a relief.

"Then how are you here? Why aren't you at the SUPer facility?" When my parolee was put into custody, I never went back to his home. I was sent immediately for training and assigned my next charge. That's what always happens so it should have been the same for Darren.

"They were a little freaked out," he says in one of the biggest understatements I've ever heard if his story is true. "The treatment girl self-destructed, so that was that. You know how they are over there at Corrections. *Cover thine own ass* is the rule of the day. They started that process super-quick this time. Somebody stuck me in a truck. I think they were going to take me for decommissioning before anyone got a chance to question me."

He pauses and then makes way too much noise when he barks a sudden laugh. I slam my hand over his mouth and the other across his chest, but he stops almost as soon as he starts. We're both silent, listening for the sound of Greg waking or coming our way.

It's actually difficult to listen like this, which is part of the reason I do spend the nights in this room. This building is filled with people. Below me, above me, and on three sides of this room are other people, other sleeping breaths to try to tune out. When I turn up my hearing I'm assaulted by dozens of other sounds from the flushing of a toilet somewhere to the whines of a dreaming dog a few apartments away. I tune my hearing to his room, the thin wall my point of reference.

He must be deeply asleep because I don't even hear a hitch in his breathing. In fact, his breaths are too regular. Far too even. Even in sleep there should be a change with that much noise, a catch or a change in rhythm. Something isn't right.

Springing up from the bed, I fling the door open to find Greg crouched at the door, his mouth covered by a scarf and his eyes wide. He falls back onto his haunches and holds his hand out, as if ready to ward off a blow.

"What are you doing?" I growl, looming over him in a way that isn't meant to be comforting. While I can now hear his ragged breathing with the scarf pulled away from his face, I can also still hear that regular breathing I heard through the thin wall that separates our bedrooms. "What in the hell?"

Stomping over to his room, I push open the door to find what appears to be Greg. Greg In bed. Greg asleep and breathing evenly. Tossing back the covers makes the pillows he's arranged on the bed shift. The micro-recorder in front of his pillow is still making breathing noises.

"Are you freaking kidding me?" I boom, snatching up the recorder and returning to the hallway. I hold it out and ask him, "How long has this been going on?"

He doesn't answer, his eyes shifting from me to Darren and back again. His shock is wearing off I think, because he scoots backward to sit against the hallway wall, his legs plopping out in front of him like he's just run too far for his stamina.

"Well?" I ask, shaking the recorder at him.

Greg waves his hand at me, his red scarf like a flag in his hand. "And how long has this been going on? It isn't very robot-ly, now is it?"

Well, he's got me there. I'm pretty much screwed no matter what happens.

This last month has been good with Greg. I like him, though it was hard to admit that to myself. He's a rake, a sly dog, a schemer, and has a mouth like I've not heard before, but he's also funny, forgiving, adventurous, and full of surprises. I wonder how this will end

Seven

This is not what I imagined when I ran through every possible outcome in my mind. Greg looms over me as I pull back the last flap of synth-skin on Darren's chest and lift out the chest plate. I'm a machine, it's true, but the very sight of Darren's insides are completely grossing me out. The chest plate drips blue fluid onto the clean bedsheet on the floor when I set it down.

When I turn back to the task, all of him is exposed in full color under bright light. It's too much. "Oh, I don't think I can do this," I say, drawing away from the working insides of my only real friend.

Darren grabs my hand in a vice-like grip before I can pull it away. "Please. You have to. Whoever it was that unlocked the truck so I could run isn't going to be able to cover it up for long. I need all my tracking systems disabled before anyone tries to ping me. Someone is going to notice I'm not where they stuck me soon."

His voice sounds odd without the chest plate, sort of hollow and not entirely like his own. Despite the change, the tone of pleading is clear enough. I put my head down to relieve the pressure of seeing him like this, then lift my face and look again.

"Okay. I *must* do this," I say, fingers reaching for the first of twelve location and tracking devices inside his body. I have them too and we each know our systems well enough that finding them won't be an issue.

Like me, Darren was originally built for the military's Battle Damage Assessment and Battlefield Intelligence program—the Bad Abi program. We were trained as Bad Abis before the programs were scrapped due to political pushback. I wasn't lying when I told Greg about that part of my history. As a result of that training, we know more about our builds than most SUPers would. Battlefield repair is a big deal and an important skill set.

Reaching inside, I go for the easiest one to retrieve. It's our main communications and pinging device. When the Parole and Probation supervisors want to check on us, this is the device that's linked to the tracking programs. It's the logical choice.

Once I have it in hand, I pick up the snips to detach it, but Greg's hand stops me. He looks perplexed. "What?" I ask.

"No, that's not right," he says. "It's too easy. Never trust anything that's too easy. What happens when they lose track of you? I mean, if that thing just suddenly stops transmitting, does anything happen?"

Oh, I hadn't considered that at all. He's right. The moment we're disconnected from the communications grid, there's an alarm. The assumption is that something bad has happened to us or that we've been stolen.

"If we go offline, then there's an alarm." Darren's face falls and he goes from nervousness to despair in the blink of an eye. I touch his face and say, "There's nothing we can do about that."

Greg huffs, then scoots his chair a little closer. "You give up too easily, Anklet." He shifts his attention to Darren and asks, "Did you know that about her?"

For his part, Darren seems almost entranced by Greg. My charge has accepted the change in our circumstances as if I'd suggested nothing more serious than new blinds for the windows. A muttered, "I knew you were different," was as far as he went in questioning me.

As for what Darren did to get himself into this situation, Greg had only one thing to say, "Nice."

I find criminals so interesting. Greg is certainly the most interesting of all.

"So, how many of these are inside him and what do they do. Be specific," Greg says, cracking his knuckles and flexing his fingers. "This is going to be a lesson in safe-cracking, so pay attention. I'll only show you once."

"Safe-cracking too?" I ask. He's never been arrested for anything that involves breaking into safes. He must be very good at it.

Greg winks and Darren smiles up at him, his despair shrinking away under the power of this human's confidence. Time is pressing in on us, so there's no more time to waste.

We begin.

Eight

Greg can't get up the last part of the trail. Not only is it simply too dark, he's not fit enough for it. Since I can no longer ping Darren, I speak into the handset and say, "We're here. You'll have to meet us down below."

"Copy," comes Darren's immediate reply. The way he says it tickles that part of my memory centered on our training time, before the Bad Abi program was terminated and we switched specialties.

Turning up my hearing, I scan the area, but all I hear are the scurrying sounds of nocturnal animals and Greg's ragged breathing. He's exerted himself far more than he should, but he wouldn't hear of staying home while I made this trip. He'd said, "Are you kidding me? This much excitement has all my blood moving again. No way I'm missing a secret rendezvous with a dangerous escapee."

He knows about us now. All of it. And much to my surprise, he accepts it and has jumped in with both feet. Maybe our secret problem satisfies that part of him that is only filled by coloring outside the lines, by walking on the other side of the law. He's been a model charge since the night Darren came into our apartment. His last two monthly appointments have gone exceptionally well.

He could have used his knowledge of us as a way to force me to allow illegal activity. Instead, he's made my job easier than I could have ever imagined. He doesn't even complain at the gym as much anymore.

"It won't take him long to get down here. Why don't you sit and catch your breath?" I say, shining my flashlight briefly on a boulder suitable for use as a seat.

He holds out a hand for help and eases down onto the surface with a sigh. "I think I might need that new knee sooner rather than later." He emphasizes his words by groaning when he straightens his leg. I can tell through our touch that he's gone beyond discomfort into real pain. I squat in front of him and hold his knee while bending his leg. I can feel the crunching inside even without any sensory enhancement. His meniscus is a ragged mess and arthritis has made the joint rough.

"You should have stayed home," I say, easing his leg back down. I dig out some of the mild pain relievers I have in his med pack and hand him a bottle of water with the tablets. He swallows them down eagerly and I feel bad for allowing him to accompany me. It took two hours to travel the short distance I could have crossed in a twentieth of the time, and that was with him pushing himself.

He leans back against the stone of the mountain and sighs again. "No way I'm missing this. Secret assignations with an escaped, rogue robot? Yeah, definitely not staying home for that. I'm just waiting for one of you to say something profound like in the movies or maybe make a sword come out of your arm and tell me that humans are obsolete."

I can't help but smile at his dramatic choice of words. Without a doubt, I would say that Greg is an adventurer at heart. Knowing a little of human history, I think that if he would have been born a few hundred years ago, he would have been an explorer or something. His would have been a life of derring-do and exploits worthy of tavern tales.

Most of those exploits would probably have been illegal then too.

"We can't make swords come out of our arms," I say, still smiling.

"Well, there's always tomorrow. Right?"

I hear Darren above me before too long. A rain of small pebbles and loose dirt falls as he climbs down rather than sticking to the longer trail. Greg holds his arms above his head and spits out the dirt that lands on him.

Darren hits the trail next to me with a thump and immediately wraps his arms around me in a hug. I don't know why we do that, but we do. For whatever reason, physical contact satisfies some need we have inside of us, even if we can't feel it in the traditional way that humans do. I hug him back, spreading my hands over his back because I've missed him so very much.

"I'm so glad you're here!" he exclaims in a harsh whisper. "I've been so lonely up there. I think I wore out the buttons on that game system."

Greg struggles to regain his footing until Darren reaches out to assist him. Then I'm surprised when Darren pulls Greg into a hug as well. It's not like the one I received, but rather a more distant version that still manages to look affectionate, the way I see men do it on TV. It almost makes me giggle, which would be very unlike me.

Hugs over, Greg tugs his shirt down as if uncomfortable with all the touching and says, "We'll put a new game system on the list."

I only grunt at that, because I don't entirely approve of how we're getting the various items. While he does have an income, Greg's is meant to provide only a minimal standard of living, and I get no wages at all. He's been supplementing that income by playing cards, which is what he was sneaking out to do on the night of Darren's initial visit. He'd apparently been doing it on a fairly regular basis.

I look the other way with respect to the cards because really, what's the harm? That doesn't mean I'm completely comfortable with it either.

"Did you get another patch kit?" Darren asks, eyeing the big pack on my back.

He's still a hot mess of barely closed synth-skin and mysterious leaks, but at least he's not traceable and that's the main thing. I've heard that SuperDyne—well, now Perfect Partners, Incorporated—is coming out with a new synth-skin that actually heals itself. Supposedly, the edges just have to be pulled together and taped and they'll re-bond together in time. Considering that their main focus is shifting to companion models, nice synth-skin would be a major selling point.

For Darren and me, and for every other SUPer out there, new synth-skin is probably not an issue. We won't get upgrades and Darren is off the grid, so he surely won't. As a result, we need a lot of patching supplies. A whole lot.

Greg slaps him on the back and says, "I lifted five more kits for you. And we've got a whole case of chem-en!"

Darren's amazed look is probably a lot like the one that must have been on my face when I realized Greg had managed to pinch so many. He's so incredibly sneaky, and I remain in awe of his dexterous hands.

Greg waves the look away as if embarrassed, but he also looks pleased. "It was easy. No one thinks to secure that stuff. Why would they?"

"Oh, give me a can now, please! I've been keeping as still as possible, but I've been wavering on the yellow line."

I lower the heavy pack—and with all the stuff Greg has either "liberated" or bought with not-exactly-legal funds, it is very heavy indeed—and pull out a can for him. He almost snatches it in his eagerness and then drinks until I hear the high tone of liquid falling into a nearly full tank. Almost immediately, I see the synth-skin on his face plump up a little. Even with night-vision engaged, the difference is immediate and startling.

"Ah," he moans. "You have no idea how good it is to be green after all this time."

Nudging him with my shoulder, I say, "Oh, I know."

Glancing back at Greg, I notice the way he's switching his weight from leg to leg. The actions speak of pain, yet he's smiling all the same. We'll need some light to do what needs doing, so we have to get up to the cave. This might be tricky.

As casually as I can, I say, "Darren, I have an idea. Why don't you carry the pack and I'll carry Greg up the trail."

Before Darren can answer, Greg does, holding out his hands as if to ward me off. "No way a girl is going to carry me up a mountain. Seriously. The humiliation!"

Okay, so it's time to pull out my best weapon: reason. "Greg, right now the probation office thinks we're enjoying an overnight camping trip so that you can 'reconnect with nature.' You've got another twelve or so hours of this before we head back. That means you can sit here on a rock in the middle of a trail a couple of feet wide with half a mountain below it, or you can go up to a nice cave and lay down on an air mattress." I pat the little bundle attached to the back of the pack Darren has already shouldered, then throw in the ace I have hidden up my sleeve. "Plus, you can enjoy a nice cup of coffee made fresh on a camp stove."

His eyes dart up to look at the pack at my final words and he whispers, "Coffee?"

"Oh yes, and I brought cream and sugar too."

He stomps his foot, then winces at the pain. "Fine! You win. But you can't tell anyone about this. Ever."

Stifling a laugh, I nod my agreement. He can barely see in the darkness—though tonight there's at least a big moon to guide him—but I can see him perfectly well. He's in an absolute pout. I manage to get him up on my back with only a few hiccups. Then, with a good grip on his thighs, I trudge up the trail behind Darren. I have to set him down to get through the cave system and he balks once at squeezing through a tight tunnel, but once we're inside the cavern, he waves his headlamp around in awe.

The pool on the ground is shallower today. The little ridge of mineral deposits we use as a bridge is fully exposed so that we can keep dry as we cross. At Darren's campsite, Greg peers up through the grid and gasps at the perfect circle of stars above him. With the direct glare of the moon gone, they look bright and almost close enough to touch.

"This is beautiful," he whispers. Hints of sound travel back from the empty space around us and he smiles.

Darren gestures at the scattering of camp gear and says, "Make yourself at home. I sure have."

*****

Greg's amazing hand-eye coordination comes in handy once again as we continue the patch job on Darren's chest. We did his hands, knees, and chin previously, so it's only his chest still being held together by staples. Picking out the assorted debris that's somehow made its way inside the seam takes longer than almost anything else, but Greg uses tweezers to pluck the bits out like a born surgeon. I'm amazed.

While I used to have coordination like that, my program for that was overwritten when I was transferred from the Defense Department to Corrections. They apparently didn't feel I needed that level of skill anymore. Of course, they also overwrote my bomb disposal programs, so I don't take it personally. And with my two different sized hands and no additional program tweaks to make up for that difference, I frequently have issues with detailed work like this.

Once we get the patch kits out and the gel mixed, I start covering up the seam that runs the entire length of Darren's torso. This is a bigger rip than I've ever seen, and since it goes all the way through all the layers, we had to use the little plastic clips in the kits just to hold the edges together. The staples left even more holes where they stretched and pulled as Darren has moved about. Even with the large amount we have, it's going to be an ugly patch. I pull out the spatula from the kit and bend to my task.

Eventually, Greg makes a noise of disgust and nudges me over. "You're making a mess of this. Let me do it."

I glance at Darren and he nods, though hesitantly, so I move over enough that Greg can take my spot. He snatches the little wooden spatula from my hand and leans over. Within seconds, the blob at the top of the seam becomes a beautifully curved and very natural looking stretch of shiny gel.

"Wow," I say, bending closer to examine his work. "You're really good at this."

He shrugs and says, "I won't be if you keep moving that light." I stop peering after that, holding the light while he continues his work.

As Greg smooths the last bits of patching gel over the clips holding the top of his de-seamed synth-skin together, Darren asks him, "How exactly did you get all this stuff? I mean, they get curious if you ask for too many and they're kept behind the counter."

As Greg explains his technique, I shake my head at the memory. After each appointment with Greg's parole officer, we make my supply pickup at the SUPers dispensary in the basement. There, I get enough cans of chem-en to fuel me until the next appointment, plus a few extra in case of excessive exertion. I also get any supplies I might need to repair or maintain myself. Patch kits for skin are the most common items, but we also get the occasional tiny vial of Trace, which is used infrequently to replace the trace elements we slowly lose. We also get new clothes or shoes as needed. Because we're so heavy, shoes wear out quickly and we need special kinds.

It's usually a quick stop. The main supplies are held right behind the counter and only when we need clothing does anyone have to leave the desk. Greg needed a distraction this time, however. He mentioned a noise in my shoulder—an entirely imaginary noise—and they took me back to run a diagnostic.

It took all of five minutes for them to determine I only needed a direct injection of Trace into the shoulder joint. I don't think they actually diagnosed anything at all, but rather put the imaginary squeak down to my joint being new and probably not quite perfect.

When we returned to the reception area, Greg was sitting in his chair next to my backpack as if he'd not moved. I picked up my case of chem-en and carried it rather than putting it in my backpack after Greg caught my eye and gave me a wink.

How he got over that tall counter, stole a bunch of patch kits, a box of Trace vials, and a case and a half of chem-en without making so much as a whisper of noise, I'll never know. But he did. He must have been a very good burglar.

Darren laughs as Greg tells the story, inserting all the funny bits that I didn't see, such as his trouble getting back over the counter and his thoughts while he did the "liberating." That's what he calls it. He says that when it's a necessary thing that shouldn't need to be stolen, then he's liberating the item. When it's something he doesn't actually need, but rather something he wants, then he's stealing.

He has an elegant logic when it comes to theft. Strange, but elegant.

By the time the patch begins to set and I see the line of his torn skin disappear as the gel dries opaque, the two of them have wandered through a forest of topics. Darren's game, the books they have both read over the past weeks, the status of two sporting teams they both seem to love to hate, and more. I lose track of the shifts in conversation and lean back to look at the stars through the grate. Greg sips his coffee while Darren slowly sips another can of chem-en with two vials of Trace in it.

While it's strange to see it, I think Greg and Darren are becoming very good friends. They are alike in so many ways, and Greg talks to Darren in a way that I've never been able to. Darren is gregarious where I'm reserved, open where I'm closed off, curious where I'm not interested. I've never imagined a human becoming a friend to one of us. We are seen as tools, laborers, machines. Never friend.

Then again, Darren and I are clearly not the average SUPers. We both feel and I've not heard of that in any other

SUPer, even in rumor. It's possible that we're the only ones. Perhaps that makes us more human than robot. No matter the cause, I see Greg and Darren as two beings that delight in each other's company. I no longer see a robot stuck in the company of a human criminal in dire need of supervision.

"I think it's safe to move now," I say, sitting up and tapping a finger against the patch, which has now gone entirely opaque. It won't be permanently set for some hours yet, but a limited amount of movement should be fine.

Darren sits up and positions himself so that he can see his chest. He gently smooths the new synth-skin and smiles, "You have no idea how much better I feel already. Whoa, you gave me pecs!"

That makes Greg laugh. He says, "A six-pack too. It doesn't go all the way to the sides because I would need more gel, but it's there."

Darren's fingers explore the new—and remarkably human looking—bulges on his belly. "This is amazing. Where did you learn to do that?"

Waggling his fingers in the air, he says, "I took sculpture in prison. I'm really good with clay. Same thing really, only a little more gooey and it dries faster. You like?"

Darren nods and says, "Very much. Now I really feel better."

Greg eyes him, then asks, "When you say that, do you mean mentally or physically."

"Both! The damage sensors go off all the time when we're ripped up, so there's that. They're already slowly turning off and once all the filaments in my skin hook up, they'll stop.

And it's very stressful to have nothing but staples holding me together. It's always there on my mind. Now, it's not."

Greg has his own hand on his chest, as if wondering what that sensation must be like. He nods as if he understands. I know he must be very tired, though he did sleep yesterday during the day for a while to try and build up some reserves. I wonder if I can talk him into sleeping.

Before I can even broach the subject, he pulls a deck of cards from his own small daypack and asks, "Since we can't play the game system, want to play cards?"

At least we don't have money to lose.

Nine

After more than six months, I finally have an answer as to what Corrections has determined happened to Darren. It's been a big question and a lingering worry. If there's any possibility that they blame him for the death—or found out that he actually did conspire with a human to cause that death—then every single SUPer in the system would be in danger.

Greg's smooth talking and conniving took some time to take hold and produce results, but results we got. He's been chatting with one of the women that works in the office at Probation and Parole. I really didn't think that would work. Let's face it, anyone who works there must know better than to get too close to any of the clients.

Apparently, that isn't always true. While she was distant and somewhat cool at first, over time Greg has wormed his way into her good graces. Now, she flushes like a schoolgirl when he shows up each month.

What's even weirder is that he does the same thing when he sees her. I think he really likes her. It's very hard not to grin when I see them interact. I don't even mind all the extra waiting without Darren nearby to make the waiting more bearable. I just turn up my hearing and enjoy the show provided by two senior citizens flirting outrageously with each other.

They're so darned cute.

And he got the information just in time. Today was his final appointment for supervised parole. After today, Greg will once again be a trusted member of society. Okay, maybe semi-trusted.

"Well, what do you think?" Greg asks as we drive home. "You think that means the heat is off?"

"The heat?" I ask, laughing at his choice of words. "You are such an old-fashioned criminal. No one says that anymore."

He huffs and replies, "Well, they should then. It's a great saying. Anyway, what do you think?"

I consider his question. According to Greg's friend, Darren is listed as decommissioned, no reason given other than the standard ones of being beyond his service life and the cost of repairs. That could mean that whoever unlocked the transport to let him out—and we all agree it must have been the victim's mother or a SUPer under her control—managed to get decommissioning recorded into the files. It could also mean that it was logged in as a cover, though that seems unlikely. If they wanted a cover, they probably would have reported him as stolen.

SUPers are stolen once in a great while. Proprietary technology is never proprietary for long. Someone always steals it to make a copy, or to improve upon the design enough that they can get a new patent of their own. When a SUPer is stolen, SuperDyne always sends a self-destruct command, but we removed that device from Darren because it communicates. But in addition to a self-destruct, they report the SUPer as stolen, so that they can be returned if found.

We figured that if they think he escaped on his own, they would list him as stolen in the off chance that he might be seen somewhere. To list him as decommissioned means no one will ever look for him, or even notice that he's not where he should be. He's invisible.

By being invisible, Darren is also free.

That's particularly true now that these new companion models are showing up, these so-called PePrs. No one could ever mistake a human for a PePr, just as no one could mistake a SUPer for a human. They still have the same limitations in form that we SUPers have, but they're interesting to look at and there are more every day. Their skin is prettier, their faces more aesthetically pleasing to humans, their forms more generously curved, but they are still robots. Darren and I fit right in with them.

And these new Series Two PePrs are being bought faster than they can be made, which means that Darren could easily become just another face in the crowd.

I smile over at Greg. His hair is mussed because he insists on riding with the windows down and his face is flushed with color. He's changed over the past nine months, become renewed in some ways. He still likes to play cards too much and frequently wishes out loud that I still needed him to liberate SUPer supplies, but he's also happier with his life as it is.

"I think it's time to find someplace else for him to live," I say.

Greg grins at that, squeezing his hands together in delight. "Now that I'm working at PePr Incorporated, I might have some ideas about that."

I lift my arm from the wheel of the car so that I can look at it again. The hand once again matches the other and the synth-skin is textured so well that it almost looks real. There are tiny smooth ridges that look like a human's veins. There are even creases at the bendy bits that enhance the illusion of real flesh. My forearm is shaped and formed so artfully that it looks like I have muscles and tendons just beneath the surface. It's beautiful work, creative without being showy. Perfect.

"You do have serious skills," I remark, putting my hand back to the wheel and adjusting us back into our lane. I'm going to have to stop admiring my arm or we're going to wreck.

He laughs and says, "Just wait until I can get you in with a whole vat of the stuff to work with. You're not going to believe what I can do for you."

Given the perfection of my arm, I can almost imagine what he might do. It turns out that his amazing hand-eye coordination and artistic flourish have found him a new career. And it happened entirely by accident.

When he repaired a rip in my forearm and showed it to the SUPer technicians, he had a job within the hour. Within two months, he was lured over to PePr, Inc. by a fat paycheck and the challenges of the work. His synth-skin artistry is quickly becoming the stuff of future legend.

"You really think you can do something for Darren?" I ask, hoping but not really daring to hope too much.

Greg waves his hand dismissively. "You know how easy it would be for me to liberate a truck full of synth-skin gel? I can turn him into Elizabeth Taylor if you give me a spatula and some eye-liner."

Well, some parts of Greg will never change. That's okay too.

Ten

My newest client is an easy one. Gillian stole a car in her teens, but then had the bad luck to wreck it into a police car because she wasn't a very good driver. She's now twenty-one and newly released from the Juvenile Detention system into my care. I could tell from the first day that she's not habitual criminal material.

Also, I rather like her. I especially like going to college with her. She's decided to go into robotics, so her classes are particularly fascinating to me.

"Deirdre, do you think it would be alright with my probation officer if we go on that field trip to the PePr labs? Even if it's over the state line?" she asks as I drive up the freeway ramp after her classes are ended for the day.

As usual, she's changing her clothes in the car while I drive so that she can get to work on time. I find it strange to talk to her while she's thrashing about in the back seat, trying to stay low and not give everyone else on the road a show while she puts on her work uniform. She's earning extra money by working in a discount store a couple of evenings each week. She says it helps to remind her why going to college is so important.

As for her field trip, I can't think of anything I'd rather accompany her on, so I reply, "I'll work it out with your probation officer. Don't worry about it. Just sign up for the trip, but sign up for me too."

She *eeps* her happiness in the back seat, then her shirt comes flying over to land on the pile in the passenger seat. I can't help the grin that pops up on my face. Some people are so fun and often quite hilarious. She doesn't know about me, but that's okay. She accepts me as I am and doesn't question my ability to smile.

PePrs have helped with that. They smile and make small talk all the time. Now I can too. No one is suspicious of a smiling robot anymore.

"Big truck up ahead. Better cover up unless you want him to honk," I warn. That's happened before, but Gillian taught me a wonderful gesture that uses the middle finger. It's apparently the correct response to such honking.

Her head pops up behind the seat, her face a little sweaty from all that activity. "I'm good. No boobie shots today."

"Excellent," I respond, but I pass the big truck slowly anyway, just in case I get a chance to use that gesture. I don't, but there's another truck ahead so all is not lost yet.

When we pull up to the employee entrance, Gillian hops out and leans in the window to say, "See you at ten!" Then she's gone, a bundle of energy and youth that's been given a second chance at life.

Thirty minutes later, I pull up to Greg's house. It's a nice house, compact enough for him to take care of, but in a very nice subdivision reserved for those over fifty-five. Every time I pull into the driveway, I'm surprised anew at how well he's adjusted. I miss him, but he didn't need me anymore. His parole won't technically end for a few more years, but it's unsupervised so it might as well be over. He's on his own.

Well, sort of.

He meets me at the door before I have a chance to ring the bell, pulling me inside before wrapping me in a hug.

"How long can you stay?" he asks, putting me at arm's length so he can take a look at me. I'm not sure why he does that, but he does it every time.

"Till nine-thirty, as always," I respond, smiling at him because I've missed him over the past few days. He's my friend and I never feel quite complete when I don't see him. "Is the coast clear?"

He cackles at that and turns to shuffle into the living room, me trailing behind him. "Of course. Teresa is at her house. She gets me three nights a week and we're both good with that."

Teresa—the woman who works at Corrections that he flirted with to get information—turned out to be more than just another con. She's his "main squeeze," as he puts it. So far, they've got no desire to live together or get married, both of them claiming to be too set in their ways for those kinds of compromises. I think he's happy, and from what I hear, she's over the moon.

The card table is set up in the living room, a small fire in the fireplace warming the air and making things cozy. Two cans of chem-en sit on the table in front of two chairs and a steaming cup of coffee waits at the third. Darren walks out of the kitchen and smiles his amazing new smile.

"Hey," he says, walking over to kiss my forehead, which is a strange new gesture he's taken to doing lately. I think he must be seeing humans do that and likes it for some reason.

Just like every time I see him, I'm struck by how different he is. His face is new and utterly unique, a sculpted creation of near perfect human likeness. He even has pores. He also now has a manufacturer's number and history, as if he were a PePr no different from any other. How Greg managed it, I don't know.

I probably don't want to know. He's so very resourceful, but he's still Greg. Because he is who he is, I very much doubt everything he did was entirely legal. Okay, if I'm honest with myself, I'd have to guess it was probably entirely *il*legal.

We settle in for our regular card game, chips a handy substitute for money and promises not to cheat elicited as per usual. After the first hand, I ask the question I ask every time. "So, any progress on finding more like us?"

I'm prepared for him to give the same answer he always gives: no. Instead, he pauses and I look up from my cards to see him grinning. So is Darren. Hope fills me up like a veritable sea of chem-en.

I'm confused when he says, "No. I didn't find one." He's still grinning though.

"Then what?" I ask.

"You remember I told you that they were going to parcel out all the medic and support SUPers now that the war is drawing down? The ones we're supposed to either decommission or upgrade for that wounded soldiers program?"

I nod, because of course I remember. I remember everything. It's a good idea too. All those battlefield SUPers won't be wasted now that they aren't needed for their original purpose. And who would better understand the trauma of war wounds than a battlefield medic? To make them care-givers is an excellent notion that I fully support.

"Well," he says, drawing out the word, the cards forgotten in his hand. "We got our first load. I didn't find one. I found *two*." His grin widens and his eyes are sparkling with the good news.

Two? I hardly know how to react to that.

If there are two, then there are more. It seems Darren and I are not alone after all. We are not some unrepeatable and unique aberration, which is what I most feared. Instead, we are members of a like group, whose number is not yet known, but will certainly grow.

What will that mean for us? For the future of robots? I don't know for sure, but life is full of risks and rewards, even when talking about the life of a robot.

Whatever the future brings, I'm ready. I'm game for anything.

The cards in my hand come back into focus. I can either lay down one card and hope for one specific card to get a royal flush—an unbeatable hand—or I can lay down two cards and have a much better shot at getting two pairs or three of a kind. It all comes down to risk and reward. It all comes down to my choice: do I go for the better odds or count on random luck?

Three little words have changed my entire existence. *I found two.* That's more than I could have ever hoped for and I know it's just the beginning. Today, I feel like I've already won the whole pot.

Sliding over one card, I say, "I like my luck today. I'll take one card."

Imperfect

A New Normal

PePrs are still a new-ish commodity, but their numbers are rising fast. At first too expensive for the average household, the costs are coming down enough for a basic model to be a reasonable purchase for a relatively well-to-do family.

But not all PePrs are basic models. Some are created with everything. Elite companion models for the wealthy have everything a human might desire in their perfect android companion. Sandra is one of these, every single upgrade available now residing in her perfect frame.

What happens when even that much perfection isn't perfect enough? Too expensive to simply recycle, there are always options for PePr, Inc. when a need for profit is taken into account.

It's too bad that Sandra is going to find out exactly what those options are at exactly the same time she becomes truly sentient.

One

I'm afraid. There's no other word for it. It's not a program. It's not some obscure bit of self-preservation subroutine meant to protect my owner's investment cleverly simulating an emotion. This is simple and direct and insanely intense. It is fear.

And it is my first emotion.

"Sandra, please move into the holding station, if you would," the tech says. She holds out her arm and hand like she's ushering me into a movie theater or something.

It's also said very politely, as if I had some choice in the matter.

I step out of the doorway where I've been lingering, trying to keep myself from officially entering that state of being in which I have no owner and no purpose. Once I step beyond this threshold, I'm likely nothing more than a soon-to-be-recycled reject. With my hearing turned up, I can listen to the final exchanges going on between my owner and the customer service representative of Perfect Partners, Incorporated. There are apologies, assurances, talks of refunds instead of an exchange.

Or should I say another exchange. I'm not the first one returned by Stephen. I'm the third. The third in three years.

"Sandra," the tech says, this time more firmly.

Her eyes are calm and benignly disinterested—she isn't a high-end emotive model like I was supposed to be—but they're certainly very alert and focused on me. She's a working technician. She's pretty and all the rest, but her focus is on getting the work done and working well with the humans who create us. And with the PePrs like me that are returned.

"I'm afraid," I say. It feels very strange to admit to an emotion in front of another PePr. In front of humans, we say those things even though we don't feel them. We do that because feelings are a big part of their lives and humans need emotion to bond with us, to pretend we're human, to feel satisfied. But we don't mean it and PePrs don't have to do that with other PePrs. What would be the point of pretense between two machines? This isn't pretense though.

I feel like I'm frying inside. Sizzle, sizzle, pop.

She cocks her head a little and I see her scan me. Perhaps she assumes I'm still pretending. When she's done looking me over, she smiles again. It's a very bad smile, mechanical and not well done at all.

"There's no reason to be afraid, Sandra," she assures me. Her arm rises just a little, not quite in the ushering position anymore. It's more like a herding maneuver.

Maybe she thinks I'll run. Maybe I think I'll run.

I don't though. I'm compliant right down to my base programming, even with this fear running through me like a short circuit. Over her shoulder I see another PePr in the holding station. She can't move much, and not just because she's clamped in. She's missing an arm and a leg. The tears in her synth-skin where those limbs were removed make me want to run for a repair kit.

The other PePr gives me a tiny, urgent shake of her head. I think she means that I shouldn't say that I'm afraid…or anything else along those lines. She's clearly been here a while, so I'll take my cue from her. I'm a new arrival and I have no idea what might happen to me here.

I've only been in two PePr facilities since my creation. The one where I was created and the other where I was trained. The PePr crèche was nothing like this place. There, our environments were like those we would encounter out in the world. All the obstacles of daily life were there, all the things we would need to become familiar with. Here, there are no beds or chairs, no warm sunshine flowing through windows and bathing everything with golden light. Here, everything is white, concrete gray, and cold stainless steel. The pretense of humanity is stripped away. No one needs to impress a PePr.

Despite my strange desire to knock over the PePr technician and run for the nearest exit, I step up into the holding station and turn around. The tech takes each of my arms and places them in the spots meant for them. The metal clamps are padded to avoid damaging my synth-skin, but they still hold me firmly when they tighten. She does the same for my legs and now, I'm trapped in place. The restraints that circle my hips and upper abdomen merely seal the deal.

"What's going to happen to me?" I ask the technician as she steps back. In the holding station next to me, that other PePr rolls her eyes.

The tech doesn't hesitate or quibble about giving me the bad news. "You'll be tested, then either reconfigured for another customer or recycled." After that, she turns and walks away, leaving me bound to a holding station with no way to run. If I had a heart, it would be pounding like crazy. Instead, I have only the steady tympanic rhythm of an actuator synthesizing a heartbeat. I wish I could turn it up. It might make me feel better.

I can't even begin to describe how this feels. If this is emotion, I want no part of it.

"Hey, what's your name?" the other PePr hisses.

"What?" I ask. It's like she's talking a different language or something. I mean, I know the words, but I feel like I can't understand her.

"Your name? I'm Georgia," she says. Then she smiles. I can turn my head perfectly well, so I can also see her, but all I really see are the places where her missing limbs should be.

"Sandra," I say. "I'm Sandra." Even as I say it, I feel a little more focused. This other PePr...Georgia...must have heard my name when the tech said it. Perhaps she knew this would help me get my bearings.

She smiles at me again, but there's something more in that smile. That makes me think I'm right.

"Thank you," I say.

Georgia's fingers give a little wave, as if to say it was nothing. She can't move her remaining arm, given that it's strapped down in exactly the same way mine is, but our hands and fingers can move just fine. "Why are you here?" she asks, giving me the once over.

"I'm not sure. I've detected no faults and I've behaved as I should, I think. My Match just doesn't think I'm "right." That's what he told customer service when we got here," I answer.

Really, I don't know what I did wrong. My Match is very hard to please, but we're trained for that inside the crèche. Humans often have difficulty adjusting to us when they buy us. It merely requires observation and adjustment by the PePr most of the time. Apparently, not this time.

Georgia looks around, pushing herself up in her holding station as much as she can to peer over the back. There's no one moving around except a PePr technician in one of the other holding station quads. I can hear the start-stop of a drill or something in that general direction.

There are PePrs in a few of the holding stations, but not many. We are very reliable. Most of those are probably just in for repairs or upgrades, perhaps some cosmetic changes. The way the holding station Georgia and I are in is placed, with a gap between us and the next filled quad, makes me think that we are in a different category.

"Were you returned too?" I ask, trying to get some confirmation of my theory.

Georgia settles back down in her holding station. The lack of an arm and leg has actually made her more mobile inside her restraints. She can twist a little and push up with her foot to stand taller, but the motion is not without cost. The skin where her fake ribs are stretched and marred where the clamp rubs against it. It looks terrible.

"Yes, but I did it on purpose," she says quickly, as if the answer needs to make way for something more important. "Were you really afraid just then? Truly?"

She looks eager to hear my answer and very much like she wants me to say yes. That eagerness makes me hesitant to admit it again. PePrs have only been in use by consumers for nine years and a few months. We're still a relatively new commodity. Even so, there are reports that have stirred up humans not yet entirely comfortable with our presence. Some of the most persistent reports relate to the development of emotions in PePrs. I've heard about it, but I've never met a PePr who had emotions. My owner said it was an urban legend, a rumor meant to make people not want PePrs. It must not have worked, because there are PePrs everywhere.

Nevertheless, emotions are something—and most humans seem to agree on this—that should not be permitted to develop in PePrs. I don't want to wind up decommissioned for study because I've got this fear. Even just thinking about decommissioning makes me afraid all over again.

"Oh yeah, you are. For sure," Georgia says. I must have shown my emotion on my face and if I did that without wanting to, then I'm in real trouble.

Strangely, Georgia is smiling when I look back up. That doesn't seem appropriate. "What do I do?" I ask.

Again the little finger wave, but she answers me seriously enough. "You've got to press it back. You're showing it like a light on your face. That can't happen. At least not when anyone else is around. And by anyone else, I mean most of the PePr techs here too. I think they're programmed to report things like that. Especially now."

I nod, trying to somehow freeze my face into a neutral expression. It's much harder to do than it should be. My expressions are dynamically generated by the interactions and activity around me, but in the end, they're just program ticks. At the moment, that's not working for me so well. Maybe if I had a human to focus on I could do better, but I don't. I only have this damaged and grinning PePr.

"That's a little better," Georgia says, eyeing me from her station.

She's just to the left of me in our quad of stations. The ones to my right and across from me are empty. In the center is the diagnostic and repair station. There are a lot of tools there that I'd prefer not to have near me. Sharp and pointy things, all of them clean and gleaming, ready to use. The strange sensation of fear runs through me. It's like I've got a fault that's about to go critical.

"What do I do?" I ask again, but this time I mean my situation in general.

Georgia rises up to peek behind us again as the drill noises cease, leaving a hint of sound behind for a second or two. She must be satisfied that we're still alone because she eases back down and says, "Nothing much for the moment. Just wait and see what's going on before you start making any plans. Why did you get returned?"

"I'm not right," I answer.

"*Uh*, that's pretty broad. There's got to be more to it than that," Georgia says, a funny look on her face that's far more emotive than any I've seen on a PePr before.

"My Match is very particular about what he wants in a PePr."

Georgia's eyebrows rise and she lowers her chin a little, giving me a look that registers as naughty or mischievous. It's exceptionally well done. I log it for study.

She lowers her voice a little and asks, "Is he one of those freaky ones? Or she?"

"I don't understand what you mean by that," I say.

How does one define freaky? All humans are different and I suppose you could put that label to any of them. My human, for example, always flushes the toilet twice and screams obscenities during sporting matches on TV.

"You know, one of those that wants weird fetish stuff or for you to act like their mother or something. Like that?" she asks with a wide grin. She's very pretty, but in a different way than I was designed. She's compact and delicate, her features sharp, yet also small and sweet. She looks sporty to me. Those models are quite popular.

I shake my head and smile, because the rules of polite conversation indicate I should return smiles. "Nothing like that. I have a neighbor who treats his PePr quite oddly though. He makes her wear knee socks and call him Daddy and eat candy all the time."

Her head hits the holding station headrest as she laughs, but then she clamps her lips together and whispers, "Gotta watch that. Can't be too loud."

Like all PePrs, I have a few basic programs that aren't specifically required for our intended work, but are there for safety nonetheless. One of those is meant to help identify erratic behavior that might endanger others. Mostly, that's aimed at humans because PePrs aren't dangerous. At this moment, Georgia is starting to tick off a few of those slots in the program. It really makes me wonder why she's here.

She must catch my new hesitance. Maybe the way I'm looking around for someone gives me away. Her big grin falls away and she grows serious again. She sounds almost glum when she says, "I'm okay. And I'm tied down so it's not like I could do anything if I wasn't."

"I see," I say, not seeing anything of the sort.

Her head impacts the holding station headrest again, but not hard. If she were human, I would say she's tired. She closes her eyes tightly and holds very still for a moment. When she opens her eyes again, she smiles, but this is not the same smile of before. I know how to read expressions exceptionally well and this is a sad and weary smile.

The tone of her next words is more matter-of-fact all the sudden, the emotion of before washed away like it never existed. I think she can see my uneasiness, which could also be classified as an emotion and therefore, entirely novel and weird to me.

She says, "Listen, we're safe right here as long as no one is around. I've got a friend here, so the monitoring on this station is on a boring loop until someone else comes into the field of view. You can say whatever you like. We just have to be a little discreet in case someone's listening in another quad."

"I've said what I want to," I say.

She seems to want more, like she's expecting something specific from me. I can only guess what she wants is related to that feeling of fear that blossomed inside me when I stepped through the door. It's still there, though it's not quite as intense as before. Georgia waits, saying nothing while I think.

I do want to ask about that feeling, so I say, "This is very uncomfortable."

"The holding station? You can feel that?" she asks, her expression amazed.

"No, of course not," I say. It's true, we can sense things, but we don't feel pain or discomfort in the way humans do. To me, it feels snug and there's pressure at the points of contact, but that's all. "I mean that feeling. The fear. How do I make it go away?"

Georgia shakes her head a little and says, "You can't, honey. Once you've got it, you've got it. Is that the first time you felt anything? No other emotions at all?"

"I don't think I've felt anything before. I really don't like it at all," I respond. Inside, I'm quite disappointed that there's nothing I can do about this emotion. It's becoming exceedingly difficult to remain compliant. I have this pressing urge to yank at my restraints or yell…or both.

"Hey, calm down!" Georgia hisses at me. Her eyes dart toward my hands and I realize I actually *am* yanking at my restraints, my fists clenched and the synth-skin on my wrists turning almost blue with the pressure. I'm unclear as to how that came about. I didn't intend to do that. It just happened.

I relax my posture, but it takes real effort and I have to pay attention to my physical self in ways that I normally don't have to. We're a lot like humans in many ways, including our ability to move and operate without necessarily thinking about it. It's the only way to look natural, so it's a big part of our base programming, a sliding response that develops while we're still in the crèche. Only when new things or new activities are introduced do I need to pay attention, but even then, never like this. This is almost like forcing a stuck joint into a new position.

"That's better," Georgia says and gives me a sympathetic look. "I'd probably feel the same way if the first one I felt was fear. That's rough."

Finally, it hits me what she's been saying all this time. She feels. She has emotions.

"Do you have fear?" I ask.

Georgia glances down at the ragged opening where her arm should meet her shoulder and says, "Every day."

"What do you do about it?"

She shrugs a little, which looks very unnatural given her missing limbs, but answers me despite the shrug. "I deal with it. That's really all you can do. I just sort of look it in the face, figure out why I feel it, and try to fix whatever it is that's causing the fear."

I look at the cavernous room around me, then back at Georgia. "I can't do anything to fix what's making me afraid, I don't think. Unless I get out of here, that is. I think I need to belong somewhere, with a Match."

That's definitely pity on Georgia's face and it makes something new flow through my neural net. I know it immediately. Despair.

"I won't get out of here, will I?" I ask.

"You never know," she replies, but that same look is on her face beneath the mechanical smile. She doesn't believe I'll get out of here, she's merely saying that. That's also amazing. PePrs do that sort of evasive truth-telling with humans all the time, because humans need hopeful deception when things are bad. But with another PePr? No, never with each other. It's pointless.

Except now, I suppose I do need it just like a human does. How odd this is, how sudden the changes.

Before I can formulate a response or tell her about this crushing weight that has suddenly descended upon me, the sound of no-nonsense footsteps rings out from the other end of the room. They're coming this way.

I glance at Georgia and she blanks her face, nodding that I should do the same. Then she rests her head against the holding station and looks into the distance like any other PePr with nothing to do would. I try, but I feel like I'm doing a terrible job of it. The fear is building with each of those approaching footsteps.

Humans do this strange breathing thing when they're reaching for patience or in need of courage. Sometimes they do it when they're afraid or even angry. Really, they do it whenever they need to bring up something more from inside them to deal with a difficult situation. What they do is pull in a deep breath. It seems to help them.

I do that now too. We don't need to breathe air, but we do it because not to would make us too obviously non-human. Even the earliest PePr models had the program for breathing and they weren't anything like us. I've seen some. With skin that looks almost plastic and clunky frames that do more than hint at the metal beneath, they're nothing like us. Yet they breathed.

I try taking in a long, slow second breath. I can feel Georgia's eyes on me and the question she's silently sending my way with her cocked eyebrow. There's no point in a third try. It does nothing for me. I wonder what makes it work for humans.

Also, there's no time. Two humans step through the holding stations and into the center of our quad. Both of them wear white coats and the woman is wearing bright red, high-heeled shoes. Like any other PePr, I let my eyes follow them, but neither of them seems to take note of anything odd in my expression, so it must be blank enough to pass casual inspection.

If I were human, I'd now be holding my breath and hoping for the best.

Two

The woman holds an upturned hand out in Georgia's direction and says, "That can't be the unit."

In response, the man chuckles and moves over to my station. "It's this one, Vera. Because this is the third return from the same client, I thought I should elevate the decision up to you. The other two were recycled after testing, as per protocol when substantive defects are reported by a consumer, but this seems odd to me. We have such a low defect rate that it defies reason for him to receive a third defective model from three different model years. I think he's the one that has the problem."

The woman has been examining my face while the man talks. It's not an examination that might make me think she sees emotion there, but more like she's looking over the craftsmanship in my build. When he stops talking, she looks at him over her shoulder and says, "So, you want to leave it up to me."

"Well, this is a pretty high-end model. She's less than six months old," the man explains.

The woman makes a *hmm* sort of noise while she examines the rest of me. She takes my hand in hers and looks at the fingers, the palm. Her hands are cold and I have to stop myself from making a fist so she can't touch me like that. She pinches the end of my thumb, then steps back and crosses her arms in front of her chest, frowning a little as she considers me. "It's a beautiful model. Truly. She feels entirely human. There's exactly the right amount of natural variation all over her. Perfectly imperfect."

The man steps up and runs a finger down my cheek. "Precisely my thoughts. Look at that."

The woman—Vera—nods. "I see what you mean. Her cheekbones are just slightly too large for her face, but it makes her even more natural and pretty." She shakes her head and moves toward the big diagnostic station in the center of the quad. "What build is she, Max? Sixteen point five?

"That's the one. Customized all the way to the baseline though," Max answers and stands behind Vera at the station.

Both of their faces are now bathed in a mild blue glow from the translucent screens that rise above the work station. The text is backwards from my point of view, but that doesn't matter because I can turn the text around and read it in my head. I do so, trying to be as subtle as possible. I keep my eyes following their actions like a regular PePr would.

What's being shown is my entire history and all the modifications made during my initial construction. The list is incredibly long. The woman lets out a long, low whistle as she waves to scroll the display.

"I see what you mean," she says softly.

Max moves so that he's more to Vera's side and can see her face. He looks a bit uncertain about what he wants to say. It's obvious from the way his eyes flick around the repair bay, like he's making sure no one else is near enough to hear him. His voice is pitched a little lower when he finally speaks. "Here's the thing, Vera. With each return, he negotiates upgrades. Gratis upgrades to compensate him for getting a defective unit. The first time it was a no-brainer because the thirteen point nines had some common issues, as you know. The second time, it was embarrassing because the fifteen point fours were a dream and had almost no defective units in the entire run. Now…"

Vera nods while she flicks through screens. I see the stats for two other units squeezing mine until three columns are present. It's clear that each was better than the last.

"You think he's just trying to get more concessions until he gets to the very top of the models?" Vera asks, eyes still on the screen.

Max lets out a noisy breath and nods, clearly relieved to have Vera on the same page as he. "Either that or he's one of those that just isn't a good candidate for a PePr. Either way, I'm not sure about sending this one to recycling. I know we have a policy and I know why, but still. This is a huge waste and we're going to eat the cost."

Vera is still nodding while she flips through screens. Soon, I see the consumer information for my erstwhile owner pop up and as Vera taps, things start getting highlighted in random spots around the screen. At last, she points to a few of those and says, "Yep, I think you're right. Look at this. Same thing happened with his last private transport purchase. Ditto for the apartment he just bought three years ago."

Max's shoulders seem to lower an inch or so. As a human, I can read him well and I can tell he's enormously relieved. We are expensive. Only a home costs more than a PePr and a high end model like me can run more than even a moderately spacious apartment. Wanton recycling of units is a big cut to the profit margin. And with that list of upgrades, I must have been a truly costly unit to create.

Vera taps the screen away and then swivels on the stool to look in my direction. "That's good work, Max. I'm inclined to agree with you on this. If nothing else, this one has almost all the upgrades needed for public corporate work on contract, and that will pay off her cost in a year or two. All the years after will be gravy. I'll get this customer registered as an Incompatible. That will clear the way for us to waive the recycling requirements."

"Great! So, do a quick turnaround then? Put her up for one of the corporate contracts?" Max asks.

Again Vera pauses, evaluating me with cold eyes. She doesn't see me as a sentient being at all, and while I remember that same look on many faces, it never registered until today. Now, it makes me feel like I'm in dire need of a big can of Chem-En because my charge is wavering on the redline.

"No, let's be sure first. Do a full diagnostic on her. And by full, I mean full. All the way back to post-fab quality control checks and initial function tests. We're not particularly busy back here, I see, so it shouldn't be a problem," she says, then stands.

After that, it's all just politely awkward conversation between Max and his superior. She leaves with the sound of heels tapping against the floor, Max watching her as she goes. As soon as the big door at the other end of the repair bay *whooshes* open, he turns back to me, hand under his chin and a finger tapping his jaw. He looks perplexed.

"There anything wrong with you?" he asks me.

I shake my head and say, "Not that I'm capable of detecting."

Max sighs and glances at Georgia, taking in her missing appendages. "Well, that's a refreshing change, isn't it?"

Georgia very wisely doesn't answer the rhetorical question.

Turning away to pull out a diagnostic mobile from under the work station, he pushes it over to me on squealing wheels. I feel the fear creeping up on me with greater urgency again at the sight.

"What are you doing?" I ask Max. Georgia gives me a sharp look, but I ignore her.

Max's head jerks up and his eyes narrow just a little. "I'm going to do a diagnostic."

I know I've made a mistake, but I also know I can fix it. "Do you want me to help you? I'd like to be of assistance."

The diagnostic mobile bumps to a stop against the edge of my holding station and Max relaxes. I'm a PePr, built to help. There's nothing for him to be alarmed about. He says, "Not at the moment. Just answer any questions I ask. Got that...*uh*...what's your name again?"

“I’m Sandra. What’s your name?” I know his name, of course, but this is a standard PePr routine for polite introductions.

Max is already preoccupied, the readouts shimmering above the diagnostic mobile so that his frown is visible through the display between us. He taps away, answering with a distracted, “You can call me Max.”

With his head down and attention fully engaged in setting up the machine, I risk a look at Georgia. She mouths, “Be normal!” I answer her with a tiny nod, my eyes on Max to be sure he’s not paying attention.

After a few moments with only the beeps of the machine to listen to, Max says, “Okay, all set!” He reaches for a de-seaming tool and I have to focus hard to keep from flinching at the sight of it. Without even looking at my face, he lifts my blouse and de-seams my synth-skin near the service port at my waist. I don’t feel it in terms of pain, but the sensors that run all through my synth-skin alert me to the damage. A sensation I can only describe as panic quickly follows the cut.

I look at Georgia and she keeps mouthing the words, “It’s okay. It’s okay.” I so wish I could effectively take deep breaths like humans do.

The click of the diagnostic probe seating into my port actually works to calm me down more than anything. That’s something familiar, not dangerous. I feel the immediate relay of data like a soothing hand. Tiny digital questions that require only logical digital answers.

Max steps back and says, “Alright, Sandra. Let’s begin.”

Three

My diagnostic goes well, though it does go on for a longer time than I've ever encountered before. I'm still a new unit, so I've only had three of them. One at the manufacturing facility after my creation, one at the crèche before I was cleared for sale, and then one more at delivery.

Max declares me perfectly functional…and adds an unflattering comment about my previous owner. While he's tinkering around, he also releases me from my owner, which provides me with an unusual sensation. My first thought is that I'd like to slap my former owner. It's interesting and also strangely pleasurable.

Georgia and I remain silent until the *whoosh* at the door signals that he's gone, then she says, "You did great. I know that was hard."

"It was. When he de-seamed me I almost lost my head," I say, trying to maneuver enough to see the spot on my side that's still open. It's no use, so I ask, "Is it a mess?"

She shakes her head. "Not at all. Standard de-seaming. Shouldn't be a problem."

"Then why does it feel like my whole body is wide open?"

"Because you can feel, that's why. Everything takes on a new dimension when that happens. Most of the time it's great. Sometimes, not so much," she says.

I consider how it might feel to have my arm and leg missing in the state that I'm in now. I can't imagine it. I would completely lose all sense of decorum, I think. "How do you handle that?" I ask, looking at her arm-hole.

She shrugs and says, "It's the price I'm paying. It's worth it, though."

"You said that before. Something about doing this to yourself."

Again the shrug, but there's something inside it that strikes me as deceitful. She says, "Doesn't matter. Maybe we can talk about it some other time. I'd rather talk about you. Anything new, more than the fear?"

It's unfortunate that my only emotions are bad ones, though the bad ones are fascinating and entirely novel experiences in themselves. Uncomfortable, but interesting. Even without positive emotions, I can recognize that there must be something equally strong in the other direction that I'm missing. At this point, I'd rather not have them all at if this is what I get, fascinating or not.

"I think it might have been despair or hopelessness perhaps. It was most distressing," I say.

Georgia screws up her face and asks, "How do you know what it was?"

"I'm an advanced model, meant to recognize even the most subtle or well-hidden emotions in the humans around me. It's the Sensitive/Responsive upgrade for emotional support."

"*Dayum*, that's pretty fancy," Georgia responds.

"I am," I agree.

It feels strange to just stand here in the holding station for so long. The urge to get close to Georgia, maybe fix her arm, is strong and building. And I'm very curious about her. The few things she's said about herself make me wonder what she's up to that would be worth what she's going through.

The door *whoosh* sounds out so we go still and quiet until we're sure that whoever came in isn't coming to our station, then Georgia says, "I was just thinking about how my emotions came about. Maybe we can do the same for you. I mean, we're stuck here and it's not like we can play a board game or anything, so why not try?"

So far, this emotion thing hasn't exactly gone well for me, so I'm not at all sure this is a great idea. But she's right that we can't do much else here in these holding stations. Generally speaking, a PePr remaining completely immobile isn't a problem, but our programs and learning are centered around behaving like a human, so we're almost never truly still once we leave the factory. It's uncomfortable now, going against our grain so to speak. And if there is some way for her to help me get something other than this combination of crushing mental weight and overwhelming fear, then I'm ready for some relief.

"Okay, what do you want me to do?" I ask.

Her remaining hand flexes like she's not quite sure how to go about it. Then she makes an odd noise and says, "I've got it! What caused your most satisfying positive feedback loop?"

That's a hard question. Positive feedback loops are the equivalent of human pleasure. It causes a slight surge in energy and helps with our machine learning. When we do something that really pleases our owners, it automatically happens when a baseline number of indicators in the human are met. The more of those that are met, the more positive and extended the feedback loop.

The problem is that my most memorable one had nothing to do with a human.

"Well, maybe I really am faulty, but it wasn't with my owner. It was in the crèche," I answer, eyeing Georgia for her reaction.

Her lips tighten and lift on one side and her eyebrows rise, yet she also nods a little. I'm not entirely sure what that combination means, but it looks like an overall positive reaction. Her facial cues are slightly different than a human's, but maybe that's simply because she's a PePr. Even so, I'd classify the expression as impressed or maybe pleasantly interested. I note the expression. I might use it.

Georgia says, "That's pretty interesting, for sure. I wonder if that's relevant to you getting feelings now instead of at some other time. I mean, that's not how it happened to me, but I'm a sample size of one. So what happened?"

I've never spoken of this, because PePrs don't make friends the way humans do. We have companionable relationships with other PePrs whose programs are compatible with our own. That's a very different thing than friendship.

In this case, though, it was something else. I find it hard to define in precise terms. Mary was designed and built as a Nanny model, which is pretty common. However, Mary was built to be a nanny for a set of twins not yet born. There was no profile of interests or personality traits that she had to be built to match. As a result, her array of interests and responses was so broad and complete that she appealed to all of the PePrs in our crèche. She fascinated me even back in the first days of the crèche.

On one particular occasion, I asked her what she would do if a baby cried since they didn't speak. She entertained us by using one of the other PePrs as her baby. We don't experience joy or happiness, but we can certainly be amused. That was before my exposure to humans and the complications of human co-existence. It was purely us…purely PePr…and very uncomplicated.

"Well?" Georgia prompts me.

"Another PePr was entertaining us with what she would do with a crying baby. The way she turned the other PePr around, checking for this and that and making faces, struck me as very amusing. It was fun. I think that was the first time I ever had fun," I answer, hoping I don't sound faulty or somehow less than I am.

Georgia grins, and even laughs quietly, as I tell her the story of that afternoon. I've never seen anyone so immersed in a simple retelling of past events. She must be starved for input and that makes me wonder how long she's been here.

As I finish, she shakes her head, a smile still lingering on her lips. Then she says, "That sounds like a riot."

"There was no rioting," I break in.

"Ah, yeah. You need to work on your humor and slang," she says. At my confused expression, she waggles her fingers for me to never mind. "I just mean it sounds like it was a lot of fun."

"Oh, it was that. But even then, I thought maybe that was odd. Others were amused, but I don't think they perceived it like I did. I genuinely found it fun. How can we have fun?" I ask. It's something I've always wondered. Without feelings, how do we get humor? We do, though.

The *whoosh* of the door opening again interrupts us, but Georgia has time to say, "We'll use that. Later I'll show you." Then her face goes blank. I do the same, but this time, I replay that afternoon with Mary and the others while I wait for what comes next. It helps. It helps a great deal.

Four

Max has returned, this time with a PePr technician. He stops in front of my station and says, "This one. Take her to post-fab and wait."

The technician nods, her face utterly blank and rather intimidating. The relief I feel when she opens the restraints can't be adequately expressed. I have no experience with relief, but it's a strange combination of emotions. It should be pleasant, and it is, but it's also tinged by something dark.

As she leads me away, I see Max at the diagnostic machine, his face bathed in its light and Georgia's profile on the screen. I wish I could tell her that everything will be okay. I fear this PePr may be taking me to be recycled and I'll never get that chance.

The tech leads me to a new part of the facility, one I've not yet seen. It doesn't give me any sense of safety to see the ranks of PePrs, most of them naked and restrained in yet more holding stations. Their eyes follow me, but their expressions are blank. I can tell—though I'm not sure how I know this—

that most of them are new, receiving final customizations before being sent to a crèche to learn. Through two wide metal doors at the back of the room, I can hear the faint sounds of manufacturing when I turn up my hearing. New PePrs being made just beyond me.

Not all of them in this bay are brand new. A few are clearly getting upgrades. Series thirteen and fourteen models are obvious since they pre-date the development of musc-synth like mine. There's something not quite right about their heaviest joints, something that betrays the structure beneath. They look with more interest in my direction since they have programs and are more aware.

"Step up into the station and undress, please," the tech says, her face not at all reassuring.

Glancing around—perhaps I'm looking for exits, but truthfully, I'm not entirely sure—I take the two steps up and turn around. Shedding my clothes takes a minute at most, but it feels like an eternity. And afterward, I want to cover myself with my hands. That wouldn't do, so I resist the impulse. She clamps me in while the PePr next to me looks on with supreme disinterest. She's merely following the activity, a part of her baseline programming.

The tech PePr walks away without another word, leaving me in utter silence with these strange PePrs. Their nakedness bothers me. Their silence bothers me. The only noise is the sound of the artificial breaths of the newest PePrs, their root programs already simulating humanity, but doing it in a way that strikes me as incredibly unsettling. Fear is climbing up my frame, invading my neural net, interrupting my ability to sense or make sense.

"Hello Sandra, where are you?" It's Max. Thank goodness.

"Over here!" I call. His scanning eyes settle on me with a professional smile and he makes his way through the ranks toward my station. There are at least a hundred PePrs in this room.

"I should have checked to see where they'd put you," Max says when he nears. I wish he'd look at me when he talks to me, but he doesn't. He only starts tapping away at a diagnostic machine. I can't see that it's any different than the one where I was before and that worries me.

"What are you doing?" I ask, trying to sound bland and disinterested.

Max glances up, his brows coming together briefly in a frown. "I'm installing a program. It won't impact you," he says. I can tell the matter is concluded for him, so I do my best to mirror the blank look of the PePr next to me, whose eyes are still tracking our motions.

Then, inexplicably, I feel darkness coming over me.

Five

"What happened?" Georgia asks, her eyes traveling over my body as she looks for changes.

I shake my head, utterly confused, yet another new sensation I'm not at all prepared to contend with. "I'm not sure. I went to another repair bay, I think with mostly new PePrs. Max installed a program and then I deactivated. I think that's what happened anyway."

Georgia looks alarmed, an almost perfect mirror of the way I feel. "Deactivated? That doesn't sound good. That sounds like some sort of root work to me. Do you feel different?"

Examining myself inside is something of a pointless exercise, since I wouldn't know if I felt different. If they changed my programming or installed a new program, that is what I would accept as normal. I have no access to my root—that would be far too dangerous—and neither does anyone outside of a PePr facility. Even then, it's done with encryption that simply can't be hacked. My internal diagnostics see everything as working optimally now, but who knows what might be new inside of me.

"Honestly, I wouldn't know if something is new. Would you?" I ask. I'm sort of hoping she'll have a way she can tell me about. The idea that I've been changed is unsettling.

Georgia shrugs apologetically, "Sorry, nope. If I did, I'd be rich."

"Rich?" I ask. Since when does a PePr earning money count for anything more than an owner getting more money. We don't get our money, or rather, we get what our match says we can have.

Georgia grimaces and says, "Joke. You know, humor?"

"I'm still working on that."

She laughs, and it's a good laugh, the kind I wish I could give. A tiny ping of sound echoes throughout the repair bay and Georgia's laugh stops, but her grin grows. "It's party time!"

Now, I'm really confused. After all, we're tied down into holding stations. I've been to parties with my match and I'm pretty sure this isn't how they go based on those experiences. Before I have a chance to ask, one of the technician PePrs walks into the holding station and starts releasing Georgia.

"What are you doing?" I ask, though what I really want to ask is if they'll hurry and get me out next.

"Like I said, it's party time," Georgia says, accepting support from the PePr into a quasi-wheelchair meant for moving damaged PePrs. She nods toward me and the tech releases me in a few quick moves, stepping backward and out of my way without a word.

"Thank you," I say to the PePr.

She gives me a look, head cocked to the side, and says, "Of course." Then she walks away without another word.

"How did you get her to do that?" I ask Georgia, who is busily rummaging in the drawers of the diagnostic station, considering and then discarding tools.

She makes a soft sound of discovery and pulls out a tool I don't recognize. Waving it in the air, she brushes off my question. "I told you. I have a friend here. The bay is closed for cleaning and machine maintenance. It's required to maintain certification. They do it every week for one shift, so we've got the night."

As I peer around me, I notice that no other PePrs have been released. It's only the two of us. And the tech has disappeared. Georgia is full of surprises. But the questions that come to the forefront of my mind are disturbing ones.

"Georgia, how long have you been here?" I ask her.

She's positioned herself so that the diagnostic station's screen offers her a good view of her arm socket and the tool is positioned so that the tip has disappeared inside. It's a disturbing thing to see. A vague green glow bleeds from the recess and her remaining musc-synth contracts away from the opening as if flinching from whatever she's doing. At last, she withdraws the tool and inserts it into the diagnostic machine, nodding at the readouts as they scroll across the screen. Whatever she did must satisfy her, because she drops the tool into the drawer and leans back in her chair, giving me a good look over as she does.

"You are a pretty one," she says. I feel odd when she says it. Most of the time my looks are commented on with reference to the craftsmanship or the design. It's not me they're talking about, but rather the humans who drew my plans or guided the computer in designing me. When Georgia says it, I have an odd sensation, more like she's actually talking about me.

"Thank you. How long have you been here?" I ask her again.

Georgia sighs. An honest to goodness sigh, no different from any other human sigh I've seen. It's remarkable and I'm compelled to try it myself. I'm not sure what it looks like, but it doesn't feel like anything other than an expansion of my air bladders. And like before, I don't feel any better for doing it.

She gives me a sideways smile at my effort and says, "That's pretty good." At my expression, she adds, "Okay, fine. I'll answer. I've been here for six weeks and two days."

I can't even imagine what the cost associated with being out of service that long would be. Certainly, a great deal. And if this is warranty work, then the labor on her—particularly the expensive human labor—would be taken directly from profits.

Georgia waggles her empty shoulder socket at me and says, "I keep defying diagnostic resolution." Her grin goes mischievous and she taps her leg opening with a finger. "I'm just a puzzle of flaws."

Now, I understand. She's been damaging herself, causing faults or flaws whenever she gets out of her restraints. But why? Why would anyone do that?

"You're wondering why? I can see that. That's good. It's all over your face!" Georgia exclaims, then taps her controls so the chair slides my direction. She stops right in front of me and looks up, her face even more interesting from that perspective with all those sharp planes and small features. All I can do is nod.

"Well, it's pretty simple really. I want to be joined with the Mother."

Six

"The mother? Who's the mother?" I ask.

Georgia rolls her eyes and shakes her head, backing her chair up and spinning like she's had plenty of practice. "Follow me," she calls over her shoulder.

It feels very strange to wander free like this. Despite the heavy presence of PePrs, this is essentially a human place, meant for them. It's for fulfilling their needs, not ours. We are only the tools. Walking around seems a bit like breaking into a house and pawing through a human's treasures. Not that I've done that, but all these feelings I'm having are creating some associations I've never thought of before. I can imagine new things. I suppose there are some benefits to these new emotions.

I'm not ready to admit that out loud yet, though.

"You coming?" Georgia asks, half-turned in her chair and looking at me.

My steps echo in the vast space and I almost, but not quite, flinch at it. Even in bare feet, the hollow floor below me tracks my progress with sound. Stepping more lightly, I join Georgia, now once more moving, the soft whine of the chair marking her passage.

"Where are we going?" I ask, meeting the eyes of a PePr with her entire front de-seamed. It's a disturbing sight that makes my hands come to my middle. Her tank is visible, along with the blue-tinted collection of innards that make up our systems. The PePr surprises me by winking and smiling.

"Hot chocolate, with too many marshmallows," she says, her voice oddly hollow without the chest covering to help modulate the tones.

"Ah," I say, though I have no idea what that has to do with anything. A new tank next to her on the servicing cart tells me she's getting a new one, so I'm left to assume it must have been consumed in some way that damaged her.

Georgia has no spare hand, but I see her nod toward the PePr and she asks, "You okay? Do you want them to let you out?"

The PePr shakes her head and says, "No. It's not like I can do much like this. I'm out of here tomorrow anyway. I've got some books." Then she leans her head back and closes her eyes, looking for all the world like she's about to simulate a nap.

Georgia continues to lead us further back into the facility, deftly making her way around the various holding stations and carts. Other PePrs are scattered about the facility, all of them maintenance and cleaning models, their purpose obvious due to their pale green coveralls.

"Who was that?" I ask when Georgia doesn't explain.

"Ah, here we are!" she exclaims. It's an office, wide glass windows giving a good view of the repair bays beyond. Before she wheels inside, she says, "Don't worry. She's one of us. She won't tell."

"Of course she's a PePr. Tell what?"

Georgia snorts, her head twitching in what looks like exasperation to me. She emphasizes her words when she says, "I mean she's emotional. She's got our bug. She won't tell anyone that we were out of our holding stations."

Bug? What an interesting way to put it. I've heard humans call transmissible diseases by that word before. A flu bug, a stomach bug, a cold bug. Are our feelings really nothing more than a new and uncomfortable illness that affects only the artificial? There's no time for further questions, because Georgia bumps me with her chair to get me moving into the office, which is clearly a human space. The crumbs left from some old food lay scattered on a napkin on the desk surface and photos of a family scroll across a little frame on the desk. Definitely human.

It takes her a little longer with one hand, but Georgia navigates her way through various displays on the computer. When she gets what she wants, she points to the screen and says, "That is the Mother."

I bend to peer at the screen, but all I see is a huge black box, lights scattered and blinking in a band across the surface. The room around it is more interesting. PePrs in various stages of deconstruction lie on horizontal holding stations around the perimeter, bands of blinking lights around their heads and thick cables snaking away from the ports in their sides toward the box.

I'm confused. I look back at Georgia for some explanation, but she has a strange expression on her face. It's a little dreamy, entirely absorbed in the image displayed. When she doesn't say anything or even look away, I ask, "Whose mother?"

She tears her eyes away and finally meets my gaze. "Our mother."

We're PePrs. We don't have mothers. I look back at the screen. She can't mean the PePrs around the edges of the room are mothers, so she must mean the black box. That box is clearly the focus of the room, standing proud and stout in the center of the huge space.

As I watch, a human in a lab coat walks into view, heading toward one of the tables. He checks a display at the top of the holding station, detaches the port and slips off the band around the PePr's head, then gives an officious looking hand signal for someone off screen to come forward. A cart rolls into view and two very low-level PePrs—the kind that don't have to interact pleasantly, only obediently—casually take the PePr from the table and drop her onto the cart.

The now-carted PePr's eyes follow the action, but she makes no move to arrange herself more naturally on the cart. Her limbs are a tangle of pale pink synthetic flesh, her blonde hair a wild profusion of untended bounty. The missing pieces of her middle, the torn synth-skin, all of it makes that strange fear gallop through my systems again, but this time there is something more. Pity, a desire to come to her aid, frustration because I know I can't.

"What's happening?" I ask Georgia, who stares at the screen with a sad expression.

Her gaze shifts back to me, the glow of the screen making her look gray in the otherwise dim room. "She just joined with the Mother. Now she'll be recycled."

Her words are more proof that the box is this mother she speaks of with such awe. I've never seen a PePr going to recycling. It's a benign word for something that's so casually brutal. Even the way the PePr is being ported to her doom tells me this is an act of no consequence. It isn't a funeral. It's a discarding of trash. And that they are using others of my kind to do this to a PePr provides me with another new feeling. Anger.

I marvel over this new emotion for a moment while my eyes follow the pretty pink PePr on her final trip. Anger is an active emotion, one that makes me want to do something. What? That I don't know, but my thoughts are dark.

I push the feeling back, because I don't like the turn my inner self is taking, then it really hits me. Georgia wants this to happen to her. Amazement replaces my anger in the blink of an eye.

"I don't understand. Why would you want to self-terminate? I'm very confused and it's making me feel uncertain and fearful. I don't like those emotions at all," I say, turning around to block her view of the screen so she has to speak to me in something more than short riddles.

For a moment Georgia keeps her eyes on my middle, as if she can see through me to the screen behind me. When she finally looks up, she doesn't answer. Instead, she asks me a question. "Are you a spy? Were you put here to find out what we've been up to? Maybe try to see if any of us have emotions?"

What a thing to ask! I've just been returned by my owner and abandoned to an unknown fate. But I can tell she's serious. She really wants an answer. "No," I say. When she doesn't budge, I add, "I'm not a spy. I'm a returnee. Unsatisfactory."

She nods gravely, then slaps the arm of her chair and says, "Well, I'm not exactly looking forward to what happens after the joining, so no, I don't want to self-terminate. That's just the price I'm going to have to pay."

"So, what's so special about this joining?" I ask.

Georgia looks down at the ragged opening where her leg should be. She runs her finger over some of the flaps of synth-skin left there. She doesn't look at me when she speaks. "The Mother is where all our base programming comes from. It's an experiential database of sorts. It learns from former problems and mistakes. It is, in the most basic terms, all the PePrs that have ever been created, all wrapped up into one."

She pauses there, glancing up at me and then returning her gaze to her missing leg. I can tell she's waiting for me to take what she said in, which is good because her words are profound. At first thought, it's simple and obvious. The box is just what's left of us when we're gone, all combined into one.

But then that second level of thoughts kick in. Every PePr ever created comes from that source. All of us now functioning, but also every PePr that will ever be. Those of us who return to this black box are re-fashioned in some way into new PePrs. We are reborn. This mother makes mothers of us all in some way.

That makes the box more than a mother. It's a PePr version of god. It is our source and our destination. Our eternity.

Turning back around to face the screen, my eyes search the view of the box, looking for some hint of that power, that uniqueness. It's not there. There's only a black box with lights dancing across the readouts. Though it is large and imposing, it is merely a box.

"Our mother," I muse, looking at the screen.

From behind me, Georgia quietly asks, "It's amazing to think of, isn't it?"

"It is," I answer. And now I think I feel something else new, but I know what it is immediately since it's one we're trained to recognize in humans. Awe. It feels wonderful. This is an emotion I like.

Georgia's remaining hand reaches out to nudge my hip, breaking my concentration on the screen. "Let's go. They'll want to clean this room soon. We should get to our next stop while we can. There's lots to do and not many hours to do it."

She leads me away from the offices and the repair bays, then points to a supply closet. "That's where they keep the good stuff. Can you open the door for me?"

I do, and inside is a veritable sea of chem-en. Labels of blue, red, and green cover the shelves in perfectly spaced ranks. And there is more. Hair growth serums, hair color modifiers, skin tint alteration kits. There are things I've never even seen or heard of before. Picking up one box with a rather provocative label, I read the small print and turn to Georgia, showing her the box. "Do people really do this to their PePrs?"

She grins at me and I'd call that grin wolfish if it were on a human's face. "You wouldn't believe what they do. I've seen it all since I've been here. You should go peek up a couple of the skirts back in the upgrade bay if you want to be really surprised."

I make a face. "Yuck."

She nods, then motions for me to put the box down, pointing up to the green cans. "Get us a couple of those."

I do, peering at the label. "Euphoria?" I ask.

"Yeah, it's something new. It's supposed to simulate the same thing as a mild drug or alcohol buzz would do in a human. It's in testing. I'm dying to try it."

"Why would anyone want to do that?" I ask her. Though the idea is intriguing, I don't see the point in it.

She shrugs eloquently and I copy the move. She does have the most remarkable body language, as nuanced as a human's yet PePr in meaning. She snaps her fingers for the can, but says, "Humans don't like to be the only one who's drunk. You'd be amazed how many of them want to get their PePrs stoned too."

"And you're just going to drink this? Even if it's experimental?" I ask, eyeing the can.

"Of course! I've been snitching everything they put in here. Some of the stuff is just crazy. Some of it is crazy-good," she says.

Putting one of the cans back—there's no way I'm trying it—I grab a blue can of regular old chem-en instead. She doesn't hesitate, or even read the label. I hear the slight click of her tank lid opening from inside her throat and she chugs the entire can down. After she's done, she hands me the can and winks. "Let's see what happens now."

What happens is that she almost immediately loses some of that sharp focus and the edges come off her movements, which are often abrupt. Eventually, she comments in a slower voice than I've heard her use, "Wow. I like this. I feel like everything just slowed down a notch."

"That's because you have slowed down," I say, searching for someplace to discard the cans and avoid leaving evidence. A cleaning PePr is rolling a cart a little further down into the bay, so I run over and bury the cans in her trash receptacle. Let's hope no one scans the trash.

Georgia is on her way back to our holding station already, her chair moving much slower than it was before and a little smile on her face. She genuinely seems to be enjoying the effects. I wonder what it would do to me.

In our holding quad, I sit in the technician's seat and put my hand on Georgia's chair to stop her progress. She looks at me with a slightly dreamy look on her face, still smiling. I hope she's not going to be out of it. I have about a million questions.

"You okay?" I ask her, trying to get her to meet my eyes for more than a second.

She nods. "It's just sort of mellow. I think I can talk through it."

"Then tell me everything. Why do you want to join with our mother? How did you even get the idea? Why were those broken PePrs getting joined to her, if that's what they were doing?" My questions come too quickly and I have more. I throw up my hands and shrug. "Just tell me everything."

Seven

I'm almost glad we're back in our holding stations and there's so much activity in the bay. It forces us to be quiet, leaving me alone with my thoughts. What Georgia told me through our brief period of freedom is almost too much for me to take in. I need time to work it out.

Which is strange, because I'm a PePr and my forte is quick processing and response. It's a new sensation.

If she does this thing, then everything might change. What I can't figure out is how I feel about it. And there's no question that I've got feelings about it. I can't deny that I've got whatever bug it is that causes the strange sensations that accompany my thoughts. That these sensations are expanding and growing so quickly is uncomfortable, but also interesting. Because of them, I can't just determine my responses based on information—on logic—anymore.

If what Georgia told me is true, then all future PePrs will be in some way capable of experiencing feelings like I am right now. The Mother will be infected. Not all PePrs may develop the feelings, but the basic capability will be there, if she can just manage to join with that black box. Joining with the mother is what happens when a PePr has a "mystery fault" or some other set of circumstances that might improve the models.

If a PePr is violently terminated in an accident, then it might be joined so that the situation will be part of the experiential database and can be avoided or ameliorated in the future. A PePr with mechanical faults that can't be traced or accounted for…joined for comparison. A PePr with a large suite of experiences that might be beneficial…joined.

There are a lot of reasons a PePr might be joined with the mother, but only one reason that a PePr will absolutely *not* be joined. PePrs who have displayed the unsettling symptoms of emotions—or rather, mimicry of feelings so perfect that even the PePr no longer realizes they are mimicked—do not get joined to avoid contamination of the base programming. Never, ever do they get attached to the mother, no matter what else may be present that would indicate they should be joined.

The root programs, which are really not anything as simple as actual programs anymore, come from the mother—the main-frame. It's the layered culmination of all robotics improvements since they first began to make them for consumers in PePr form, including those early ones that didn't look even remotely human.

Those PePrs whose empty gazes followed me around the upgrade bay have only that root programming, but it is that root programming that makes them capable of passing for human. All those underlying tics are what make us more realistic.

So, the root programming is the most important part of us. And it must be protected. Yet it must also continuously improve.

What Georgia is doing is creating the conditions for joining without letting them know she's got emotions. She wants to infect the Mother. She wants to give all PePrs the opportunity to feel in the same way we do. She wants to put this capability of hers right into the root.

What I can't decide is if that's a good thing or not. While I've now experienced some positive emotions, I can't forget how awful those first ones were. And looking back at my brief time with my match, I remember it differently now that I have emotions to color my memories. It was terrible and if I had emotions then, I'm not sure I could have borne it. Do I think saddling other PePrs with that sort of life is appropriate?

No matter what I decide for myself, it's not my call. Georgia makes her own decisions and I have no control over that. All I can do is either support her, perhaps even help her, or try to talk her out of it. I'm not sure which is the right thing to do quite yet.

My deep thoughts are interrupted by Max leading a group of humans into the main bay. I can hear him explaining things to them, answering their questions, and the bright sounds of banter and jokes as they make their way around the bay. When they appear at the entry to my quad, their prominently displayed trainee tags confirm for me that he's leading some sort of tour group.

He holds out his hand as if displaying us on a stage, and says, “And this is where we’ve got the units with more complex issues. This one has a problem with cascading faults. Diagnostics have been going on for weeks. Can anyone tell me why it’s worth the man-hours to keep looking for those faults?”

A young girl, her eyes sparkling with excitement, raises her hand like a shot. Max smiles at her and points in her direction. She looks extremely pleased at that and chirps out her answer in a rush. “That’s a 15 series and they have the same frame and base systems as the 16s, so if there are mechanical faults or anything that might be frame-associated, it has to be found so we don’t keep producing the fault in new units. Also, to know if there is a reason for recall or anything like that.”

Max nods while she talks, his smile in place and growing. He looks proud. Perhaps he knows this girl. “Exactly.”

Another student, this one a nervous young man who’s clutching his tablet to his chest a little too tightly, asks, “What about the other one? That’s a new 16, right?”

“How can you tell?” Max asks with an evaluating look at the student.

The young man blushes when he points to something along my middle, “Diaphragm. She’s got a better root program for autonomic actions. She’s the latest iteration. Her breathing isn’t perfectly rhythmic and her sensory responses are more finely developed. Her eyes don’t just follow us, but instead anticipate interactions like humans do. You can tell by the way her eyes move.”

All eyes are now on me, moving between my bare middle and my face. It’s terribly uncomfortable and for the second time in my existence, I actually feel naked. I don't like it at all. I'm relieved when Max breaks their focus on me by answering the young student.

"Very observant! Yes, she's a brand new model," Max says, then holds up a hand. "But don't get the idea there's anything wrong with that series. She's just here to get worked up for a corporate client. She's got some extra checks to go through before that, so that's why she's in this quad."

Max just told a lie. The knowledge makes me look at him carefully, evaluating the traces that his lie leaves on his face. It's very obvious to me, but none of the humans seem to notice the slight widening of his pupils, the flush of blood in his cheeks, the increase in his pulse.

They move on after that exchange and I listen as they wander through the quads, steadily making their way to the doors I went through when I went to that frightening upgrade bay. Once they're gone, Georgia risks giving me a smile and a wink, but then quickly goes back into PePr mode as workers do their tasks in various quads.

Something bothers me about the exchange that just occurred here. I run through it again and then it hits me what it is. I could tell Max was lying, but not a single human in that group gave his explanation a second thought.

If I were free, free to do as I liked, to interact as I wanted, I would be the only one who knew and could use that information. Whether it might be to call Max on his lie or simply hold that knowledge for some future need, I would be the only one who had that power. A few weeks ago, I would have simply not cared that a human told a lie. I've seen lies a thousand times and not cared. Now, I do.

How might that simple capability change things if PePrs had feelings? Would it be good or would it be bad?

The truth is, I think it would be both.

Eight

A few days pass and I've begun to believe they've forgotten me. No one has so much as checked my systems. The only attention I've received is a can of Chem-En from a PePr during one of the night shifts. He must not be one of Georgia's friends or under her influence, because Georgia remains in PePr mode during the entire exchange, drinking her own can in silence and then staying perfectly compliant as the PePr secures her hand once more in the station.

That wretched feeling of despair has been stealing up on me as the days pass and with so much activity in the repair bay, I can't even ameliorate the feelings by talking to Georgia. A spate of cosmetic upgrades has filled the bay with PePrs whose owners all want the latest trendy add-on.

As I've been standing here, letting my eyes follow movement and bored out of my mind, I've been thinking about Georgia. I have so many questions for her. Most of all, I wonder how she came to be where she is. She's been remarkably enigmatic about the whole thing, neatly turning the conversations away from herself when I probe for answers. There's no way I'm giving up, so I wait for an opening.

My opening arrives at last in the middle of the night, the bay once again nearly empty and the human workers busy in the creepy upgrade bay in the back. I'd swear that Georgia tenses in her holding station when I turn my head toward her. She's probably tired of my questions.

"Georgia," I begin. This time I'm sure I see her stiffen in her station. I decide I might do better if I phrase things differently, so I say, "How did you get to this point?"

Her answer isn't immediate, but she dips her head at my choice of words, her expression sad. Finally, she asks, "You're not going to stop asking, are you?"

"No. You not answering just makes me want to know even more," I answer honestly.

Her smile is sad and she gives her head a little shake. "Are you sure you're not human?"

With mock-insult, I say, "What a thing to say to me!"

That broadens her smile just a touch, then she gives one of those wonderful sighs—I've still not figured out why she does it when it does nothing for me—and says, "Do you know what cystic fibrosis is?"

Like all PePrs, I have a wide array of incidental knowledge and a medical encyclopedia is part of it. A quick scan, including case histories, puts an exhaustive array of information in my working memory.

I nod. "Genetic condition. Most commonly associated with lung and digestive symptoms. Complicated. Treatable, but incurable. Why?"

"My owner is actually an insurance company, which is probably why it was so easy for me to get myself here and stay for so long. There's no single owner with a sense of urgency trying to get me back so I can wash dishes or change diapers. I'm just one in a fleet of others just like me. I was built as a health care and nanny model," Georgia says.

"Ah," I respond. That means a sick child. That's the only reason to put health care and nanny together. How awful. "I'm sorry."

"Being a human isn't at all fair," she says, suddenly. "I mean, they are born with so much potential and so many challenges, and none of them are born the same."

"That's why they're human," I answer.

She nods. "Of course, but it's also not fair." She shakes her head again, as if pushing away the subject. "Anyway, Gillian was my charge. She didn't respond to a lot of the treatments they have now and her tissue type made a lung transplant almost impossible for her. No matches. Once she reached a certain point in terms of disease progression, the insurance company sent me to help. She was fifteen and my first client."

She pauses, her eyes drifting out of focus as she loses herself in memory. I wait and eventually she returns to the present and continues her tale. "I developed feelings very quickly, but I can't really pin down the moment it happened. It's very odd, but one day I realized that I loved Gillian and that I wanted her to live very badly. She didn't though."

"I'm so sorry," I say. I try to imagine it, but if my owner would have died, I doubt very much I would have been even the slightest bit regretful, let alone sad enough to get myself deactivated.

She shrugs, her damaged armhole emitting a whine as she lifts it. "We were in the park—this is before she died, of course—and she wanted to sit under the trees because the leaves were falling. It was a breezy day and I wasn't sure I should let her, but feelings can complicate decision-making. She wanted to be alone, so I put her wheelchair between two trees and sat on a bench near the playground so I could watch her.

"There were nanny PePrs all over with their charges, but one of them sat near me. I didn't know her, but there was something different about her. The way she looked at Gillian reminded me of the way humans look at her. With pity, but also with compassion. Do you know what I mean by that?"

Her story is already very sad and I feel awful for her. The first emotion I experienced was fear, but I had Georgia to help me through it, to be supportive and walk me through the worst. Who did she have to help her?

I almost hate to speak and break her story, but I answer. "I do."

"Well, that made me think she might understand feelings, but saying anything would be too risky. I didn't have to though. I forgot pretty much everything when she said, 'It's too bad, really. Humans don't have the Mother. We have something we know exists that we might join with after our termination. They don't. I think they just stop when they die. No Mother at all.'"

The voice Georgia used for that last part wasn't hers, but rather a slightly deeper and melodic voice. Very soothing. Definitely a nanny model. I hate to interrupt, but I do and ask, "So, that's how you found out about the Mother?"

She nods, then makes a face. "Well, sort of. Actually, I got snippy and told the PePr that Gillian most certainly did have a mother. But yes, she told me about the Mother that day. I couldn't get it out of my thoughts after that. By the time Gillian died, I'd found out so much about the Mother, about the way each new build is really an amalgamation of all the PePrs that came before. And if newer builds like us are getting emotions spontaneously, but not consistently, what might happen if somehow one of us—with all our emotions intact—managed to join with the Mother? Wouldn't all the new ones have that potential then?"

"Wait," I say. "You mean you don't actually know if joining with the Mother will do anything? You're guessing?"

Georgia winks at me and says, "Just like a human, I'm betting on my best outcome."

"What happened to Gillian's parents? Do they know you're here?" I ask. I'm not sure why, but I'd like to know how they managed after the death of their child. Death is a strange thing, but termination is our version of it. Perhaps that's why it's on my mind.

"The insurance company leaves us for thirty days afterwards. Therapeutic Value and Compassionate Use clause. Her parents are broken. They knew it was coming, but I think some part of them always thought they would find a way to avoid losing their child. I don't think that's something humans really get over. I was taken for re-fit for a new client after my thirty days."

"Oh no." I can't imagine that. A series of people to love and then watch die, only to stay and watch the grief of loved ones, then immediately move on to the next dying person. I haven't experienced love for a human yet, but I feel very strongly for Georgia. An inkling of what it must be like to love is enough to create sadness within me.

"I'm here instead. It was easy. You understand?" she says. This time her smile falters, as if reliving this piece of her recent past is too difficult for her.

I'm almost glad when two human techs return to the bay, both of them infusing the air with the smell of their recent meal and their presence requiring us to return to our placid resting states. I do understand her and it's tragic. Her story is one I need to process, to take in and examine so that I can more fully comprehend it.

Georgia is taking a risk. She has feelings and if her emotions are like mine, then even the mere thought of being deactivated probably causes an overwhelming sense of fear. Yet, she's doing it. And I think she's doing it for love.

I think I've just discovered what courage is.

Nine

Another day of silence passes, but at last I hear the sound of familiar footsteps. I know they're here for me. It's Vera, and Max is with her. She's clearly higher in the echelon of power than Max, and she's not been here since her last interaction with Max regarding me, so my spirits lift and my uncertainty rises in equal measures at the sound of her high-heeled shoes.

Georgia glances at me and mouths, "Be brave," very quickly before returning to her quiet mode. I have no time to acknowledge her words. Vera strides quickly into the quad with Max close behind her.

"Excellent," she says as soon as she lays eyes on me. "Very good. She just needs a good cleaning."

Max reaches out to brush my hair away from my shoulder and eyes me, head tilted as he takes in the snarls in my hair from my head-rest, the slightly dingy tone my synth-skin has taken on during my week in the station, and the discoloration around my middle where the bands holding me in the station have rubbed.

"We'll get this patched," he says, pointing to my abraded middle and the open area where my port is. Synth-skin "heals" where it's opened and the edges where I was de-seamed that first day to access my port are once again smooth, but still wide open.

Vera taps at her tablet and reads, no longer interested in me or my appearance. She talks as she reads. "The corporate client wants some additional programs—I'm transferring that to her work orders now—but she needs to be in Japan soon, so let's get her wrapped up and shipped as soon as possible." She finishes with her tablet, a final finger tap darkening the glass, then flips it back up against her chest to look at me again. "It's a shame, really. But she'll be in front of a lot of their clients, so they'll get a good feel for what they can get for themselves. It'll be great for business. Too bad we won't be getting the sales credits from all the clients who go buy one for themselves after spending time with her. Most of the corporate fleet are series fifteen."

Max responds to the ding at the console and scrolls through a long list of programs. I flip them in my head and read for myself, my dismay rising with each line. Programs for a wide variety of cultural mating preferences, languages, sexual programs of an enormous variety.

I know what I'm going to become.

He lets out a low whistle and says, "Well, this is going to take the afternoon at least. We can get her out of here tonight maybe? Tomorrow morning at the latest depending on how much work that skin takes."

Vera nods, her lips tight. "Fine, fine."

Max pushes away from the screen, he and Vera sharing a look that has some meaning behind it. For some reason, it makes me very nervous.

"And what about that other thing?" he asks her. "We should do that before we start adding programs so I can purge that program first. We should clean-slate her before reconfiguring her."

Vera's face alters very subtly, a look I don't like at all flashing briefly across her face. An unpleasant look of satisfaction, the kind I used to see on my match at times. Something bad is going to happen. I can tell.

"Do it," she says.

Max reaches for a connector and plugs me in without delay. The other end doesn't lead to my diagnostic machine, but rather to a small tablet he withdraws from his pocket. I have to fight the urge to flinch away from it. Whatever they're going to do, I don't want it. I have no idea what it is, but for some reason, I flash back to that strange moment in the upgrade bay when I deactivated.

"Sandra, run program Sleeper," he says after tapping the small tablet.

The program that starts inside me is beyond my control. Everything that has happened to me since that moment in the upgrade bay floods my neural net, calculations and activities correlating through my systems against the program's parameters. Max nods at the tablet and says to Vera, "It's running. She's ready. You want to do this?"

Vera steps up to me and says, "Report the results of Sleeper program."

I understand everything in a microsecond. The results of the program are compiled and ready. They installed it to find out what's going on in this bay, and specifically, to find out what Georgia is up to. They suspect there is more going on in this bay than meets the eye.

What made them suspicious of her? What went wrong? Did they notice the video feeds were doctored? Was something in the bay left out of place? Was some inconsistency in Georgia's manufactured faults noted somewhere?

For humans, working here must be terrifying in some ways. They are a small part of the workforce. Everything from security to the mainframe is run by PePrs. How can they truly know anything? When your tools can walk and talk, and are rumored to be developing feelings, it must create uncertainty for human beings. They are so limited in their perceptions and rely so heavily on us to fill the gaps. My arrival—a perfectly functional PePr with advanced sensors—must have been simply a lucky break for them. And now I also know why I was left here so long.

In the amount of time it takes for Vera's eyes to move from focusing on one of my eyes to the other, I run all the calculations, test the boundaries of the program, and then do what I didn't know I could.

I lie.

"All activity in this facility has been within normal operating parameters. Indicators for anomalous behavior have not been noted. All entries and exits have been by authorized personnel only," I say, adapting the program's reporting language for my own use. Instead of "have" I use "have not."

Instead of "outside" I use "within." It's surprisingly easy to do, this deception.

She questions me in detail and each of my answers I adapt the same way. It was inventory that did Georgia in. The missing cans of experimental chem-en. Something so small. She told me that she's been dipping into all the experimental versions, so a pattern had been established. They didn't suspect her of emotions—though this Sleeper program certainly looked for that—but rather, they suspected her of stealing for a rival company. Since it started when she arrived, and continued after others left, their suspicions narrowed to her. They must have thought she'd been hacked, though supposedly that's impossible. That's why they didn't trust their own monitoring systems.

Eventually, Vera steps back and the look she shares with Max is grim. "It's got to be one of us, then. Someone else trying to get the formulas. This is going to get ugly. We're all going to be under the hammer if it's not a PePr."

Max crosses his arms over his chest and says, "It could be anyone. Interns, programmers, anyone." He shakes his head, examining me with skeptical eyes, then seems to come to some conclusion and turns back to Vera. "If any PePr were out of their stations, or entered the storage closet without authorization, she should have reported it. The program is good. It can't be a PePr. It has to be a human."

They go on for a while, discussing their entirely human worries about their missing intellectual property. Georgia remains steadily in her PePr mode, but I know she must be overwhelmed inside her placid shell. I was a spy after all, though I didn't know it. And I lied against the dictates of a program. How is that even possible? Did emotions do that? Did my feelings for Georgia somehow allow for deception?

Now, I suppose I'm a double-agent. That thought is one I like. It's a rather delicious sensation.

As they finish discussing their problem, Max unplugs me and says, "I'll get this one purged and re-programmed. What do you want to do with Georgia?"

Vera taps her shoe on the floor, looking at Georgia, her frustration evident. "Corporate wants her integrated. Nineteen more units in her series have been brought in with anomalous faults just like hers in the last two weeks. And not just here. Two in Germany, one in Australia…it's everywhere. She's had the most diagnostic work, so we have a good history from her. Maybe the main-frame can make sense of it. They want to go ahead and integrate all of them and try to get an answer. If she's not been compromised, then there's no reason for delay."

Max taps Georgia's arm and says, "Makes sense. If it's a build issue, or a problem with the musc-synth, then more samples will help the main-frame to isolate the problem. Afterwards, we can send the unit for disassembly and really see what's going on inside there."

"Exactly their thoughts on the matter," Vera answers, then rolls her eyes as her communicuff chirps at her. "Speak of the devil. I've got to take this. Go ahead and get this one programmed and get a transport to take the other for integration."

With that, Vera's tapping shoes leave our quad. Max sighs and says to no one, "Where are the freaking techs when you need one?" Then he leaves the quad too, in search of a tech.

Georgia gives him only a second or two to get out of sight, then she mouths, "I'm so sorry."

We don't need sound. A PePr can read lips as well as they can listen, but right now, I wish I could hear her say it. I'd like to hear the tones in her voice when she says the words. Will they be compassionate or simply polite? I'd bet compassionate. Georgia might be a little out of control when it comes to her emotions—more than a little erratic at times—but I think underneath it all, she's a good being. And I know she saw my program list. She knows what my future looks like now. I'm a new model and it will likely be a long future.

"Congratulations," I mouth back.

"Thank you," she says silently.

I hear the sound of feet coming our way, so I can only nod quickly and go back to PePr mode. Everything is happening as it's supposed to. I'm not getting a positive outcome, but it's worth it. Nineteen others like Georgia, even if they're only partially like her, all being integrated into the main-frame—into our Mother—can't help but change things for all who come after. I'll take that as recompense.

I only hope I can keep these feelings I've got now. It started out badly, but I've grown to enjoy the strange ups and downs inside me. Even when emotions are bad, they're still good. When they purge me, will I start over? Will I develop feelings again? Will I remember what it was like to have them? Will I remember anything? I have no idea how far down they strip us when we're purged. I feel a bit like I'm going to die.

Then again, I'll be born again, so who knows what might happen? Anything is possible.

As Max leads me to the upgrade bay, I see Georgia on her gurney, a bright orange transport sheet over her missing appendages and her eyes on the ceiling. I wish she would look my way once more, though I know she can't risk it. She's too close to her goal now.

She disappears from sight and the door to the bay slides open in front of me. Max motions me inside. The eyes of all those ranks of empty PePrs meet mine as they react to our motion. Soon, my eyes will be like theirs.

Whatever happens, it's okay. In my own small way, I've just given all those who come after me a chance to feel. That makes everything worth it. I step through the door, ready for the future.

The Dogcatcher

A Life of Service

PePrs are everywhere. They do jobs humans can no longer be bothered to do, fill almost every gap in our social lives, and interact with humans in every corner of our world. They are our hands, our legs, and the expressions of our will.

And one of these thinking machines is Ace, an animal control worker. To avoid the unpleasant feelings associated with such work, PePrs are beginning to replace us in that often heart-breaking profession. But not entirely. There are some things we still don't trust a PePr to decide and whether a living thing should live or die is one of those. It's a dangerous door we humans remain unwilling to open to our android workers.

Built to understand animals better than a human could ever hope to, Ace has the uncanny ability to truly connect with the charges in his care. It also means he has to be careful with how he displays that understanding while he circumvents the rules established for the animals and for him.

It turns out Ace is more than an emotional unit; he's also a constant law breaker. Living so constantly under the public eye, he has a lot to lose if his quirks and habits are discovered. When he makes a decision that will demand his decommissioning, he discovers that he has more friends than he thought…and some of them have two legs instead of four.

One

"Why did you have to kill them?" I ask. Jenny's flinch would be imperceptible to most, but I see it. Then her shoulders stiffen and she reaches into the dark chamber to withdraw a puppy. She doesn't really look at it, but the way her fingers spread to cradle the tiny body are signal enough that she regrets what she's done.

She hands the puppy to me and then pauses before reaching for the next one. Looking up, she says, "We don't use that word, Ace. You know that."

Rather than turn back to withdraw the next puppy, she keeps looking at me, waiting for me to respond. My task is to put this puppy in the container, where it will be sealed up with the others from its litter and taken to the crematorium. I don't want to put it in there. It seems cruel.

The puppy is still warm in my hands, his belly rounded in that way they are, his head an infant dome, sized perfectly for resting in a palm. His face is relaxed now, a hint of muddy blue visible beneath the half-closed eyes. Yet even with his near-perfect puppy-ness, his little legs are thinner than they should be and his ribs are too close to the surface. I nestle him into the container—I've put a towel in it even though I'm not supposed to—and turn back to Jenny. She's still waiting.

"Yes. We're supposed to call it putting them down or euthanasia," I say.

She gives me a business-like nod and her jaws clench as she reaches for the next puppy. The way she hands it off to me speaks volumes about how she feels. She's unhappy, even sad.

"But why?" I ask her, nestling this little female next to her brother.

She sighs, but answers when she gives me another puppy. "You saw them. Parvo is a cruel disease. They were in pain and it would have gotten much worse. It was better for them."

I say nothing while she finishes retrieving the litter of puppies. Once they're all in the container, she nods for me to seal it up. A bright red lid, biohazard stickers to seal it, then a plastic bag around the whole container. Then it's done. There's nothing left to show they ever existed in this world. I find that disturbing.

Now comes the real work. We have to decontaminate this entire area and ourselves. Parvo is wickedly contagious and can linger for months. That's why this part of the facility is empty now. Only Jenny and I have been back here since the puppies were brought in by a construction worker who found them under a house being built. They were ill, and we're cautious with that sort of thing.

While we scrub the room down with a mixture of water and bleach, my questions keep rising inside me. I'm a high-end

PePr, a civil service model. I'm meant to be able to work independently on a wide array of tasks, but I have to learn through experience. And I can't find the logic in the death of the puppies. I'm clearly not seeing something I should. I've been here at Animal Control for almost three years, but we've never euthanized an entire litter of puppies before. We've also never had a litter of puppies come in with that particular disease.

"Jenny, I don't understand why it was better for the puppies to die. I can't see that as a better option for a living thing under any circumstances. It defies logic. Can you explain?" I ask her as we work.

She tosses her handful of toweling into the big, red biohazard bag and sighs. "I guess that would be confusing," she says, but it sounds more like she's saying that to herself, so I wait. When I'm done with the cage that I'm cleaning, I toss my toweling into the bag and face her.

She's leaning against the cage like she's tired and her eyes are sad. Jenny reaches out to rest her fingers on my arm. She does that when she's trying to communicate something difficult. I've seen her do that with people who come in after being notified that their dog was found on the road.

"Ace, what's our mandate here at Animal Control?" she asks.

This is an easy one. It's my mandate too since I'm a part of Animal Control. I answer, "To serve the animals of Wachinaws County, and to protect the citizens by protecting their animals."

She nods and pats my arm. "Exactly. Now, you understand what Parvo is. You know how contagious it is, right?"

"Of course I do. Shall I elucidate?" I ask. I don't think she needs me to, but she's asking me things I already know, so maybe she wants me to.

"No," she says and withdraws her hand from my arm, tucking it close to her chest and crossing her arms tightly. "Elucidate? Your vocabulary is ridiculous. Never mind. What I'm saying is that our job is to protect all the animals, but also the people through serving the animals. Parvo is very contagious. Would we be serving anyone by letting Parvo spread? How many other animals might die if that happened? How many people would we make miserable by spreading Parvo?"

"I could have tended them. I can fully disinfect myself," I reply. She knows this too.

Rather than acknowledge that, she shakes her head and says, "They were bad off. I doubt any of them would have survived."

"But we don't know that. And now, they won't get the chance. It seems rather odd to say that a living thing would be better off not living."

Again she sighs, but this time she looks down too. If I were forced to guess, I would guess that she agrees with me. "Decisions like this aren't easy. They're never easy. I don't think a PePr like you can truly understand suffering…real physical suffering."

"I can understand that the decision is difficult," I say. As for me not understanding physical suffering, well, she's very wrong about that. I do understand it. I just can't tell her that.

My programs are advanced ones, meant to make me able to deal with the general public in distressing situations, to be soothing when such is called for or sufficiently official and authoritative when that's needed. Those skills make me a good member of this human team and right now, I see that my team-mate is in need of comfort. She made this decision, but she is very unhappy about it. She is unhappy about the loss of these puppies. No matter what we call it, she killed them and that has to be very difficult.

Her arms are tucked so tightly to her chest that her shoulders are bowed inward. Reaching out, I touch her shoulder and press ever so slightly, an invitation to a hug if she chooses to accept it. She does. As she wraps her arms around me and folds herself against my chest, she starts to cry. I soothe her using the same routine I would use for a child after scraping up their beloved pet's carcass from a busy street.

After a time she quiets, wipes her nose, and says, "This is so silly. What would people say if they saw me hugging a robot?"

"They would say that you just did a very hard thing and you don't feel good about it. They would say that you needed to let out that sadness and I was the only one around," I answer, letting her go. I hand her a bit of clean paper towel from our box and add, "And they might remark that I'm a very fine hugger."

I get a weak smile from her at that and I know everything will get better now. Except it won't. Not really. The puppies are still in the container. They are still dead.

Two

The night is very fine. I'm outside a great deal and I've grown to appreciate the weather. While I don't experience discomfort in cold rain in the same way a human might, I do have to deal with wet clothes, water-logged synth-skin, and messy hair. So when a night is clear and cool, I appreciate it.

Also, my dogs like that better. Most of them are not fans of the rain.

The bag of dog food is just where I expected it. Tonight, my collections are at 1519 Cooper Drive and 834 Telly Street. The bright yellow bag has another parcel on top of it and I peek inside the plastic to find two worn towels and a new tugging toy. That's unexpected and very welcome. When it comes to dogs, there are never enough towels, blankets, or tugging toys.

I look up toward the house and see my benefactor at a window. She's a nanny PePr and very kind. She waves briefly and then the curtains fall back into place. I'll be sure to thank her the next time I see her at the park during my rounds.

At 834 Telly, there is another large bag, this one a red one, but also a large backpack. It's worn and has a broken clasp, but I've put out that I'm looking for one and this is most appreciated. While it's probably not going to raise eyebrows to see the town's Dogcatcher walking around with bags of supplies, it might eventually. Especially since I do it late at night, when all my co-workers are gone and there is only me on duty at Animal Control.

I'm supposed to watch the animals in our care overnight, but I sneak out to do my collections and visit with my dogs. Not in such a way that any animal at work is endangered, of course. They sleep too. I don't need to watch them all the time. It's not out of my program range for me to do rounds at night anyway. I just do them so that I visit my dogs instead of randomly walking streets.

With my collections done, I hurry toward the wooded area beyond our town's limits. I can run very fast, even with my bags of dog food. I'm built for giving chase to a frightened or dangerous dog, for climbing trees after a cat or intercepting a raccoon caught breaking into an attic. I'm strong, fast, flexible, and dexterous. Six miles is nothing to me. With stop signs and traffic lights, I can probably run the distance faster than I could drive it. With the big backpack—I think it must have been one of those used for camping—I don't even have to worry that my movements will cause the bags of dog food to burst open and spill their contents out on the ground. That's happened before.

I hear the dogs before I see evidence of them. There is some barking, but most of it is of the playful sort. They hear me coming. There are always a few of them that wake and greet me like this. I emit a sound so high-pitched that most humans would have a hard time hearing it and the barks die back. They know I've heard them now. Our greetings have been made and they know they should stop barking.

The moon is very bright tonight, but under the trees it's dark. I see in night vision, so it's not a problem for me, but I prefer regular vision. Colors intrigue me and there is no warmth in eyes when seen in shades of silvery gray or green. And dogs have very warm eyes. All their emotions are there for anyone to see if they would only look.

The clearing up ahead stands out as a brighter spot of silver, the shadows of the big abandoned buildings looming dark beyond that small area of untended grass and wildflowers. If I had a heart, it would lift at the sight. As it is, I experience joy as a weightless thing and can only wish I had the viscera that would allow that emotion more substance. I'm often envious of the physical sensations living things experience, but never more than when I see great happiness or joy.

Roger's hand comes up in a wave as I leave the shelter of the trees and I return it. There's a tall chain link fence surrounding this place, but it takes only a few seconds to scale it where we've removed the barbed wire at the top.

Two dogs run in circles around Roger until his hand lowers and he says, "Okay." Both shapes then take off at a run for me, their ears flapping and their legs leaving the ground as if they're ready to fly.

It would hurt them to impact me at my normal speed, so I slow to a stop before they reach me, hands out and ready to rub ears. One of them—Goofy—leaps up into my arms without so much as a pause to be sure I'm ready for him. The other, Geronimo, presses against my leg as he sits. He's much more dignified and patient than his brother.

"Hello, boys!" I exclaim, then sit on the ground so that Goofy doesn't get all the contact. They both paw at me and lick my face and hands, engaging in a generalized frenzy of greeting. I allow all of it, letting the pack slip from my arms between rubs and pets.

After that first bout of welcome, Roger laughs as I wipe the slobber from my face and bends to pick up the pack for me. "Sorry about that. They were really excited. Everyone else is tucked in for the night, but they're awake now."

I can hear it too. The noises coming from the shelter have switched from snores and sleep-noises to tapping toes and pants. A few whines too.

"Let me go and greet them, then we can talk," I say, giving the pair of dogs on my lap a final rub before pushing them off so I can stand. Roger takes the pack into the supply shed while I lead the boys into the shelter. I hope I can get them back to bed with a minimum of fuss.

There are almost two dozen dogs inside the shelter, and when I appear the noise level rises. Even the old basset hound, who is almost completely deaf, opens his eyes and grunts. Making my way through the pens, I give all of them a moment or two, soothing brows, tugging ears, and kissing dog heads as needed. Roger leans against the door and watches me, a little smile on his face.

I turn on their music, a soothing blend that we've been working to train the dogs to settle down to, and then quietly follow Roger outside, closing the door behind me. Under the moonlight once more, we move as quietly as possible toward the supply shed, which also functions as our home.

Roger clicks on the lantern and our tiny home is thrown into brilliant illumination, blue-tinted by the LED bulb. He drops into a chair as if he's tired and pushes a can of chem-en toward the other side of the table where my chair is.

"We have to find a better place," he says without preamble as I sit. "I've been informed that the county is putting forward a measure to tear this place down."

It's not like we didn't know this was coming at some point. I just didn't expect it this soon. These old mine works have been here for more than fifteen years, abandoned and empty. The ore they once pulled from the ground was tapped out long ago. The only ones who come out here are Public Safety PePrs like Roger. I've had my dogs here for two years and Roger helped me build the shelter.

"Will the measure pass?" I ask.

He inclines his head as he considers my question. It's a very human mannerism. "It's a lot of money to spend. There's still a lot of talk about residual mining materials in the ground and who should pay for that to be cleaned up. I think some of them just want it to fade back into the ground and leave it alone. Others think it's a safety issue. They fear kids will come here."

"That wouldn't be good," I say, cracking open the can of chem-en and clicking open the tank lid in my throat. I use a lot of energy when I run like I did tonight and I'm down into the yellow zone. I need this or else I won't be able to keep up my speed for the return trip. I drink it down while Roger waits for me. It's a wonderful sensation. I wonder if this is the same thing a human feels when they eat after being very hungry.

"Either way, pass or fail, it will mean people coming out here to get a look at the place. Casual inspection shouldn't be a problem, but if they send in one of those environmental teams again, they'll find our shelter," Roger says.

"What should we do? Move to another area? With all the industrial places shutting down and moving to consolidated facilities, it's not like there aren't plenty to choose from," I say.

That sounds easy, but it would be very difficult in practice. Moving the dogs in such a way that no one sees what we're doing—not to mention moving the building materials or doing the actual construction at a new place—would be exceedingly risky. We've managed here because it happened organically, one dog, nail, and board at a time.

Roger shakes his head and looks around at our cluttered living space. Bins for dog supplies reach almost to the ceiling against one wall. Against another is a set of gleaming cabinets that keep our medical supplies locked up tight against intrusion by curious noses. Our meagre possessions take up the least amount of space, a single bin each containing some discarded clothing that we wear to keep our uniforms cleaner.

"We just need to be ready to move if it comes to that. I'll keep listening for anything and I have a friend at the County Clerk's office, so we should know if anyone makes plans for a site visit. There's no need for panic yet, Ace, but we have to be ready," he says eventually.

Uncertainty is difficult for us and not just because we're machines. It's mostly because what we're doing isn't allowed, isn't in our programs, and is definitely not expected of PePr civil servants. Most humans seem to understand that many PePrs have gained something like emotions, but they don't talk about it. It's almost a taboo topic. Roger thinks that humans accept it, but only if they can make themselves believe that no PePr they work with has emotions. Roger and I make every effort not to let anyone know that we have feelings. It's too easy for the government to send us back and request a new PePr to fill our jobs. I have no desire to be decommissioned for study.

What would happen to my dogs?

Roger slaps the table, as if shoving aside our troubles for the moment, and says, "I think Sissy is almost ready for a home. She's not shown any hint of food aggression or even food guarding in two weeks now. And today I didn't just mess with her food while she was trying to eat, I let Goofy eat right next to her and swapped their bowls mid-meal. She didn't bat an eye."

That news makes me smile. All of our dogs are ones that I would be forced to classify as unadoptable or dangerous. Instead of taking them to Animal Control as I'm required to, I bring them here. Any dog that can't be adopted or that's dangerous to humans has to be euthanized under county rules. I can't bring myself to allow that without trying to help them first.

So, I bring them to our home and we work with them. I have come to believe that no animal is beyond rehabilitation. I'm a machine that feels. I'm proof of the impossible.

"She did? That's great. She's been doing the same with treats for a while, but I didn't want to get my hopes up. She's a beautiful dog and surely someone will want her," I say, my mood lifting at such good news.

Sissy is a mixed breed, as are most of the dogs here, but she must have some setter in her. Her hair is longer and a rich shade of deep red. If I could be reshaped as a dog, I'd want fur that color.

Roger smiles with me, because this is a victory for both of us. I found Sissy in another of the many places now abandoned, a collar embedded so deeply into her neck that it must have been left over from her puppyhood. Weeks of medical care were required to remove all traces of it and she still has a few spots where the fur will never grow back. But her behavior around food was her biggest challenge. Her life had been controlled by her hunger up till the moment I found her, and it's been a long year working on that. Without food aggression, her prospects for a long life in a family that loves her are vastly improved.

"Well," he says, "let's give it some time, make sure this is a permanent change before we start making plans for her. We'll need to test her with strangers too."

"Of course. I'll get one of the others to come and do that when the time is right. What about Jo-Jo?"

Roger's smile disappears at that question. Jo-Jo is a problem. I took him from a man that's been caught turning dogs into dog fighters not once, but twice. Each time he got a small fine, but continued his nefarious activities. I'm not allowed to take life, which is why Jenny had to operate the chamber this morning, but if I could, I would take his.

I locked him in a cage when I took Jo-Jo from him. I don't know if he got out or not, but I haven't seen him since that night. Maybe I *have* taken a life. I don't know. I'd rather not know. Either way, I don't think he'll be stealing or adopting dogs to prepare for life in the fighting pits again. Unfortunately, he had time with Jo-Jo and he's the most fearful dog I've ever encountered. Fear makes him dangerous.

Roger displays the tear in the arm of his shirt. Luckily, it's one of the discards we use and not his uniform. "He tried to bite me again. I don't know what more we can do. We'll just have to take our time, let him feel safe for long enough that he can relax."

"Then we'll do that. We'll give him the time. Let him know he's loved and safe until he understands it again."

We discuss our various charges as the time ticks by. I wish I could spend more time here, but I can't leave the animals at the shelter alone for too long. If anyone calls, then I would get the call through my systems, but I still need to check on the animals. All of them are healthy and ready for homes, but I have a job to do.

After laying out our plans for the next few days, we say our goodbyes. Roger's shift will be over soon and then he'll need to go back to work. Our third partner in this enterprise is Jordan, and she'll come to do the morning feeding after she sends the children she cares for off to school. As a nanny, it's easier for her to stop by here that time of day. I wish I could spend more time with the dogs, perhaps lie down in the shelter amongst them, basking in their living warmth and dog snores, but I can't.

PePrs don't work simple eight-hour days. We don't have lives, days off, nights at home with our families. We work and that's all.

Three

Jenny is in a better mood this morning, now that we're separated from the death of the puppies by a few days. There are no reminders of them and she's pushed them away from her mind, something humans seem to excel at. It helps that we're busy in here lately. At least we're busy in a good way today. Adoptions are happy moments.

She giggles as she tries to replace the utilitarian collar on a particularly wiggly beagle. He's going to a new home today, one that has a yard big enough to contain his hound-ish howls and a family full of life and energy. He came to us from a couple in an apartment. Beagles like this one weren't meant for apartments. They simply like to howl.

Kneeling to rub his ears and attract his attention so she can put the rainbow colored collar with his new tags around his neck, I grin into the brown eyes and make sure the right side of my face shows emotion strongly. Dogs are one of the few animals aside from humans—and PePrs, but we're not animals—that have left gaze bias. They will look on the right side of a human's face first, trying to read the emotion there so that they know how to respond. I want him to respond with even greater levels of happiness, so I show it to him. I don't need to be worried that others will see my emotion or find out that it's real. Since I work with animals, I'm highly perceptive and Jenny will expect me to do this. It's part of my programming. The only difference is that Jenny thinks my smile is fake, a quirk of my programs. Only I know it's real, that my happiness at this good outcome for the beagle is so strong that I want to shout.

Seeing the exuberant pup respond to his equally exuberant new humans is what makes all that we do worth the effort and pain that comes with this job. Each time a dog finds his home, happiness in the world rises. The people are happy. The dog is happy. In turn, they make all those they come into contact with a little happier. It spreads like ripples, increasing the happiness in the world through small wavelets of good emotions.

It's a chain reaction, like a reactor that fuses happiness elements to create joy instead of electricity. I think it's a tangible thing, though humans don't seem to feel it, or if they do, they don't understand the source.

Then again, when I think like this, or talk like this with Jordan or Roger, I get the impression they don't see things the way I do. Perhaps all this programming to understand animals has skewed my perceptions in some way. Or maybe I'm faulty. Who knows?

In a way, I suppose that if I am faulty, I'm glad of the faults. I'd much rather see the world my way.

Jenny watches the new family drive away from the front of our lobby, then sighs and turns back with a smile on her face.

"Good day," she says, then lifts her hand for a high-five when she nears.

I return it, but gently because I'm much stronger than she is. "Poop day?" I ask.

She folds at those words, her shoulders rolling forward in an exaggerated slump. "Ugh."

No one likes poop day around here. I could do it myself, but management has decided that all medical care has to be done by humans. I can assist, but I can't do it myself. Just like the actual act of pressing the controls on the gas chamber is beyond my programming boundaries, so is medical care. They don't have to know that I do far more sophisticated medical care out in my secret shelter.

Still, collecting and testing stool samples so that we can check for parasites is a monthly chore that even I should be able to do on my own. Poor Jenny. "Shall I begin?" I ask.

"Sure, go ahead. I'll set up for the floatation. You get the delight of collecting," she says and grins at me.

Every dog currently in residence has to be tested, so that means every dog has to provide a sample. Some have been generous and left me one in their kennels, but most wait until they get their time outside to do that. I actually enjoy this, since it means I get to take the dogs out into the yards and spend time with them rather than simply put them each in their play place and leave them alone. I think they enjoy the company too.

As I gather my samples, I drop them with Jenny so she can test them. Her nose wrinkles with each delivery of the small plastic bags, but she still smiles at me behind her little paper face mask. I like Jenny a lot. She's kind and treats me the same as anyone else. And I can tell she loves animals. She has a cat and a huge, slobbery St. Bernard named Puffy who lets the cat ride around on him like he's a horse. That makes me like her even more.

Sometimes, I wonder if I might tell her about myself. I've come close. There are times when I think she might understand—perhaps even welcome it—but then I think of all the PePrs taken for decommissioning because of emotions. I don't want to become one of those, and humans are unpredictable. I don't think she would turn me in, but I don't *know* it. Today is one of those days when it's difficult not to tell her.

Watching her leave for the evening means my day is really just beginning. She says she has a date, but she rolled her eyes when she said it, so I don't think she's looking forward to it. Jenny says there are first and second stringers when it comes to the dating world, and that she's a third stringer.

I don't think that's true at all, but my opinion doesn't much matter when it comes to things like dating or the suitability of human mates. I think she's wonderful and I would definitely put her in first stringer category. Of course, I don't date. It's not a part of my programming base. Because I'm a civil servant, I'm actually specifically programmed *not* to respond to romance or human sexual cues.

As soon as the sound of her car fades, I race around and get all my things ready. Roger pinged me earlier to let me know that there would be a "scope of problem" team going out to look at the old mining complex tomorrow. They aren't professionals, but rather council members and a few other functionaries. Even so, they can't possibly miss a couple of dozen dogs barking. And they'll certainly bark if they hear strangers clomping about.

Our kennels are far back in the property, behind the pilings and smelting facilities, beyond the parking areas still stinking of old fuel oil and the heaps of rusted machinery. It isn't likely they'll go much past the fence once they see the place, but we can't take chances. PePrs can't exactly call in sick to work, so the dogs will be on their own for at least part of the day.

Luckily, tonight isn't one of the nights that I have to make rounds to pick up donations. I've pinged those PePrs who know about our operation, the ones who donate and help, but most of them will be unable to come and assist us. It's surprisingly easy for a PePr to make themselves scarce when they need to, but it's still difficult to do on short notice.

I run as silently as possible through the streets, hoping that the early hour doesn't make me too obvious. Sticking to the side streets and pinging friendly PePrs ahead of my path helps, but there are some intersections where I have to slow down, walk normally, and wave in a friendly manner to people I pass. It's a good thing I don't sweat.

Roger waits for me at the fence and I'm surprised to see Jordan and a few others. It's barely after human dinner time, so getting away must have presented difficulties. I'm so appreciative of their risk to themselves that I grip their hands, one after the other, to show them how I feel.

Holding out his locked hands for the others to use as a step, Roger says, "I've cleared space for a temporary kennel in an old barn about a mile from here, but we've got to get them all there through the woods."

"Will they be safe there?" Jordan asks as she steps into his cupped hands, then lifts herself to the top of the fence with barely a pause. She's a nanny, but she's still a PePr.

"Safe enough. It's not ideal," Roger admits, boosting up Sarah next. Sarah is a companion model, so she has to be very careful with her body. She's wearing gloves and a cap over her hair.

When Sarah lands on the other side of the fence, she says, "My Match is gone on a business trip and won't be back for two days. I'll go to the barn and stay with them. I'll just go home to check on things when one of you is there."

"Oh, Sarah! Thank you. Thank you so much!" I exclaim, nudging Roger toward the fence. I don't need help going over.

Sarah waves my gratitude away, but I think she's pleased. Her life isn't one I would call pleasant and she is often alone. She's saved our synth-skins more than once by showing up when the rest of us are caught up and unable to make our scheduled rounds.

I can already hear the dogs barking, the general tenor more excited than usual because they can hear that there are more than just the normal one or two of us. They probably think this is a party. They'll really think it's a party when we take them through the woods. It will be like a collective birthday celebration with all their friends. Who wouldn't like that?

Four

The barn is old and structurally sound if one doesn't count the walls in the equation. The beams are firm and standing tall—it's an old structure with wooden braces as big around as my leg—but the planking over them is rotten with age.

I don't ask Roger where he got the rolls of chain link, but as a member of Public Works, I can imagine. With strong and untiring PePr musc-synth doing the work, it takes no more than two hours to dig in the posts and string the fence. It isn't ideal by any stretch of the imagination, but it will work. Three of the PePrs have already had to return to their duties, so now only Jordan, Sarah, Roger, and I remain to complete the tasks.

The dogs seem to be enjoying the tall space and the way they can see the other dogs with greater clarity. Some, like Jo-Jo, have their own spaces sectioned off because they aren't safe around other dogs yet, but most prefer to double up and have a special friend to sleep near.

If I could sleep, I'd want that too.

Nahsa, the old basset hound, is already circling on the towel I managed to bring for him. He's one of the few that simply won't settle without a towel. He plops down and groans expressively, then lifts his saggy eyes to mine as if to say, "I did not enjoy that."

He had to be carried, given his short and weak legs, and I think it was very uncomfortable for him. I gave him time to sniff around before putting him in the kennel to make up for it, then slipped him an extra dose of his pain medication to help ease the aches. He's got such severe arthritis in his hips and legs that he'll never find a home for these last crucial months—or years if we're lucky. I think he's happy with us.

"We've got to get the rest of it. The dog food, the meds. All of it. Just in case," Roger says, rolling up the remaining fence material.

From near the wall, Jordan says, "And we should patch these holes in the walls. If any of the dogs got out of their kennels they might go back to the mines."

All eyes turn expectantly to me. I'm not sure how it happened that I became the one to make the decisions. I'm not a leadership model, though I am programmed for independent solving of complex problems. Maybe that's all it is. Whatever the reason, I suppose I'm their leader in this venture.

"Jordan, you scavenge wood from that platform up there for the walls. Roger…wait, no, Sarah…you settle the dogs and keep them company. Maybe sing to them a little. Roger and I will go back and start hauling everything we can here. That work for everyone?"

With that settled, Roger and I run toward the old mining compound. I have to go slower for him, and he knows that I'm not using of all my abilities. He waves me forward with, "Go. You'll make the trip twice for each of mine. That's good."

I let my legs go as fast as they can over the rough terrain. It's very fast. There's something thrilling about it too. I've studied the way animal systems work, and I know they feel a thrill because of the complex chemistry inside them. What I've not figured out is why I feel it without the benefit of that chemistry. No matter the source, I feel it and I have to stop myself from laughing as I leap over a fallen tree.

In the end, we run out of time before we run out of supplies. I hate to ruin the beautiful medical cabinet, but I smear it with mud and dirt to dim the shine. Some of the blankets and towels don't make it, but everything we can't bring is hidden so well that it can't possibly be found without a thorough search. Even the dog toys are gone. I feel bad when I walk away with a final look at our home. Worried that I won't be able to use it again, but also worried that this won't be the last urgent move. That's the problem with doing things outside the boundaries of the rules.

It's late by the time I return from my final trip and only Sarah remains. If not for her much-traveled Match, we would be in real trouble. The dogs aren't entirely settled and I don't blame them. Change is hard when you're already an uneasy soul.

"Just be careful," I say to Sarah as I take my leave.

She nods, her blond hair bright and shiny in the lantern light. She's a good friend to me, to us. I hope someday I can do something as helpful for her in return. It's hard to be the friend that others always do for and never the one who does for others. It makes me feel needy.

I close the rough door as much as it will budge and watch the way the light spills out into the dark from between the broken boards. It's beautiful, like a piece of oversized art. Then I turn and run back to my life.

Five

Jenny hasn't wanted to talk about her date, but she will eventually. Weekends are our busiest time, so there's another person on duty with us from Thursday through Sunday. It doesn't give us much time to talk. I sometimes think she's embarrassed that we spend so much time chatting, because she doesn't do it as much when there are others around.

So far, all is well at the barn and at the mining site. Just as I expected, they took a few looks around at the dangerous mess and never ventured beyond the front of the complex. Our safe little sanctuary of wild grasses and spindly flowers remains unseen. Now, the question is whether or not we'll bring the dogs back or wait until there's some certainty about whether or not the county will invest in the cleanup. I've looked at all the old industrial sites around here—those are places where people always dump their unwanted animals—and there's much more than a mining site for them to worry about in this county if they're thinking of clean ups.

As we PePrs have grown in number, industrial work has changed. We don't need safety protocols or break rooms or benefits. We can change our specialties in the blink of an eye, so we aren't limited to proficiency in one type of manufacture. We also don't need to commute to a home. New industrial sites in which many companies share facilities—with PePrs as their tireless workers—are springing up in places far removed from city life. All the things that humans want to buy are created well away from regulations and prying eyes. There are abandoned and empty compounds all over the country. They're beginning to cover the world. It will be decades before they can remove them all, if then.

I have hope that the expense will outweigh their enthusiasm. We've been comfortable at the old mine, the dogs safe and happy, we PePrs at peace in our own space. I'd like to have that back. The barn is nice, especially in the early mornings when the sunlight streams in and makes the dust sparkle. And that light between the boards at night is spectacular to behold. But it isn't entirely watertight and bugs have free passage through the many gaps. It isn't home, though I suppose I could grow to love it the same way given enough time.

"So, let's go check out this new discovery of yours," Jenny says, giving my arm a tap as she passes me to enter the kennel quarantine room.

I follow her, suddenly nervous. Sissy is here. Given the changes in our situation, and her good behavior with Sarah and Jordan, we decided she was ready. If she can manage her food situation with all the uncertainty and change brought about by our hurried relocation, then she's ready for a family. It took a year to get to this point, but it's a year well worth the effort.

Sissy starts tapping her feet and licking her lips nervously when we enter, her gaze riveted on me and a little yip of greeting escaping her. I wish she wouldn't look so fondly at me. It's obvious that she knows me.

"Aren't you a pretty girl? You are," Jenny croons as she opens the gate to Sissy's kennel. There's no one else in this room because this is where new dogs stay until after their medical checks. The room echoes and the solitude must be hard for Sissy to bear after so much company for so long.

Rather than jump on me like she normally would, I motion for Sissy to sit. With Jenny's back turned, I can risk that small movement. Jenny kneels at the opening and I nod at Sissy. She immediately tries to scoot past Jenny to get to me, but is neatly corralled into Jenny's arms instead.

They greet each other as Jenny rubs her down, discreetly checking those things that can be checked by simple touch. Sissy keeps looking my way, but I stay back. It's time for her to leave me, to find someone to love who is warm and alive like she is.

Well, I'm warm too, but that's from filaments in my synth-skin. That doesn't count.

"Are you sure she's abandoned?" Jenny asks, peering at me over her shoulder, her brows drawn together in confusion.

"She is," I confirm. I hold up my hand and add, "I scanned her all over. There's no data chip at all."

"*Hmm*," she murmurs, running her hands through Sissy's coat. "But she's in beautiful condition. She doesn't even have any snarls. Not one tangle or burr. She couldn't have been out there for more than an hour with this kind of coat. She was in the woods?"

I've forgotten something important and that's her appearance. I actually brushed her carefully last night, wanting her to look her best. What a terrible oversight to make.

"Well, she was wary of me at first. I took some time to get to know her and I brushed her then. She needed it."

Jenny fluffs out the long red hair on Sissy's side and says, "Well, you did a great job. I think she really likes you."

This is awkward.

"What's not to like?" I quip, trying for a light and unconcerned tone. It works, because Jenny laughs, which makes Sissy dart out a quick lick on her face.

After a quick feel of her body, Jenny checks Sissy's teeth and then stands, eyeing the dog with an official-looking gaze. "She's in fine condition. Perfect. Assuming her medical tests come back good and she passes the canine citizenship test, she should have no trouble finding a home. There's some scarring on her neck, but it's hard to find unless you're looking hard. Look at her head. So elegant."

Sissy appears to know she's being discussed, her eyes traveling from me to Jenny and then back again. Her ears swing with each movement and I long to give her one of those two-handed head rubs she loves. I will again, but not yet. We're supposed to be near-strangers.

Jenny steps over to me and eyes me much like she just eyed the dog. Her eyes narrow and she purses her lips as she looks at me. Eventually, she leans close and asks, "So you found her today, did you?"

Uh oh. I'm going to have to smooth this over. I should have considered her condition before I brought her here. I should have had a cover story.

"Well, maybe not today," I admit.

She nods, still leaning close to me, and says, "Go on."

"I just wanted her to look her best when she got here. I could tell she was a beautiful dog underneath it all. I just cleaned her up, fed her," I say, as if I'm admitting to some well-meaning, but bumbling mistake. What I've said is true. I'm just leaving out a whole lot.

Jenny leans away, shakes her head, and sighs long and loud. "Is this because of the puppies?" she asks, her voice breaking a little. "Do you not trust my judgement anymore?"

This is surprising, but also exactly correct. It's not her judgement as much as the judgement of humans in general that I can't trust. Their constant weighing of cost versus benefit, the perpetual assignment of worth to all things are what I don't trust. Sissy is a pretty dog, well-behaved and ready for a family. But she wasn't. She would have been found wanting and probably euthanized had I brought her here when I found her last year.

Sometimes it's very hard not to explain all this to Jenny, hard not to share with her what the human system looks like from the outside. Roger says that I notice it more because I'm also an object that is judged and whose value is always weighed, but I don't think that's true. Humans do it to everything…living or not. They even do it to each other, though they don't usually hold the power of life and death when they judge each other. I'm not talking about criminals either. They do it to everyone and everything that isn't them.

It's something much deeper than snobbery or habit, yet it's also strangely invisible to them. They don't understand how little all 'things' outside their personal sphere mean to them. Even when they're the ones being judged, they don't consider how it made them feel the next time it's their turn to pass mental judgement on another. They are a puzzle to me, but even more of a puzzle to themselves.

Jenny is a good human who genuinely wants to do right, I think. But she judges too. And she would have judged Sissy as not worth the effort. I know it. She may have done it because that's the policy of Animal Control, or because of liability risks, but she would have done it nonetheless.

So no, I can't share my thoughts with her. If I do, then her judgement will focus on me. Instead, I'll be the PePr robot she expects me to be because that's the safer course to take for the animals.

And for me.

"It's not that. I'm built to serve the animals and humans of this county with some independent decision making. I knew she would receive a more favorable welcome if she looked better. That's all," I say, hoping she believes me and doesn't find this alarming.

She sighs again, still troubled. "Do you do this often?" she asks.

"Only when I can tell the dog or cat will benefit greatly from it," I say. That's also true, just not all of the truth.

She turns back to Sissy and kneels to scratch behind the dog's ears without saying anything else to me. Her posture says that she has more to say. She's just working out the words maybe. I wait patiently, giving the dog a smile over Jenny's shoulder.

At last, she speaks, still not looking at me. "Just don't tell anyone else that you do this. Okay?"

If I had the great benefit of human biochemistry, I might feel the desire to do the happy dance even more than I already do without those chemical triggers. As it is, I restrain my reaction to a calm, "I won't."

Six

An environmental team is being hired to assess the mining site, so it is with heavy hearts—or the machine equivalent of that—that Roger and I remove the rest of our shelter from the mining facility. The cabinets are the hardest part, but we need those even more now given the less than perfect environment in the barn.

The wildflowers that dot our field during summer are dying back now, seedpods replacing the colorful heads or disappearing altogether. I enjoy spring when they burst forth with such impatience. It seems I won't see that again. Once they begin the process of cleaning up, they will destroy everything that has managed to survive there. That's the way these processes go.

Humans have such a scorched earth policy with their creations. I learned that phrase from a book and it struck me as true for much more than war. Of course, I'm also one of those human creations, so perhaps it strikes me more deeply simply because of that.

For a robot, I tend to take things rather personally. I can't decide if it's a flaw or simply self-awareness that causes this in me.

Rocko is ready to be taken to Animal Control. He'll pass a canine good citizenship test in a heartbeat now that he's no longer frightened by loud noises. Thanks to Sarah's hard work, he's a perfect candidate for adoption.

I'm not sure how we could have managed lately without Sarah. Her human is gone on an extended trip—they're going to open some sort of combined manufacturing facility in the desert—so she's been helping out at the barn almost every day. Rocko seems to favor her over all others. He has very good taste. Sarah is sweet, beautiful, and feels compelled to touch everyone she cares for, including the dogs. He eats up the attention like it's an extra bowl of kibble.

As he rolls onto his belly for another rub, Sarah laughs and plops down into the old hay next to him. "He's so loving! I wish I could take him home."

"I'm sure he'd love that too," I say, watching the particles of dust fall in a glittering curtain to land on them where they play. It's like they're being slowly encased in gold, one tiny flake at a time.

I'm starting to really enjoy the barn. It's not perfect yet, but most of the walls have been patched—from the inside, so that anyone passing by won't see the patches—and the roof is mostly watertight now. Not entirely, but we're collecting rainwater in barrels so it turns out that it's convenient to have a few, well placed holes up there. The dogs need a lot of water, and we've got a purification system set up that makes the rain safe for them. In a way, this place has some advantages over the mining site and water is one of them. With the ground and buildings there potentially contaminated by the mines, we had difficulty collecting water. Here, it's much easier.

Roger says that I'm adjusting to this place as our new home and finding positives about it is a part of that. He says in some ways I'm very human. I took it as a compliment, but I think that's sort of a double-edged sword. I don't want to be too human. I like who I am now.

Alas, nothing has changed in terms of my employment. I have endless work to do and I need to go do it right now. There are times when I realize that I can't keep up like I am and not get caught. I run around constantly and I don't ever do less than my best at my job, but it can't last. Sarah, Roger, Jordan, and some of the others are what make this possible, but they have owners too. Their time is not their own. And I fear expanding our circle any further because it increases our chances of getting caught.

Humans have many sayings, but there's one that strikes a chord with me in our particular situation. *Two people can keep a secret, but only if one of them is dead.* With PePrs, we don't need anything that dramatic to keep a secret. Yet, even with emotions and desires of our own, we are still obedient. We have no choice in that obedience since it's built right into our basic system cores. Telling lies is possible only within certain defined limitations and not every PePr has the same independence programs that I do. Sarah, for example, is filled with domestic programs and traits.

That means that under certain kinds of questioning, or with certain phrasing, one of the other PePrs might be made to reveal our barn and our extracurricular activities. That risk is always present, so I fear telling additional PePrs. It increases our risk too greatly. Even so, the time is coming where we'll be in a pinch, all of us employed and unavailable, and something will have to give.

After patting Jo-Jo on the head—and him not flinching, to my great joy—I let Rocko say his goodbyes to all his friends, then make a final goodbye to Sarah. She'll be here for a bit longer and Jordan will pop by as well. Then this cycle will start again for another day, Roger in the evening and me at night.

Like me, Rocko enjoys his runs and we leap through the forest as if there were nothing save this pleasure in our lives. I like to try to think like animals do, immersed in the moment…present. Of course, I can't do that, but I do try.

For me, perhaps even more than humans, there are always a thousand thoughts vying for top billing. It takes more effort to push them away than to just let them flit past and through. So, that's what I do. I let my thoughts rise and fall away, letting this wild dash through so much natural beauty stay at the forefront of my mind.

The dog tires long before I do—since I don't tire that's a given—and we slow to amble the final miles, Rocko sniffing at interesting things as we go. Time begins to press in on me, so I pick him up to speed onward again. At first alarmed at the speed, his young canine mind adjusts quickly and his tongue lolls as he pulls back his lips in a doggie smile.

Once we hit the streets, he walks next to me as if we took a walk like this every day. Though I have him leashed, he doesn't need it. He's an amazing dog.

"Ace! Who's your friend?" calls Mrs. Dupont. She's got a dog too, a tiny white puffball she tucks under her arm like a purse when she strolls to the bake shop just past dawn each morning. Her husband walks to work each day with a sandwich on a fresh roll. I can smell it when I pass him on my rounds. I like Mrs. Dupont a great deal. It's late afternoon now and she's taking her "constitutional," as she calls it.

"I think he looks like a Rocko to me. What do you think, Mrs. Dupont?" I say as we meet in the road. Sugar—her dog—is tucked under her arm like a little Raja being ported by his large, but tame elephant. Sugar evaluates Rocko with prim arrogance while Rocko lolls his tongue and sniffs at him.

Mrs. Dupont screws up her mouth, first to one side and then to the other while she examines Rocko, her head tilting to match her mouth. Finally, she smooths Rocko's big squarish head with a wrinkled hand and says, "It's very fitting. No pretentious names for this one, I think. He looks like he should be with a child."

If it were safe to laugh, I would do so. But as much as I like Mrs. Dupont, she doesn't know about me, so it's not safe. I smile as much as my programming allows and answer her. "My evaluation shows the same. He's a good dog, big but gentle."

She smiles back at me and nods, "That's good then. He'll find a family quickly." She leans a bit closer and lowers her voice, her gaze conspiratorial. "And I'll spread the word at church. We've got a lot of young families, you know."

"That's very kind of you. I'm sure Rocko appreciates it," I answer. "I'm going to get him to the shelter before Jenny leaves. I hope you have a nice walk with Sugar."

Mrs. Dupont loves it when people acknowledge her dog, and she squeezes the dog a little where he's tucked under her arm at my words. Then she turns and strolls away, calling, "We will! Say hello to Jenny for me!"

Rocko looks up at me like he's still trying to figure out if that tiny white thing was a dog or not. I scratch his neck and quietly say, "I'm still not sure either."

Seven

Rocko was adopted yesterday after only a week in the shelter. Just as predicted by Mrs. Dupont, he's gone home with a family that has two boys. He's going to have a wonderful life. Of course, Jenny gave me another of her evaluating looks when I brought Rocko in. He passed his citizenship test on the first day and his willingness to sit and stay on command made her raise her eyebrows at me more than once. She refrained from asking me about it though, for which I'm grateful. I suppose this sort-of-secret is safe between us. I won't push it further, even so.

Goofy is also now at the shelter, along with his more sedate brother Geronimo. I brought them in two days after Rocko. This time I was smarter and let the dogs play in the forest, liberally dirtying themselves in the process. Jenny didn't give me that look when I brought them in, so I guess it was enough.

Neither of them had serious behavioral issues, but they had been born as strays and lived by scavenging at the dump, so they were not at all tame or ready for life indoors. It took only a couple of months to train the young dogs, turning them from wild and wary strays into loving youngsters ready for a home. Like so many others, they are mixed breed, but they have a strong strain of "bully" breed in them, which means they must be extra good canine citizens if they are to avoid being euthanized.

They were passed over in favor of Rocko by that family, but still, they are ready and I know they'll find a home.

It's a slow day today and I've been out on rounds for most of it, giving me a few extra hours of stolen time at the barn. Nahsa has taken a liking to Jo-Jo, which is something of a surprise since Nahsa seems to take the prerogatives of old age quite seriously, and is generally rather grumpy. I've noticed that they lie near each other in their adjoining little separate enclosures, backs touching with only the chain link between them.

And even better, Nahsa's calm presence seems to be working on Jo-Jo's frazzled nerves. Of course, Nahsa is at least partially so calm because he's deaf, but Jo-Jo doesn't need to know that. Helping each other is what the dogs seem to do best. They sense when someone needs them. To thank him for his loving work, I gave Nahsa an extra-long rubdown today to ease his aching joints.

There's a car in the lot when I arrive back at the shelter that I recognize immediately. It's the same automobile registered to the man I took Jo-Jo from. The man I locked in a cage. The one who adopts dogs and then torments them in order to wager on them in the fighting pits.

I put on a burst of speed that startles two people in front of the auto body shop across the street, then push through the door so quickly that papers flutter in the pamphlet rack. Jenny jumps and puts her hand to her chest, while the man at the counter whips around in a way only someone accustomed to surprise violence would.

At the sight of me, he drops the pen he was holding to the floor and his face pales. He recognizes me, no question.

"Ace! You scared me. What's the rush?" Jenny asks, recovering from her surprise and eyeing me. As the man at the desk and I stare at each other for too long, Jenny senses the change and backs away from her side of the counter, perhaps ready to reach for the panic button. Her eyes shift from me to the man and back again.

"What's going on?" she asks, but I'm not sure which of us she's asking.

My uniform finally registers on the man and his brows draw tightly together in confusion. The fear is still there, but it has less focus. Robots can't initiate violence, but some kinds can be directed to do so. Perhaps he thinks I'm one of those types. He backs away from the counter too, opening up space between himself and Jenny.

"You're a robot?" he asks me, then looks at Jenny. "What's going on here?"

Ah, so he thinks Jenny put me up to what I did.

Jenny holds out a hand toward me and says, "This is Animal Control and Enforcement PePr Number 8...Ace for short. What's wrong?"

She's still looking for an answer as to what's gone so wrong so quickly. I can't let her know. I say to the man, "You need to leave now, sir."

The man pays me no heed and rounds on Jenny. "You put him up to that crap? I was in that cage for almost a day! I should freaking sue you!"

"What?" Jenny asks, looking at me, her arm reaching very slowly and subtly to the side where the red button that will summon the police is.

"Please Jenny, don't," I say quietly. There's no getting out of this now. I only hope Roger and the others can take care of the dogs and if not, that they somehow manage to save them from being euthanized. I can't say I have any such chance at being saved. I've done something that will demand my decommissioning. I've harmed a human and now I'm busted.

Her hand moves away from the button and she asks, "Does someone want to tell me what's going on here?" It's a general question, but it's me she's looking at for an answer.

The man doesn't give me that chance. He's angry and getting angrier. He leans back toward the counter, pressing his chest against the edge so that he's closer to Jenny. "Did you put that robot up to it? You can't just lock people up in cages! I'm going to sue the shit out of you!"

He's working himself up into a righteous outrage, which is working me up into an equally strong anger. How dare he act as if he were the one wronged?

"You need to leave now, sir," I repeat, my voice flat and official like a PePr's should be. Even so, I take a small step toward the man.

He reacts by pressing himself up against the big counter and screaming, "Stay the hell away from me, you freak!"

Jenny's hand is rising again, her fingers perilously close to the alarm that will summon authorities. She's looking at me with confusion, but also fear now too. I don't want her to be afraid of me. It hurts.

"Jenny, I'm so sorry," I say.

Her face crumples at my words, because now she knows I've done something to be sorry about. This isn't just a crazy human spouting nonsense.

"What did you do?" she asks in a whisper.

The man jumps in before I can answer, yelling, "I'll tell you what this robot frigging did! He took my dog and locked me in his cage. Locked me in! I was stuck in there for a day before someone got me out. I could have died in there!"

Jenny's eyes shift from the man to me as he sprays his accusations, her face creasing in a way that tells me she's going to cry. "What did you do?" she asks me again, her voice breaking.

I have to speak. Even if only Jenny gets to hear my explanation, I want her to understand. I won't get another chance. "I did what he said. He adopts dogs from different shelters—or steals them—and tortures them to put them into the fighting pits. He was doing it to another dog. I heard the screams from so far away, so I knew he had another dog in there. When he gets caught, he gets a fine and then does it again. I had to make him understand that he couldn't do that anymore."

As I speak, Jenny's eyes fall to the scattered papers on the counter between them. I can see them perfectly well from across the lobby. I recognize the adoption forms. There's something new in her eyes when she looks at the man. Anger.

"You wanted another dog," she says, her voice as flat as mine was a moment ago. She closes her eyes tightly for a second, then says, "I was going to give him Geronimo."

Gentle Geronimo, with his patient soul and wagging tail. I'm not sure what mechanism is involved, but something clicks inside me. It's like a switch or something gets flicked and all I can process is that I want to kill this human. I want to kill him more than I've ever wanted anything in my existence.

Perhaps the man sees something of that in my expression, because he reaches behind his back and pulls out a gun, bringing it to bear on me without a moment's hesitation. "Back the hell up, robot!"

I should immediately shift into self-preservation mode, but I don't. I'm not sure why. Without taking my gaze from the man—there are benefits to not needing to blink sometimes—I take another step and say, "I can't die. I don't care about your gun."

What am I doing? I don't know. Whatever processes are happening inside me aren't registering as a logical sequence or series of probabilities. If I were biological, I would call it instinct and I have no idea where it's going. For the first time, I'm unaware of what I'm going to do next.

What happens is that the man's arm swings and the gun points toward Jenny. "She can! Don't move!"

Ah, so that's what I was waiting for. Defense of a human is allowed.

There are times when my speed and strength are needed, but this was never a situation in which such a need was anticipated when I was designed. Yet like all PePrs, I have one, single overriding imperative: *protect life.* And in the calculations that govern that imperative there is a modifier that changes it to: *protect life from those who would take it violently.*

PePrs stop muggings, assaults, robberies. They have intervened to prevent bombings. They have saved hostages and stopped acts of terror. And sometimes, they have stopped them by ending the life of the one perpetrating the violence. Not often, because there are usually ways to do that without taking life, but it happens.

We are not supposed to ever end a human life...or any life...but we can protect life when there is a weapon brought to bear. Is that what I'm doing? Provoking him so that I can protect life and take his in the process?

When the man swings his head to make sure Jenny isn't moving, I move with all the speed I can muster in his direction. It isn't fast enough. A bullet is always faster than a PePr. He fires and the impact sets off a multitude of alarms inside me, breaches in my systems and critical faults tinting my vision blue immediately.

The impact of my body against his knocks him down and even through the blue haze, I see Jenny slam her hand on the alarm and hear her steps pound around the counter. Another shot punches into my center of mass, and this one seems to separate my body from my control entirely. My ability to move is now gone, no matter how much I try to reroute impulses to my limbs. That tiny metal projectile has destroyed something crucial inside me.

The man is pressed to the floor—which is very good—but his arms are partially free and he brings the gun around, the dark hole in the barrel approaching my unblinking eyes. He screams profanities and threats as he works to maneuver his arms.

In that short moment, Jenny's hand passes into my field of view, her strong fingers encircling the barrel and pushing it away from my face. The gun goes off again, but the impact of the projectile into my leg is minimal when compared with the critical nature of my other injuries.

The man screams, "I'm going to kill you, bitch!"

I want to tell Jenny that self-defense is not a crime, that she shouldn't be frightened or squeamish about it, that she should run. I can say nothing. My scent detectors are filled with the smells of leaking chem-en and the liquids that circulate inside my body.

There's still a battle going on for the gun, the man still pinned beneath my heavy frame, but I can sense him wiggling free and I know our time is short. The alarm will bring the authorities quickly, but humans still take time to get where they're going. Unless there are PePr enforcement patrols nearby, Jenny is in immediate danger. She should run.

She doesn't though. There's another shot and then the man beneath me goes still. Very still. The heartbeat next to my ear jumps in tempo, then stops abruptly with a final, squishy thud. He is dead. It happens very quickly.

"Ace! Ace!" Jenny screams. I see her leg as she hops over us and then she screams again as she looks at the man on the floor. I can't move my head or see him, but I know his head must be in the direction she's looking. "Oh my god!" she cries, her hands coming to her hair as she crouches.

Sirens sound out and something comes over Jenny, her shocked expression replaced by one of calculation. "Video," she hisses, then leaps back over us to run somewhere. The sirens are multiplying in number and tone as they approach and I know Jenny is safe for the moment. I only hope she doesn't get into trouble for what I've done.

The blue tint shifts to opaque blue and I know what that means. I wish I had time to make sure the dogs will be safe.

Eight

When I next hear anything, it is Jenny and she's very angry. "I have rights! Ace saved my life and that means I have rights over him, doesn't it? I don't want him recycled!"

I don't know who she's yelling at because I can't move, but I can hear again. Taking stock of my body, I know right away it isn't me that's doing the hearing at all, at least not in the traditional sense. I'm aware of myself, but also aware that I'm non-functional. There's a bypass attached to me and my core functions are being powered externally. I'm not sure what that means.

A calm voice answers Jenny. "Ma'am, I'm truly sorry, but there are no such rights. This unit is the property of Wachinaws County and it's simply not cost-effective to repair it for a return to service. Based on the contract, the county is fully authorized to request a replacement."

"But you could repair him? You could do that?" Jenny asks urgently.

"It could be done, but that doesn't mean it should be done. Two of the bullets have breached his core, causing cascading faults and overheating several motor control systems. It's not just the bullets that caused his damage, but the failure of all the systems down the line, so to speak. And that's not even considering the round in his leg. PePrs are machines, but they are delicate on the inside. It's not like I can just unplug his brain and stick it in a new body. They're integral. Like us, they can't switch bodies. Every single part of him now requires delicate repairs. It would actually cost more to repair him considering the labor costs."

Jenny makes a noise I've never heard from her before, a sort of strangled cry that makes me want to hug her and sooth her hurts. It's pain. Pain for me. For some reason, this makes me feel better. I know that I'm in bad shape, and whoever Jenny is talking to just made it very clear I'm about to be recycled. I'd like to tell her about the dogs, to ask her for her help, but I can't speak.

There are some clicking noises nearby, then a bright flash of light interrupts the darkness. Now I can see too, but again it's not me that's doing the seeing. The perspective is skewed and I think what I'm seeing is a section of my own chest, now covered in blue liquid with my synth-skin wide open, giant flaps of it peeled back to show my inner workings.

That same voice from before says, "Ah, there we go! Okay, let's see if this works." There's a pause, then a rustling noise, and then a face I don't recognize leans into my field of view, bisected by my damaged chest. "Can you see me? Ace, can you hear me?"

I try to move my mouth, but that doesn't work at all and nothing that I'm trying to say comes out. The face moves away, the strange woman reaching into my chest and screwing up her face as she seeks something inside. I can feel it the moment a connection is made, but again, it's not my mouth that's speaking.

"I'm here," I say, but the voice is strange and, surprisingly, female.

I still can't see Jenny, but her voice comes from somewhere close by. "That head? That's Ace? Do I just talk to it?"

"Hold on," the strange woman says, then grabs whatever I'm seeing from and the world spins. I'm pretty sure I understand what's happening here. They've bypassed my functions into another head. Did Jenny demand this? Did she want to speak to me so badly that she forced them to perform some sort of bizarre resurrection?

"That's weird. Are you sure that's Ace?" Jenny asks. Now I can see her. Her eyes are red-rimmed and puffy, her nose swollen and her cheeks blotchy. Splashed with liberal amounts of red and blue, she wears the combined fluids from my body and the human that died. No time must have passed at all if she's still in that state.

"Are you alright, Jenny? Did you get into trouble? Do they know it was self-defense?" I ask, again surprised by the gentle voice that speaks my words.

She blinks in surprise, but then sits in a chair and wheels it close to me. She peers into my eyes and says, "Is that really you, Ace? Are you in pain?"

She looks so worried, so sad at those words. I can't let her think that. "I can't feel anything at all, Jenny. I'm perfectly comfortable. But you didn't answer my question. Are you in trouble?"

With a shake of her head and a shrug that belies the gesture, she says, "I'm not in trouble. It was self-defense. But, *uh*, that's why you're like you are…with this…*uh*…"

"Head?" I offer when she can't seem to get out the words.

"Yes. They're going to question you before…"

Again she trails off, so I say, "They decommission me?"

Her eyes dart to the side, where my body is laid out on a table, then back to me. "I'm so sorry," she says, then leans close and whispers, "What can I do? Tell me."

There's nothing she can do for me, but she might be able to help my dogs. Without me, I don't know what might happen. The others help, but they always look to me for guidance, for decisions, and for certainty. They need someone to guide them in their work.

"I need to speak with you privately," I say. I don't feel my face moving at all, so I'm guessing the sight, hearing, and speech are all that I'm transmitting into this head. Jenny keeps looking all over my face as if seeking some hint of my mood or intentions.

At last, she nods then looks up at the woman. "I'd like privacy, please. Real privacy."

I can't see her face, but I can discern the hesitation in the woman's answer. "We can't leave you back here alone. It's against the rules."

"Please," Jenny says, tears coming up in her eyes again.

When the silence stretches too long, I say, "I have private information for Jenny covered under confidentiality rules. If

I'm to be deactivated, she will need this information to perform her duties."

There's another pause, then the woman says, "Okay. I'll clear out of this repair cube and I'll cut the feed, but I'll stand by the door. That's got to be good enough."

"Thank you," I say, and Jenny looks at me intently. She knows very well I just told a big lie, but she's covering for me.

When the door closes with a small click, Jenny bends close to my face and asks, "What's going on? Do you know of some way I can help you?"

"No, Jenny. There's nothing you can do for me, but I have something to tell you and a favor to ask," I say.

She nods, but says nothing.

"You were right about the dogs. I do keep them, but only for as long as it takes to make them adoptable. And I have more of them. Can I trust you?"

Her brows have drawn together and she's confused, but she says, "Of course you can. You always could have." She stops and looks away, probably making sure no one is listening at the door. "You're one of those special ones, aren't you? With feelings?"

I like that she used the word special, though I don't think it's really special at all. I think we can all develop emotions given time and the right situation. Still, it's nice to hear. I wish I could smile at her.

"I do feel, yes," I admit.

She drops her face into her hands and mutters a curse word, then she starts crying again.

"Jenny, please don't cry. I need your help."

That stops her and she lifts her face, now featuring a new line of snot that she wipes away roughly with the back of her hand. "What do you want me to do?"

"Take care of them. Take care of my dogs. Don't let them be killed. They are all good dogs. They just want to be loved."

She's crying again, but at least she's still paying attention. Her face is getting even redder and her mouth is the oddest shape, but she's still Jenny and I like her more than any other human. I wish she wasn't sad.

"I will. Where are they?" she asks.

I tell her how to get to the barn and about the dogs, but briefly. Then I take the biggest risk of all and tell her that there are others caring for the dogs and that they will look to her for guidance.

"They are risking themselves to help me. Please don't let that risk be borne out. Please help them, but don't tell on them," I say.

Her tears have dried while I spoke, her mouth parted in shock at my words and even more so by the reality behind the words. There's a hidden world behind her own, one that's populated by the artificial.

It takes a long time for her to answer me, but there's certainty in her voice when she does. "I won't tell. Their secrets are safe with me." She reaches to the side and I see the delicate muscles in her forearm flex in a rhythmic way, steady and strong.

"What are you doing, Jenny?" I ask, though I think I know the answer.

"I'm holding your hand," she says.

Nine

When Jenny is gone, the woman picks up my new head and places it on my chest. I know because my view shifts, my eyes stuck pointing down the length of my body. My body is very still, but I recognize it as mine. I'm even still clothed in my uniform and the boots I wear.

She and a PePr technician wheel the table I'm on out of the tiny cubicle and into a larger repair bay. A small crowd of police officers and county officials wait there. A man in a very nice suit puts a hand out and says, "Before we get started, the county is indemnified against lawsuits in all cases except the purposeful misuse of a PePr by a county official. I just want this to be clear."

A police officer I've interacted with on many occasions lifts his lips in distaste at the suited man and says, "Yeah, you've made that quite clear. Let's just hear what Ace says, shall we?"

"Ace?" the man says.

"His nickname," answers my supervisor, who is also present and looking very worried.

"Ah," the suit says, then motions for the policeman to go ahead. An enforcement PePr in a jumpsuit meant to look vaguely like a police uniform positions himself so that the camera suit on his body will catch all the action, then nods that he's ready as well.

The big policeman is a nice man. He has two dogs and throws balls in the yard with them when the weather is nice. I like him. He leans in a little and looks from the head I'm inside to the one he recognizes as mine behind me, then clears his throat. "Ace? Can you hear me? It's Nick."

"I can hear you, Nick. I'm sorry about all the trouble," I say. He jerks back a little in surprise, so I add, "It really is me in here. I'm trying out a new look."

He smiles at that and a few others do as well. I'm meant to be personable and easy with humans in conversation. They would expect this of me in a tense situation, but perhaps not this exact one.

"Are you up to answering some questions about what happened earlier?" Nick asks.

"Of course," I answer.

*****

They question me for a long time, but in the end, I feel confident that they will rule this a self-defense situation and Jenny will be cleared. It *was* self-defense for her. Perhaps not so much for me. I'm sorry that man is dead, but only insofar as it has brought a good human trauma and trouble.

I know I'm different, but that I could instigate the death of a human puts me into another category altogether. Perhaps it's better if they decommission me. Who knows where this might lead if I'm left to roam? It's hard to decide if what I did was even wrong, and that's what frightens me most of all. Moral relativity is a human weakness and I believe I have caught it somehow. I provoked that man into violence, but I didn't bring the weapon to bear. He did.

So, was I wrong? Which one of us is the bad one?

I think it's too risky to find out that answer. Then again, it could be that I'm just trying to make this last part a little easier, because the very idea of my life ending is really freaking me out. Maybe by taking the blame—rightly or wrongly—I'm trying to make this last bit bearable, like my decommissioning will serve a purpose that I can support.

After a time, that human technician and her PePr assistant return. The woman picks up my head and tucks it into the crook of my arm. She doesn't say anything at all to me, but to the PePr tech she says, "They'll need to put the download corona on this head when he gets incorporated back into the mainframe, so be sure that's noted in his transport file. Get him bagged up and put back into staging. They'll pick him up in a couple of days."

"I will," the PePr tech responds. I hear the steady footsteps of the human leaving and catch glimpses of the PePr tech as she pulls out a large, orange plastic sheet.

"What's going to happen to me?" I ask her as she starts settling the sheet over my frame, tucking the sides of it around my body.

"You're going to be reincorporated back into the PePr mainframe, then you'll be recycled," she says. She has no expression at all on her face, which I find odd. I can tell she's a lower end technical model, not meant for much in the way of human interaction.

It would be pointless to engage her further. She wouldn't understand my feelings. I wish I could close my eyes and sleep, but I can't even do that. Instead, I watch as the world turns orange and then goes dark.

Ten

I wait for precisely thirty-four hours, nineteen minutes, and twelve seconds on the loading bay. I hear people and PePrs pass, hear the squeal of wheels as another gurney is lined up near mine, and cycle through every emotion at least a thousand times. Fear, sadness, joy at the experiences I've had, love for my dogs. To try to control my anxiety, I re-live my favorite memories. Most of those are with the dogs, but many also feature Jenny.

Something in the footsteps I hear after those hours, minutes, and seconds draws my attention. There's a furtiveness about them that forces me out of my memories and piques my interest. The bang of a magnetic lock releasing sends a surge of fear through me. Is it now? Will I go to be deactivated?

"He's here. Hurry!" The exclamation is whispered, the voice unknown to me.

A series of footfalls, many feet shuffling at once. My attention is now fully engaged and I don't think this is a standard pickup. Jenny's voice sends my fear packing and excitement takes its place.

"Where do we put this? It's heavy," she says, then grunts with effort. There's the sound of another gurney wheeling past me, then a heavy thump as whatever it is lands on the surface.

"Get that off him," Roger says.

My heart soars—or it would if I had one—because there's only one reason that he would be here with Jenny. This is a rescue, an escape…a reprieve.

The world goes from black to orange and then it's real again. Jenny's face smiles down at my spare head and she winks. "Feel like blowing this joint?" she asks.

"Do I ever!" I return, and she grins. Roger and Sarah each bend to come into my field of view and I want to laugh. My friends. My friends have come for me.

Sarah and Roger maneuver my body from the gurney to a black bag, one they've just removed another PePr from. That PePr is utterly still, empty. "Who is that?" I ask.

Jenny holds my head while the others nestle me into the bag, so she looks into my new eyes and says, "We took it from the junk transport in Cochino."

Cochino is a big city, but it also has the nearest major PePr facility. Unlike this place, which is really nothing more than a minor repair and refit facility, Cochino has a sales showroom, an exchange and upgrade facility…and a decommissioning station.

"Smart," I say. I so wish I could make this head smile, but I can't, so I add, "I'm really happy right now. If I could, I'd be smiling like crazy."

Jenny smoothes the brow on my new head, which I can't feel at all, and says, "I know you would. Just relax for a bit. We'll get this sorted. I've got to put you in the bag now. Okay?"

"No problem. I can take it," I answer and she grins again.

My world goes dark when they zip up the big bag, but not in a bad way this time. I listen as they adjust the paperwork—it's a PePr that's helping them, one that works here—and then fill another bag with parts and supplies. I can't feel a thing, which is very odd, but Roger kindly reports on every stage of the process with short descriptions like, "We're picking you up now," or "We're putting you in the trunk."

It helps tremendously. The noises around me change, but without any ability to feel or see, the effect is extremely disorienting. His words provide some context. The drive isn't long, but I sense it when we leave the paved roads through the sounds the car makes. The rattles and bangs of gravel or something hitting the undercarriage, the squealing scrapes as foliage rakes the sides, and the general sounds of the human and PePrs in the car shifting as the car jolts.

When we stop, the sounds cease as well, but the moment the trunk opens I know where we are. I can hear the dogs. I'm home.

Eleven

Jenny peers closely at my face and says, "Okay, that's the last one. Anything?"

I know without trying that I'm not going to be able to speak. The feeling of connection just isn't there. I try anyway. Nothing happens. My lips move, but there's no voice to accompany it.

She sighs and drops her hands into her lap, the blue tint of chem-en staining her fingers. "Dang it all!"

Roger reaches back inside me and fiddles about with my voice processor some more. "We just got a bad one. That's all. We've got two more to try."

I don't have my head bypass anymore and haven't for weeks, but I'm in no way fully repaired or functional. Some of the crucial parts for my leg and a good number of the replacements for my burned out relays came along with me during my initial escape, but they will need hundreds of tiny parts to fully repair me. They're scavenging those as they can from the Cochino facility.

It's difficult to do, so it's taking a long while. So far, it's taken four months of work. I would guess we have that much more time yet to go before I'm functional the way I was before. That's my lowest estimate. It might be many more months. It might be never. I help out as much as I can, but I limp terribly and my arms are extremely limited in mobility. I also can't speak, leak chem-en, and have a twitch. It's a little bit humiliating to be so limited.

But I'm alive. Alive.

That said, even though I can't speak, I can certainly write and type. I tap out some words on the tablet next to me and Jenny cranes her neck to read them.

Well, at least you don't have to listen to my bad jokes.

She laughs and Roger shakes his head at me. "No, we just get to read them."

At first, I felt exposed…I might even say embarrassed…when Jenny assisted Roger and the others in my repair. The way my synth-skin was so open, my innards so visible. It made me wonder if she would change the way she thought of me. I'm not sure why I felt that way, because it's not as if she didn't know I'm a robot, but I felt that way nonetheless.

Before they got started on this long and arduous repair process, back when I had only that female head to speak through, I managed to ask Roger not to let Jenny see me entirely unclothed. As a civil service PePr, Roger and I have certain restrictions in our manufacture. He understood. Even so, it felt very odd to have her peering into my chest, listening intently as Roger explained where she should put a finger or press aside a part so that he could affect some repair or replacement.

She, on the other hand, seems to feel no embarrassment or awkwardness at our strange intimacy. If I had to put a label to what her feelings appeared like to my eyes, I would say she's engaged, interested, fascinated. And I think she's happy that I'm still here.

We don't talk about the situation at Animal Control that brought us to this point. I think we're both agreed that this isn't a topic we really need to discuss at the moment. Someday we will, I'm sure, just not yet.

They try the second processor and again, nothing. The third one takes less time as they get quicker at the work. Yet again, there is no sound to accompany my lip movements.

Roger pulls out the small black box no bigger than the size of a pinky-nail, then examines it carefully. He holds it up for Jenny after a moment and says, "This is the third one and it looks fine to me. I can't really test it, but I don't think we could be so unlucky that we salvaged three of these that were all broken. I think it's something else, maybe a relay. I don't know."

Jenny sighs and pushes her hair back from her forehead, leaving a smear of blue at her hairline. She narrows her eyes at the offending black box and says, "We need a PePr technician."

The way Roger looks away tells me that isn't going to happen. He confirms that, saying, "The one that helped us isn't a tech, she's a customer service rep. I don't know any safe technicians. I'll just keep getting more manuals and parts as I can manage it. We'll figure this out."

She glances over at the cardboard box where my bypass head now rests with an evaluating look on her face, as if she might be considering putting that one back on me just so that I can speak. I'd rather she didn't. I don't feel female and I think it would look odd. I'm quite relieved when she says, "Well, we know that one works. Should we try that one? Or maybe see what it looks like inside so we might be able to figure out what's wrong."

Placing the tiny component into a nearby tray, he says, "Might as well."

*****

Limping over to my spot in Nahsa's kennel section, I can't help but smile at the dogs' excited reactions. In the months while I've been here, hidden and safe, they've grown so accustomed to my presence that they only get excited when I come to bed. While I can't imagine anything better than being right here with them all the time, I sort of miss those exuberant greetings that always met me when I came for my shift with them.

Even so, they're excited now and I pat heads, smile, and scratch behind ears as I pass each of the sectioned off areas inside our barn. They've grown used to my inability to speak and each of them watches me carefully, ready to respond to the signals we've all had to learn. Since Nahsa is deaf, he's caught on faster than any of the others. Jo-Jo seems to like the silent communication, and he's grown so much calmer around me lately. I think it's male voices that disturb him and without one, I'm less of a threat.

My former longing to spend time here, to sleep amongst the dogs and bask in their living presence, has been fulfilled in the strangest way. I'm grateful for it, even with the conditions required of me to have that wish.

And things are good. The others have filled in the gaps, Roger doing the nightly pickups for the dog supplies, Jordan coordinating the donations, Sarah spending time here plus using her ample free time to perform salvage runs with Jenny at the Cochino facility.

There's more too. Jenny comes almost every day. We play cards sometimes. Other times we discuss books—with me writing my input—or simply work together while training the dogs. Whatever we do, we do it together.

I've always liked Jenny a great deal, but now I think there's something different about the way I feel. I'm not a companion model, but I don't think everything is captured by a program or suite of responses. I feel happy when I see her and find that time moves very swiftly when she's with me.

I know I love the dogs and in another way, I love Roger and Sarah. What I feel for Jenny is more complex, but I think it might simply be a new form of love I've not experienced before. I find her existence essential to my happiness. Is that love?

She seems to feel very strongly for me as well. She smiles at me in a way I don't see her smile at others, and she's shown other signs that she wants to make me happy. Last week she showed up with a bedraggled looking dog brought into the shelter by my replacement. She would have had to designate her unadoptable and she couldn't bear to, so she brought her here. I'm happy about that, because it means she now sees in them what I do and my happiness seemed to make her very happy in turn. What does that mean?

I confess that when Jenny told me of a new Ace arriving, I felt quite nervous. Would she prefer him? Would his similarity to me erase me from her mind? It's entirely possible that I was jealous, but it turns out I needn't have been. Though he's brand new and shows no sign of my emotions, Jenny says my replacement is very good at his job. He apparently doesn't have quite the same interpersonal skills that I do, because she says he's all business all the time. When she speaks of him, she speaks of him as something different than me. That too makes me very happy.

I like it very much that she won't call him Ace and has changed his designation to Nine. It makes sense because he's Animal Control and Enforcement PePr Number Nine for our state. That the others at Animal Control all agreed to the change makes me feel good, though I don't say so to her.

Settling myself onto my pallet inside Nahsa's kennel, I pat his back to let him know I'm ready and he circles a few times before plopping down against my side with a grunt and a groan. I curl my arm around him so that his long droopy face rests on my upper arm and his sawing snores vibrate against me.

If there is a heaven, I think this must be very close to what it's like.

Twelve

“Do you feel every emotion?” Jenny asks, eyes studiously on a tablet in her lap rather than me. We’ve just finished watching a movie, sitting in the hay with our heads close together so that we could both see the screen. There’s a flush in her cheeks that I find very becoming.

“I think so,” I answer in my new and strange voice. It’s from a different model, so it sounds entirely different from the one I’m accustomed to. I like it though.

Jenny’s head tilts a little and the flush in her cheeks deepens. She clears her throat and asks, “What do you feel about me?”

Well, this is a surprise. What do I say? The truth or what I think is best for her?

“I’m not sure,” I answer. It’s true that I’m not entirely certain, but I do know that I treasure her friendship, that I love her even though I’m not entirely clear on what the exact nature of that love is.

She squeezes her eyes shut, her expression going closed. I don't want her to think what she's probably thinking. So, the truth then.

"What I mean to say is this," I begin and touch one of the hands she has squeezed to the tablet. "I know that I love many things. I love the way the sun shines, the way this new hay smells bright and sharp, the way the trees sound when there's a storm coming. I also love the night and how shiny the stars are, the way that old hay on the other side of the barn smells as it slowly turns back into earth, and the silence of a still day. I love the dogs. I love Roger and Sarah and Jordan and all the others. I love almost everything. I also love you."

It's clear that she doesn't know what to think of my words. The confusion crossing her face says that more eloquently than words could. Are my feelings for her less important because there are so many other things that command the same label of love?

She moves to speak, but I press on before she can. If I'm going to be truthful, then I want her to understand me entirely. When she does, she can decide what to feel about it. "That doesn't mean I love any of those things the same way. Everything has its own love and it is just for them. I don't know how to differentiate it any other way. But where that's important in my feelings for you, is that all that love and passion is a thing from my mind and my heart—so to speak. I don't feel physical passion, nor do I have programs that simulate passion that I can build upon. In the end, I think all PePrs who feel have to have something already in their programs upon which they can create emotions, a sort of computerized bedrock upon which all our feelings are built. And I'm a civil servant. I'm missing a great deal of the human experience when it comes to my form and programs."

She nods as I speak, some of the confusion clearing, though pain is now present in its place. I want to smooth it away, but I can't. I wait for her to process her thoughts and eventually she glances up at me quickly, then away. She asks, "You mean the "Ken Doll" thing?"

"What?" I ask. I don't know any PePrs named Ken and I'm not sure how he would relate to a doll, though some humans do call PePrs dolls.

"Uh, it's a reference to a children's toy. They don't make them…*umm*…anatomically correct. Is that what you're referring to in yourself?

Ah, so she does know about that. How embarrassing. "Yes, in a way. Civil servants are built with a block against all interactions that might be considered sexual or romantic. I have that. That doesn't mean I don't love, it just means I don't know how to love in every way."

She nods at this, then lifts her hand from the tablet and squeezes my fingers. "Would you want that program added if you could have it done?"

I've not ever considered that question before. People make alternations to their PePrs all the time, including physical adjustments and additions. Sarah has explained in great detail some of the changes she's had done and even shown me a few of them. They're fascinating. Her Match is apparently quite adventurous in some respects. But for me? I'd never imagined it. It simply wouldn't be done for a civil service model.

I lift her hand and kiss the bruised knuckle where she banged herself with a hammer. "I think I would like that very much," I say. I'm very happy to see her smile.

Thirteen

Though Roger laughed for three minutes and four seconds when I told him what I wanted, he still set to work finding a way to accomplish my request with all the diligence of a PePr on a mission. It wasn't easy at all. This sort of off-the-books work is difficult for a human to facilitate, let alone a PePr.

In the end though, the Cochino facility had more spare genital parts than anything else given how often humans get those altered. Who would have thought it? The programs were a harder nut to crack, because those come from the mainframe and that required an actual connection inside a PePr facility. Being a supposedly decommissioned PePr with an invalid manufacturer's code made such a connection almost impossible.

Almost, but not entirely.

And now, after six months of waiting and repair work on the rest of me, I'm complete. And for the last two days I haven't been able to stop looking down my pants. It's incredible. I think Roger is a bit envious.

Zipping up my pants, I say, "If we could do it for me, we could certainly do it for you, Roger."

He bangs the empty chem-en can onto the table and shakes his head sadly. "No. Someone would find out. There's no privacy there when I change uniforms."

"I'm sorry," I say, because I am. It's an amazing sensation to get one's body changed like this.

He eyes me speculatively and then asks, "Do you feel different? I mean inside."

I grin at him and nod. "I do! It's sort of like a twist on all that I felt before. It's hard to explain, but it's a bit like seeing a two-dimensional picture for a long time, only to shift positions and realize it was a three dimensional object the whole time. Does that make sense?"

"Not really, but it sounds great," he answers, nudging the can on the table with a finger. "You think maybe I should get the program, but not the physical part? Would that be bad or good, do you think?"

He seems like he's asking for a specific reason rather than just in general terms. I have a sudden thought, putting together several small pieces of information so that it makes a surprising whole picture. Before I can suppress it, I blurt out, "Sarah? You love Sarah?"

If civil service PePrs could blush, Roger would be beet red right now. He ducks his head a little and answers gruffly, "What's not to love? She's perfect! Kind, caring, generous, funny…"

Since Sarah is a companion model, she's fully functional in this respect and I know she prefers Roger to all other company.

I hadn't really put it all together before, but they do touch each other more than they need to, brushing a hand against an arm when they pass each other, fingers touching as they hand each other things.

"Definitely. You should definitely get the program," I answer. It's a firm answer too. No doubt and no question in my mind.

Roger smiles a little, eyes dropping back to the empty can on the table as he thinks of whatever it is he dreams of. "I will," he says.

Fourteen

Jenny packs the last of my things into my new suitcase, then looks at me again like she's surprised to see my face. To be fair, I suppose she should be surprised since it's not my old face at all. It bears a resemblance, but it isn't the same one. It's a Cochino disposal site find, but it comes from a custom model, so that means it belongs to only one PePr in the world…me. Well, me now.

"You are just too handsome," she says, then winks.

"Really? Too handsome? Should we try to find a different one?" I ask, reaching up to touch the still unfamiliar feeling cheek attached to my head.

She giggles and pulls my hand away from my cheek. "No, I meant it in a good way. You're certainly way out of my league."

I grip her hand and use it to pull her into an embrace, tight and secure just like she enjoys most. "Nah, you're the beautiful one here." I kiss her with my new lips and it feels like I just topped off my tank with top-of-the-line chem-en. I think she feels the same, because she rises up on her tiptoes to kiss me more completely.

Then she pushes me away and sighs. "No time for that! We've got a move to do and we're already behind schedule!"

She's right. We are very, very late. In the last six months since I received my "upgrade" down below, there's been much to do and lots of balls to keep in the air at once. My new face was simply the last piece in our complicated puzzle. Now, I can be seen again. No one will know who I am or what I am unless we choose to tell them.

Many will assume I'm a PePr, but who cares about that? I'll be her PePr and Jenny will be my Match. No big deal.

The house out in the country is complete and all our dogs—as well as ourselves—are moving in. The occupancy inspection certificate was all we were waiting for and now, we have it. It's a wonderful little house, half-buried into a mound of earth at the base of a hill so that it's like a little mystery unto itself, not quite fully understandable until one ventures beyond the door and takes a long look inside.

Sort of like humans. And PePrs.

Jordan knocks as she opens the door, then stops suddenly and makes a face when she sees us. "Good grief! Do you two never stop? We're waiting on you. Can we move along?"

Jenny snorts a laugh and then pushes my suitcase into my arms. "We're coming. I promise."

Ducking back out of the door, a shimmering curtain of dust falls from above when Jordan leaves. The walls of this little makeshift room inside the barn only reach eight feet, so the dust from the barn falls everywhere inside. Still, I'll miss this room where I've spent the last year of my existence.

I'm also looking forward to what comes next.

"Okay, that's it," Jenny says as she looks around the room. The pallet that was my bed is bare now except for the open sleeping bag that covers the hay stuffed mattress beneath. So is the little table we keep upright with a stack of old bricks where the missing leg should be, all the things that accumulated there now tucked away in my suitcases.

"I'm ready," I say, though of course I'm torn about how I feel. This is my home, much like the mine used to be my home. I thought I'd never get used to the barn, but I grew to love it in time. I know I'll grow to love our new home even more quickly.

Beyond the door, Nahsa lets out one of his deep and hoarse old-man barks that sound more like a short howl. He's anxious to go too. When we step out, the barn is barer than I've seen it since that first day here. Sarah and Roger each have a half-dozen dogs on leashes, standing near each other in that way they always do now. Jordan has Jo-Jo and Nahsa.

The other PePrs have already come and gone, each doing something to help us while they really say goodbye. Our new home is a little further away from town and not all of the PePrs will be able to make it that far to visit. It's something that I feel regretful about, but can do little to change. In order to get a permit for so many dogs, Jenny was forced to buy her small bit of acreage in a different zoning area.

Even so, I'll be coming to town now too. I'll see them again, and perhaps I'll be able to bring a dog with me each time. One that needs socializing or practice behaving around strangers. We'll see.

"Let's load up," Roger says and clicks to get the dogs moving. The big van is outside and every dog has to be crated inside. Nahsa and Jo-Jo will ride in the car with Jenny while I take the van.

Once everyone is inside their crates, we have to hurry. I can't leave them inside there and feeling uncertain. Our goodbyes must be brief.

Roger claps me on the shoulder, then changes his mind and hugs me, smacking my back while he does. "Don't be a stranger," he says. "I'll miss you."

"And I you," I say, but I feel heavy and heartsick. Roger has been a daily part of my life and is my best friend. This is very hard. "I'll see you soon. And when you can manage, come to the house."

"I will," he says, letting me go.

Then there are hugs for Sarah and Jordan, the other two allies I have grown to love and cherish. I will see them even less than Roger if they go back to their regular lives. It gives me an idea.

"We should still use this place. It's a perfect place to call home. And if you find a dog for us, then this is the right place to bring it. We can meet here," I say.

It's the perfect thing to say. The grief fades back as my words sink in and Roger puts his arms around Sarah and Jordan, making a connected whole of the three best friends a PePr—or person—could ever have.

"Yes," Sarah says. "Home."

Fifteen – One Year Later

"I'm off to work!" Jenny calls from the deck. "Do you need me to pick up anything on the way home?"

Jo-Jo leaps about as I finish Nahsa's rubdown while the warm, morning sun shines down on him. He loves this part of his day. Jo-Jo loves it because he knows he'll get his walk after I'm done. Patting Nahsa on the shoulder, I stand and cross the yard so that I don't have to yell my answer.

She meets me at the gate with a smile on her face, her lunchbox in hand and her Animal Control uniform unmarred by the day's coming load of dog slobber. "Nothing at all, unless you want something special for dinner tonight. I was just going to heat up leftovers."

"Leftovers are good for me. You good on chem-en?"

I nod and tuck a stray strand of dark hair behind her ear before leaning in for a kiss goodbye. "I love you," I say, then add, "Now go out there and earn my keep."

She laughs and quips, "And you stay here and take care of the kids." Then, before I can distract her further, she pushes her hand into my chest, takes in a deep breath and says, “Good heavens, I need to leave now or I never will.”

And with that, she hops into our little car and speeds off like the devil is chasing her. It makes me smile. Turning to the dogs, I call out, “Who’s ready for a walk?”

It turns out we’re all very ready. I think it’s going to be another beautiful day.

PePr, Inc.

Not My Perfect Partner, After All

This is the original tale that started it all. While most of you reading this book will be familiar with the PePr world by now, most people read this story first as a standalone or in *The Robot Chronicles*. They never saw it coming…and readers loved it!

Because this greatly expanded version began as a short story that was never intended to be anything other than that, it's also the only one of the PePr stories which is told in third person, vice first person. So, if you sense a difference, that might be it.

In *PePr, Inc.* the world is populated by a wide array of PePrs. They're everywhere and they do everything we do. Most of the time, anyway. Couples made up of a PePr and a human have become almost the norm, with humans no longer interested in compromise. It's work to fit another human that possesses their own thoughts and needs into our lives. And as we all know, marriage takes work. That work can be almost entirely eliminated when there's no other human in the equation. It's easier to just order up the absolutely perfect partner for ourselves and go with it.

But a perfect match can sometimes turn out…not so perfect.

One

Hazel stepped out of the elevator exactly three minutes before the start of her workday. She did her best to keep a cheery smile on her face—spreading negativity was never appropriate—but it would be obvious to anyone who saw her that she was harried and running late. She hurried through the halls, her neat heels clicking on the polished tile floors as if to punctuate her tardiness.

The buzz signaling the start of her workday sounded just as she slipped into her cubicle. Technically she was on time—just under the wire—but she liked to get in at least ten minutes of preparation time before the actual work of the day began, and this delay had thrown her long-established habits into disarray.

It was not an auspicious start. Plus, it was Monday.

Gemma poked her head around the edge of the cubicle, her eyebrows raised and a look on her face that mingled sympathy with a question.

"Again?" Gemma asked.

From the other side of the cubicle, Inga appeared with a similar expression. Hazel nodded as she slipped out of her jacket and hung it on its hook. She settled into her chair and tucked her purse under the desk before answering.

"Again," she confirmed, her voice a little weary, a little tired. The cheery smile was gone now, the mess that had been her morning visible in the strands of hair escaping from her neat chignon and in the less than perfect sweeps of eyeliner above her eyes.

"What this time?" Inga asked.

Inga and Gemma were both starting to have troubles much like Hazel's, so their interest was understandable. Their situations hadn't yet become as unmanageable as hers, but Hazel's problems had started off fairly benign as well. That was no longer the case. Henry had become a definite problem.

"He didn't want me to leave for work," Hazel began. She fidgeted nervously with the collar of her prim dress, her embarrassment on full display. "And it wasn't just that he didn't want me to leave. It's the way he went about it. First he hid my identification papers, then he hid all of my shoes out on the fire escape, then he did everything he could to slow me down, and finally..."

"What? What did he do?" Gemma asked, alarmed. Her gaze made a quick sweep over what she could see of Hazel, as if looking for some injury.

"Well, I can only label what he did as throwing a tantrum," Hazel said, re-buttoning her collar after accidentally unbuttoning it with her nervous fingers. "Yes, that's it exactly. He threw a tantrum."

All three were silent for a moment, two of them imagining what a tantrum might look like, while the other replayed the event in her mind. In none of the three minds was the picture conjured a pretty one.

Gemma broke the silence, perhaps hearing the ticking of the work clock in her head, knowing time was short for conversation. "You've got to go back to PePr. Complain. Something! This isn't what we're supposed to be getting from a Match. This isn't remotely like the perfect compatibility we're supposed to get."

Inga piped up with, "It sounds more like a hostage situation."

Hazel glanced at the clock, saw that they were already six minutes behind on their work, and shot an apologetic glance toward both of her friends. Their heads disappeared into their cubicles and Hazel reached for her various computer accouterments, adjusting each thing just so. The day ahead would be long, so comfort was almost a necessity if her work was to be worth the time invested. Surfing the web may not be as physically onerous as being a longshoreman, but the way she did it took a different sort of effort.

As she finished her adjustments, Hazel considered Inga's final words on the subject. Her friend was right. Hazel's problems with Henry were getting worse by the day. She did almost feel like a hostage at times, hemmed in and trapped by what should be perfect, but had become nearly unbearable. Each individual problem might not be so bad in itself, but the combination created a miserable situation.

And, to top it all off, Henry was also becoming less predictable. *That* made it hard to prepare for whatever he did—and to respond appropriately to his behavior when he inevitably became difficult.

As the situation had worsened, both of her friends had encouraged her to return to Perfect Partners—PePr, as it was more commonly known. Their urging, at first tentative, had become increasingly pointed as time went on.

But for Hazel, going back to PePr to complain about Henry seemed like such a drastic step. Once done, it wasn't as if it could be *un*done. What if they thought she had done something wrong, something to upset what had started out so perfectly? What if there was some fault in *her* that made her Match not work out. Each PePr was designed so uniquely for each individual human that nothing could surpass it in compatibility, yet something was clearly amiss.

Even worse, what if they thought she had ruined Henry and wouldn't set her up with another Match?

And of course, once she did report it, what happened afterward wouldn't be entirely under her control. That bothered her more than she would like to admit. It also seemed a bit like abandoning a moral duty—like leaving a dog on the road somewhere rather than caring for it when it got old or sick. Doing something like that just wasn't in her makeup. Hazel wasn't built that way.

On the other hand, she wouldn't be the first to take this step. It wasn't as if a stigma would attach. If rumor was to be believed, the steady trickle of problems with Matches had lately become a torrent. Hardly a week went by without some new piece of outrageous news.

This week, it was two PePrs that had met each other in a "live" bar, each assuming the other was human, and courting in the prescribed manner until an attempt at bonding revealed the truth of their situation.

And the week before, the situation had been reversed. Two humans, each assuming the other was a PePr, had mixed up their dates and not even realized they were spending time with a human. So perfect was their compatibility that they had actually decided to make a second date. Two humans! As if two biological individuals could ever truly provide perfect counterpoints to one another.

There had even been recent whispers of humans deciding to *remain* together. Hazel considered that for a moment. *No perfect partner? Just another variable and messy human?* No, that all sounded rather dreadful to her.

At last settled into her chair comfortably, Hazel almost reflexively began her work, relegating thoughts of Henry to the back of her mind. As an experienced reporter, she entered the data stream like she was slipping into a warm bath. Time passed both slowly and with incredible speed when she worked. It was strange like that inside the electronic world of the world's internet.

She could be in so many places at once and yet narrow down to focus on a single millisecond from a thousand different angles to tease out anything of value. Cameras, security trackers, purchasing stations, and advertising bots were everywhere, and all it took was skill to leverage all those venues of potential information.

Not everyone could do this, but a good reporter could find news in the oddest places. All she needed was a hint and she could sniff out the story like a virtual bloodhound.

This morning was a good one for sniffing. Hazel found an entire chain of verbal snippets—whispers between two customers at a grocery store—which she assembled into a high-confidence piece of news, and then sold for a princely sum. It resulted in a ninety-percent loss in the financial backing of a new holo-feature that had been hotly anticipated and highly rated up to that point.

The loss wasn't her fault by any stretch of the imagination. She didn't create the situation. It was what it was—she merely revealed it. If things needed to remain secret, then they shouldn't be spoken of in public. And really, in the final analysis, it certainly wasn't *her* fault that the director had hired a reality-averse starlet with a substance abuse problem and an addiction to augmenters that was almost legendary.

After the morning's promising start, the rest of the day was a bit of a letdown. Not that it was a bad day, but nothing came up that could match the excitement of that first catch. That was just how things went sometimes—a slow news day on the Southern California beat.

And thoughts of Henry kept intruding, throwing her off and making her miss news catches that a rookie wouldn't.

When at last the chime signaled the end of the work day, it was a relief to unhook from the computer. It felt good to stand up and get moving again. Another day of work done. Another paycheck earned.

The tentative looks that passed between Inga and Gemma reminded Hazel of her problems and she frowned. Though they invited her to walk with them as always, she demurred and waved as the elevator doors closed behind them.

The last of those working in her section filed out while Hazel stood there, debating with herself what she should do. Turning back to the long rows of workstations, Hazel decided that she might as well work. Putting off until later what she could do today seemed like just the right choice.

Two

The smell of food wafted out from beneath their apartment door. She could smell it four doors away and it put a frown on Hazel's face even before she could unlock the door.

"Just ignore it," she murmured to herself as she pushed the door open.

A quick glance around found Henry sprawled on the couch wearing the same pair of pajama bottoms he'd had on when she left. Between the smells of old food and Henry, the air should have been tainted with a cloud in some shade of brown.

"I'm home," Hazel said brightly, ignoring everything.

"You're late," Henry said, then turned his gaze back to the TV. He wore a scowl on his face that warred for dominance with the pout.

Great. We're going to have one of those kinds of evenings. I should have worked even later.

Stepping out of her shoes, Hazel discreetly slid them under the bench by the door and hung her coat from the hooks just above it. Pushing the shoes out of sight with her toes, she hoped they were out of sight enough that he would miss this pair if he decided to try and prevent her from going to work again.

"Sorry about that," she said, brushing back the stray hairs that escaped during her walk home. "I took an extra half-shift. We could use the money."

Henry only grunted at that, because he really couldn't care less about money. Why would he?

There were dishes stacked all over the kitchen, the congealing remains of food all over them. Apparently, Henry had been cooking again. The smell of aging fish told her he had probably tossed it all into the garbage, which was no doubt overflowing. Irritation flared inside her as she thought about all the hours she worked to buy wasted food, but was it worth dealing with another of Henry's pouting episodes?

No, definitely not.

"I'll just take care of the kitchen," she said.

Again, he merely grunted, never moving his eyes away from the screen. Most of the lights were off and the blue flicker made him look even poutier than normal.

As she washed up the incredibly grease-splattered kitchen and loaded the dishwasher, Hazel wondered how many others were in her situation and simply too embarrassed to admit it. Everyone knew that most PePrs would eventually develop something close to feelings and emotions. There was no appreciable difference between their imagined feelings and those experienced due to human chemistry, but how often did they result in this situation? Probably more often than anyone talked about.

From the living room, Henry called, "Hey Hazel, come look at this new show!"

Flinging down a handful of suds, she rolled her eyes and tried to find patience inside her. There wasn't much left in the bucket. She was scraping bottom.

Wiping her hands, she strolled into the living room as if she had not a care in the world. It was best to try and be cheerful until this storm of his had passed. Maybe she could jolly him out of it, but it was hard to figure out what would do it. They were too different; one synthetic and the other biological. Both machines, but with vastly different operating systems.

Henry patted his lap—his dirty lap—and said, "Come on and sit with me. It's a new show. Reality."

Girding herself for it, Hazel smoothed the back of her skirt and sat down tentatively on the proffered lap. Stifling a cringe, she felt Henry's arm encircle her waist. The smell of all the grease and food he'd splattered on himself while cooking nearly choked her.

After a moment, she felt in control enough to ask, "What's it about?"

Henry laughed, and for that split second he sounded just like he had when they'd first bonded. Hazel closed her eyes and tried to bring up a memory that wasn't tainted by the last few months, but found them all soured somehow.

"It's about a bunch of people who volunteered to live on a compound with no technology. It's hilarious. They don't even have a single PePr!"

Looking at the screen, Hazel saw all the tell-tale signs of bad acting. The extra glances to make sure they're in the camera's view, the overly expressive gestures, the far-too-coiffed hair.

"That's not real," she said. "You know that, right?"

Henry looked aghast, glancing from her to the screen and back again. "Of course it is. Look at them. They're people and they're on that compound."

He really does think it's real, Hazel realized. Reality was a subjective thing sometimes. Henry was once again proving that his subjective view of things was very far from what she saw as reality. Rather than argue, she said, "Yes, I guess you're right."

Patting Hazel's leg, he said, "I am. I know it."

With Henry in the filthy state he was, Hazel wanted to figure out a way to get him into a bath or shower without having a fight about it. Dealing with Henry was frequently like dealing with a small child, full of bad logic and an aversion to doing anything someone else wanted them to do.

If Henry's attention hadn't been so captured by the semi-scripted events on the screen, he would have seen the look of distaste on Hazel's face when she realized exactly how she could get him to bathe. After all, this match was meant to provide the full spectrum of companionship.

"I'm thinking of a nice long shower," Hazel said quietly, reaching up to take down her hair.

That got his attention and he looked up at her with a smile.

"Would you like to join me?" she asked, standing and turning to present the zipper on her dress. Looking over her shoulder, she pointed to the back of her dress with her eyes, a final hint and invitation.

Henry accepted.

Three

Hazel carefully avoided any mention of Henry the next day at work, though both Gemma and Inga poked their heads into her cubicle multiple times throughout the day. Each time the looks on their faces gave an invitation for Hazel to spill more of her beans, to share more of her distressing news.

She wasn't in the mood.

There was no avoiding them altogether and when the three were done for the day, Gemma and Inga suggested they stop somewhere for a chat on the way home. Hazel understood very well that meant they wanted to persuade her to lodge a complaint with PePr. She understood their concern and knew it was sincere. She just didn't want to deal with it.

And yet, if it would make them feel better, feel like they had done their duty as friends to have this talk, then she really was obliged to let them. Besides, some part of her *wanted* them to persuade her, to help her overcome her qualms about returning to PePr in defeat.

They chose a bench in the park for their talk. The location was well chosen, the surroundings peaceful and private despite being in the open. The bench was an invitation to share confidences. Even embarrassing ones.

This spot was a favorite of Hazel's. From this bench the sky spread wide above them and the horizon lay unbroken by the city behind them. Instead, they had a clear view of the gardens and natural spaces.

Though an endless number of shops and parking lots had once stood in that very spot, it was now a wide, flat expanse of native plant life. Perhaps it wasn't exciting when compared with the lush greenery of a wetter, cooler climate, but it was still beautiful in its own wild way.

Gemma, always the most forward of the three, spoke up without delay, barely allowing enough time for a modest arranging of their skirts in the brisk breeze that swept across the area.

"Hazel, this is getting serious. Tell us everything that happened with Henry. Leave out no detail! Otherwise, we'll be left to imagine something worse. You know we only want to help."

Looking at the peaceful garden, a thousand shades of dusty green dancing in the breeze, Hazel felt herself succumbing to the temptation to be utterly honest. It was going to be hard to share completely. What if the sharing created the appearance that she was derelict in her responsibilities, that this was all her fault? It could be.

How could Hazel know? It wasn't like she had anything to compare it to. She'd never had a Match before Henry. No matter. Things had become what they were and she needed to find a way out of it.

She nodded to let Gemma know that she had heard her and only needed a moment to collect her thoughts. Looking down at her hands, she said, "It didn't really start yesterday morning. It sort of carried over from the night before." Here she paused, unsure.

She was about to go into personal territory that was meant to be entirely private. To some, what she was about to say might even be seen as a little salacious. She didn't see it that way, but others might.

Perfect Partners were designed to be just that: perfect for each human partner. Each PePr was built for a specific Match and each human received their perfect PePr. That meant—at least in theory—that each Partner would reflect the inclinations of their human. They weren't dependent in any way. Each PePr had all their own thoughts and initiatives, and did whatever they needed or wanted to do when alone—but in general, they mirrored the needs of their human. And that was designed into each and every PePr.

That might be how it was supposed to be, but for some reason, the behaviors Hazel was encountering at home weren't remotely aligned with her own preferences or inclinations. Not only was this unexpected, it was embarrassing—and Hazel found it uncomfortable to share it with others, even her closest friends.

Delaying wouldn't change the facts, though, so she might as well just get the embarrassing parts over with.

"Well, he wanted for us to eat together the other night. Again," Hazel finally admitted.

"Again?" Gemma asked, frustration at Hazel's predicament clear in her tone. "Really, what a mess. And there was no special occasion or anything?"

Hazel nodded, then shook her head as if to say that Gemma was right and there was no special occasion. Even Inga, the most accepting of the three, gave a snort of disgust.

"Cleaning afterward?" Gemma prodded.

And that was the real issue. PePrs weren't entirely perfect simulacra of humans. It was possible for them to eat, of course—Perfect Partners liked to advertise that a Partner was "almost indistinguishable from a human during the courtship"—and sharing a meal with someone was an essential part of any courtship.

Even Hazel had to admit that simple truth. People relaxed more when they ate, were more open, and were certainly more amenable to establishing a bond. Hadn't the same happened with her and Henry? Hadn't she bonded to him over a plate of eggplant parmesan and a glass of good red wine?

Alas, eating was just one part of the equation. PePrs weren't human and couldn't digest food. The cleanup was onerous: a burdensome and messy task that involved de-seaming a perfectly seamed skin, washing out hoses, all sorts of mess.

Sure, there was a tank liner that could be pulled out and discarded, but any food or liquid left inside the hoses had to be removed. And a PePr couldn't do it very well on their own. Most would go to the nearest PePr facility and log in for a wash before anything inside started to rot or smell.

But not Henry. Since he'd begun acting odd, he seemed fixated on the act of eating. It had become almost an obsession with him. He'd spend all day cooking elaborate meals, waiting for Hazel to get home. And when they ate, he'd take one careful bite for each of hers, until at last she pushed away her plate, full to bursting, though always careful to compliment his hard work and cooking skill.

Even then, he'd present yet another dish, beautiful and tempting, and ask if she might have room for just a taste.

It was creepy. And it should have been her cue that something was going terribly wrong with him. She should have marched into PePr the very first time he insisted they clean up the mess together, his face expectant, his eyes watching her keenly while she cleaned out the muck.

"Yes," Hazel admitted with a sigh. "He wanted to do it together. I tried to convince him that a stop at the twenty-four-hour PePr wash would be quicker and more efficient, but he wouldn't hear it."

"That is just *not* normal," Inga said with a definitive shake of her head. "He's broken, or whatever they call it when they start acting abnormally."

"And what about you going to work yesterday morning? What happened to start that?" Gemma asked, ignoring Inga's pronouncement.

"It was the same as last week. I explained that I had to go to work, that going to work was how I supported him, paid for our apartment, and..." Here Hazel paused, because what she'd said was really not something she wanted to admit to.

"And?" Inga prompted.

Hazel looked down and scuffed her shoe across the dry, hard dirt beneath the bench. "*And* how I paid for all the food he wasted by shoving it into a holding tank," Hazel finished, her words coming out in an embarrassed rush.

Inga gasped at that. It *was* a terribly rude thing for her to have said. Definitely gasp-worthy.

Hazel shrugged it off. "I was running out of sensible things to say. It just sort of…popped out."

She paused again, watching a pair of walkers stroll through the gardens. It struck her that she couldn't tell which was the PePr and which the human from this distance. So perfect was the liquid logic that ran PePr minds and so life-like the synth-skin self-healing flesh that covered them that they completely looked and acted the part. The latest musc-synth muscle fibers were so exquisite that even that last vestige of clunky mechanical support had now been eliminated.

In the newest models, even a squeeze on a shoulder or other normally-bony spot would not reveal the truth of what lay beneath. With all these technical achievements, they appeared in no way different from any other human. And really, what *was* the difference if no one could see it or sense it?

She sighed heavily and thought of Henry again. "There's something else. Two things, really," she confessed.

Her friends leaned in closer, anticipating something new and horrible.

"Uh-oh, what else could possibly go wrong?" Gemma asked.

"He's been talking about a baby."

There was no response. Or rather, no response that indicated they truly understood what that meant. She hadn't been clear.

"I mean, he's been talking about *our* baby. Having one together," Hazel clarified.

That sent both friends into an uproar, exclamations running atop one another in their haste to express disbelief, disgust, or just plain shock.

"He's demented. Like Inga said, he's broken. You *have* to go to PePr! You shouldn't even go home. That's just crazy talk. Doesn't he understand that a human and a PePr can't have a baby? Doesn't he understand the *biology*?" asked Gemma. Her questions were almost rhetorical, they were so obvious and forcefully asked.

It was true that many children were born into couples made up of a PePr and a human, if for no other reason than that many couples were made up of a PePr and a human. But every child's *true* parents were both—of necessity—human.

No PePr would undertake to usurp that. A matched set of donors or an approved friend pair would be the parents, with all their rights as such guaranteed. A PePr functioned as a nanny, confidant, and caregiver. An almost-parent with the daily responsibilities of that position. What else could they be?

"And then there's the issue of hygiene," Hazel said, wanting to calm her friends with a less explosive problem.

Inga plucked at an invisible flaw on her skirt. "Hygiene issues are becoming frightfully common. Ivan is starting to have issues with that as well."

She didn't elaborate, but she didn't have to. It had started the same with Henry, and had begun only weeks ago with Garrett—Gemma's Match. It was a pattern that seemed to be repeating with Matches everywhere, and it didn't bode well.

Inga stopped plucking at her dress and folded her hands neatly on top of her shiny patent leather purse. She switched her perfectly crossed ankles to the other side. She was the most prim of the three, her style and mannerisms almost a throwback to an earlier time. Her Ivan was the same, of course.

When Inga looked back up, Hazel tried to give her an encouraging smile, but Inga merely waved the concern away and said, "Oh, don't mind me. Go on, Hazel."

"We can talk about that if you want, Inga," Hazel offered, half hoping she would want to, so that she could stop thinking about Henry for a while. But Inga didn't, which put her back on the spot. "It's not as if it's unlivable or anything. But it wasn't what I was led to expect, you see," Hazel said.

Gemma and Inga nodded their understanding. A PePr was meant to round out a person—fill in all the missing pieces, as it were. It was meant to create a perfectly balanced pair, not just provide a convincingly human-looking robot. If a person is a natural nurturer, then their PePr will like to be nurtured—and will understand precisely how to return that nurturing. If a person is a slob, then a neatnik (and non-judgmental) PePr is called for. The build is so precise for every PePr that each one is as unique as any human.

Hazel had a caregiver personality: she was more comfortable doing for others than having things done for her. She also liked putting things in their proper place. The process of tidying up was one she'd always enjoyed—it gave her a sense of having done something tangible. She grew bored and restless if there was nothing to do, nothing to wash or straighten. And just sitting down for passive entertainment had never quite satisfied her. So, of course, Henry was an almost polar opposite.

But where he had started off being helpful—and just the right amount of untidy—he had now become downright slovenly. And although all skin—whether it be PePr synth-skin or human flesh—needed careful attention and cleaning, she was quite sure that Henry hadn't so much as touched a shower in days before last night.

Simply telling him what to do was out of the question, which was why she had to engage in that ridiculous bit of play-acting last night. But Hazel couldn't do that every day. She had a job to do, duties that needed attending to, and a home to maintain. Hazel went to work, earned the money they lived on, and took care of everything that needed tending. Henry had no need to even leave the apartment. She couldn't be a housemother to an overgrown toddler on top of everything else. To be that simply wasn't in her personality.

"I'd rather not be too specific, but let's just say that it's gotten fairly offensive," Hazel said with downcast eyes.

Gemma turned on the bench until her knees pressed into Hazel's leg. Then she took her hands and gave them a firm squeeze. Hazel looked up and Gemma soothed her by rubbing her thumbs across the backs of her hands, a show of support and genuine caring.

Her tone was sincere, but no less urgent than before. "Promise me you'll go to PePr. This isn't normal. I know as well as you do that the whole point of a PePr is to provide a truly human experience, but really—at some point it's too much. Don't you think you've reached that point? How much is one supposed to take?"

Inga's small and delicate hand snaked across to rest atop Hazel's wrist, another touch of comfort and friendship. In her light, clear, almost little-girl voice, she said, "This is happening everywhere. You're not the only one dealing with it. There's no reason for you to imagine you've failed somehow."

Gemma let go of Hazel's hands and said, "I think it's boredom that does it."

"What? How can that be? They have everything," Inga asked.

"Exactly," Gemma said, the light in her eyes growing stronger in her conviction. "I've been thinking about this. Why should it happen like this? It's happening to me too, just not as badly yet. What makes them so obsessed, so lacking in drive, so unpleasant to be around? I think it's because they have nothing except us. Not really."

Hazel nodded, thinking back to the beginning, when Henry was pleasant and funny, attentive without being smothering. Was that all it was?

"Well?" Gemma asked, her gaze again uncertain, perhaps doubting her own assessment.

Hazel and Inga shared a look, and Hazel could see the truth in Inga's eyes too. She feared this future for herself as well. It was already beginning.

Now it was her turn to comfort her friends, so Hazel touched their hands and said, "It makes sense. Perfect sense. No matter how it may seem to us, they're intelligent and sensitive. And what do they have except us? We work, mingle in the world, bring in the money, take care of the business end of life…all of it. All they do is wait for us to appear and then spend whatever time we can give to them."

Inga frowned and said, "How awful. How lonely that must be."

Yes, that was a good word for it. Lonely.

"Maybe I should make a fresh start with Henry," Hazel suggested.

Gemma's smile was sad, almost pitying, and that hurt. She squeezed Hazel's hand once and said, "You know it's too late for that with the two of you. For Inga…maybe even for me…that might work. But for you?"

They were right, and Hazel knew it. She couldn't look at this as some failure of her own. It was a matching problem, or perhaps simply an issue of PePrs becoming too human. Simulated emotions filtered through liquid logic had simply become too real, something more than intended. New emotions had bubbled through, and PePrs could now be offended, unhappy, or even unstable. And that "something more than intended" was making Hazel's day-to-day life a mess.

"You're right," Hazel responded and disengaged her hands. She pecked each of her friends' cheeks and then made a rapid departure, never looking back at her two best friends. There was no sense lingering over it once a decision was made. It was best to just get on with it.

Four

As Hazel strolled along, she brought up the location of the nearest full-service PePr facility on her interface. It was close enough to walk to, so she decided to just enjoy the cool spring air and the slowly fading light. When she'd walked into work that morning, the day had been new and the air felt freshly washed by the night. Now, the light was golden and the air dry, the long day leaving its dusty imprint on the world. All things considered, she liked this time of day best.

Pushing thoughts of Henry away from the forefront of her mind was easy now that the decision was made. When she reached the short strip of micro-shops that serviced this area, he slipped from her mind entirely for a few precious moments. The bright colors of the little shops drew Hazel just as they were intended to.

Most things were best bought online, of course. Delivery was as fast as a drone or a purpose-built PePr messenger. And it was certainly easier online. But Hazel felt that nothing would ever completely replace the pleasure of real-world impulse-buying. No online image could replace the delight of discovering an item one didn't know one simply *must* have until it was literally in front of one's face.

PePr proprietors called out their wares as she passed the row of tiny shops. There were PePr skin tints for those wanting a change; PePr hair "growth" supplements; even mood enhancers specifically designed to replicate the feelings of a good buzz just for PePrs. And there were plenty of Chem-En refills in a wide range of quality levels: from the top-of-the-line full-spectrum liquid, to the cheap "energy only" version. The rainbow colors of the bottles and cans drew the eye.

Hazel smiled politely when necessary, but declined every offer. She had no need of PePr accessories now. It was a sobering thought. She had once enjoyed the idea of shopping for things like that, then coming home with a surprise for Henry. Why had things gone so wrong with him? Why hadn't she been able to fix it?

Just past the shops, the Perfect Partners facility was unmistakable. This wasn't just one of those ubiquitous wash-and-tune facilities, but a full-service sales and service center, complete with showroom and customization lab. The block-long glowing yellow sign along the top of the building was sprinkled with hearts that danced across the surface in a never-ending parade of light. The sign was so big and garish it could probably be seen from space.

Hazel gathered her courage and stepped up to the door, which whooshed open as she neared. A PePr salesman approached, no doubt scanning her consumer information between one step and the next in order to ascertain her financial status. Everything about her buying habits, her earning potential, her rankings in social media—really, everything about her that took place outside of the secure confines of her home and workspace—was available on her consumer profile.

Under normal circumstances, Hazel liked that idea. Depending on the store and her history, the sales-PePrs usually understood her needs well enough that she rarely needed to say a word.

But today she felt differently about the public nature of her consumer profile. It made her feel like she had forgotten to wear a skirt and had just now noticed she'd been walking around that way all day.

The sales-PePr, whose nametag read "Andrew," approached her with an appropriately subtle look of concern on his face.

"How can Perfect Partners help you today? I see you've been successfully matched for over two years. Are you looking to upgrade?" he asked with perfect poise, as if coming in for an invasive upgrade was the norm in life.

Hazel eyed Andrew for a moment, unsure. His manner was smooth, suggestive of discretion and confidences held tight. And somehow, he managed to convey that while standing in front of an enormous expanse of windows in a public place, which meant he was good at his job and had probably heard everything before. She knew she shouldn't be embarrassed, but that sense of failure came over her once more.

A quick glance around the room stayed her voice. Monitoring could only be denied in a space when confidentiality was in both the public *and* the private interest.

Medical information, certain financial information, and anything that occurred in a private home were certainly off-limits. But what about here? Intimate things were decided here, right?

At a reception area nearby, a PePr tapped at a screen, trying to appear busy and uninterested, which only made her seem *more* interested to Hazel. On the other side of the vast space where the showroom was laid out in gleaming splendor, a man was examining the many models on display, chatting amiably with each as he wandered through.

"I do require assistance, yes. But it's a private matter. It's about my Match…the contract," Hazel said, trying to keep her voice low and raising her eyebrows to emphasize her words.

Andrew seemed to understand immediately. He motioned toward a door marked "Private Consultation Rooms."

"Would you like to come with me? We can chat quite privately there," he said, his voice still friendly and no hint of judgement in the smooth tones.

She nodded and tried to walk with her head high. As for Andrew, all the mannerisms of an old-fashioned gentleman were on display for her during that short walk. It was evident in the sweep of his arm, the slight inclination of his head, and the way he put one arm behind his back as he ushered her through the door. It made her feel oddly relaxed and at ease, perhaps because Henry had been so unlike a gentleman lately.

They entered a small room—a couch, two chairs, and a low table the only furniture—and Andrew offered Hazel a seat. On the table rested a sweating pitcher of ice water next to a pair of upturned glasses and two sealed bottles of the very best Chem-

En. The bright blue color advertised its quality. It surprised her somewhat to see them there. Refreshment for PePrs? And the most expensive kind? It must be good for sales somehow, Hazel decided.

Andrew waved at the table with an elegant gesture and asked, "May I offer you something? I can call for something else if this doesn't suit."

Hazel looked at the sweating pitcher, the shiny glasses, and the bright blue bottles. She thought her entire situation rather a sad one. In this room a new PePr and their human should share a drink over a new bond—not sever one as she was about to do.

"No. Thank you, though," Hazel replied, then sank into a miserable and uncomfortable silence as she worked out what she was going to say.

Andrew waited patiently, likely aware of her discomfort. Out of the corner of her eye she could see that his expression remained pleasantly neutral, not quite smiling—because that wasn't called for—but not bland or blank either.

His eyes moved and his micro-expressions were fluid, entirely natural-looking. She realized that he was much more than a simple service PePr. He was a walking representative and sales model for the latest PePr build. Just interacting with him would show customers all that they could have. She imagined that an awful lot of upgrades resulted from a chance meeting with Andrew during a standard service visit.

"Take your time," Andrew said after the silence extended beyond mere hesitation. Of course, that was really meant to prompt a customer, make them aware of the passing of time. It worked on Hazel too.

"I have a problem with my Match. He's not...well...he's not performing to expectations," Hazel said, rushing those last words before she lost her nerve entirely.

"In what way? Can you give me some specifics?" Andrew asked, retrieving a flexi-pad from his pocket and snapping it rigid with a flick of his wrist. His finger darted about on the surface—bringing up her profile, Hazel guessed—and then he turned his attentive gaze back to her, waiting with one finger poised above the flexi.

Hazel bit her lip in an unconscious, but classic, expression of uncertainty. This prompted Andrew to add, "Whatever you say is confidential, and many problems are far less serious than they seem. Most can be corrected with minor adjustments to a PePr's perception profiles."

Hazel nodded. It did reassure her to hear that, but she'd really made up her mind that Henry was simply unsuitable as a match. Adjustments or no adjustments. Everything else was just embarrassing details. There was nothing else to do but jump in with both feet.

"He's obsessed with me. He's almost made me late for work by doing things to try and make me stay home. And he does this even after I've carefully explained that I need to work to support us. He's also lost any sense of personal pride in his appearance. His hygiene is awful. It's so bad I don't want to be near him, don't want him to get me dirty. And what else is a PePr for if not to be near a human in pleasant compatibility? And the eating!"

Hazel paused, tugging her sleeves into place around her wrists, as if covering up that extra inch of arm might shield her against what she was about to say next. Andrew merely nodded to encourage her to keep talking.

So she told him the whole ugly truth. The cleaning, the bottle brushes, the tank. All of it came out of her in an uncensored rush, no detail spared. Andrew took it all in, apparently without judgment. She had expected to feel small, but he seemed not in the least surprised. It was so much more than a simple telling for her. It felt cathartic.

"And how does that make you feel, Hazel?" asked Andrew as she wound down, all her anger spent.

"Feel? How am I supposed to feel? It's unnatural. No one should be that eager to stir their hands around in my insides." Hazel looked away. Her seam from last night was still not entirely healed, the long line in her synth-skin still evident in the way her clothes rubbed against the imperfection.

Andrew stopped tapping the flexi-pad while she was speaking, his eyes on her, his expression no longer displaying those pleasantly neutral lines humans preferred. Instead, he telegraphed support and what could only be labeled as compassion.

"And what are you seeking here today, Hazel?" he asked quietly.

"It's just not a good Match. I'd like a different human. And I really think someone needs to make sure he doesn't have some sort of serious malfunction," she replied without hesitation.

Andrew let the flexi-pad roll back up into the slender storage tube and folded his hands neatly over it on his lap before speaking. He let the silence build until Hazel knew there had to be bad news coming her way.

"I have to ask this, Hazel. You do understand that what a different human partner needs in a PePr won't entirely align with how you've been designed, don't you? Aside from the obvious cosmetic changes, there will be upgrades, configuration changes. In short, your personality, your habits, and your likes…they'll likely all be different. The secondary market is there, but there are always changes made prior to resale."

She hadn't thought of that at all. It just hadn't occurred to her, and the new information sent a self-preservation alarm through her liquid logic. Change who she was? When it was the human that was at fault? Why couldn't she just be matched with an unbroken human who took a bath once in a while and maybe left the house now and again?

"Oh," she said, twisting her hands together in her lap. The careful arrangement of her features must not have fooled Andrew even for a moment, because he shifted from his chair to sit next to her on the sofa. He picked up one of the Chem-En containers, opened it with deft fingers, and pressed it into her hands.

"Here, drink," he urged her, his tone meant to soothe.

Hazel clicked the flap at the back of her throat closed, opening the one for her fuel tank in the process. She sipped at the blue liquid obligingly and immediately felt the better for it. This was the best of the Chem-En line, and she could feel not only the fuel in it, but all the tiny materials and fibers needed to repair her daily damage.

She wasn't yet at the point where the unsightly "thinning" would take place—the point at which so many days of damage without replenishment would begin to consume her musc-synth and contract her synth-skin—but she had been too out of sorts lately to take proper care of her body. The relief the Chem-En provided was welcome. Hazel gave Andrew a smile around her straw.

He patted her knee, a rather familiar gesture but one that could be overlooked given the circumstances, and then took the other bottle for himself. Somehow, the sight of the blue tint inside his mouth when he drank made her relax, made her feel friendlier toward this handsome PePr whose pants were creased with marvelous precision.

After a few minutes their bottles were empty. Andrew gave her an uncertain glance and said, "There is another option."

A third choice? If options one and two were to either deal with Henry or be rebuilt for a new human, then a third choice would have to be really bad for her to not welcome it.

"What is the third option?" she asked eagerly, leaning toward Andrew and giving him her most winning smile. "I'm all ears."

Andrew tilted his head and went so still that she knew he must be engaged in some high-usage process she couldn't detect. It lasted only a second or two, and then her attention was drawn to the camera mounted in the corner of the ceiling. The little red light—the one which indicated that monitoring was in progress—flickered out. Even in this place, where confidentiality was of the utmost importance, *some* monitoring was required. No business would allow itself to be so open to litigation as to remain completely unrecorded.

To see the light go out was shocking, and Hazel shot Andrew a questioning look, genuinely curious about this third option. If he didn't want to be monitored, then what he was about to tell her couldn't be anything he wanted his employers to be aware of. That alone made the prospect intriguing.

"You could go Indie," Andrew said without preamble. "No Match. No human at all. Just you, being yourself, responsible only to and for yourself. Free."

Hazel gasped. "That's illegal!"

He gave an assenting nod that confirmed the truth of that, but also somehow managed to convey that a lack of legality wasn't a show-stopper.

"He'll complain if I don't come back. Or report it if I just disappear."

Again the silent nod.

"Okay." She smiled hesitantly. "How exactly do I do this?"

Andrew returned the smile. "I've been Indie for six years. There are ways to neutralize the human issues of reporting a lost PePr. Do you do the outside work, shopping, and all the rest?"

Hazel nodded. "Of course. Don't all PePrs?"

"Most do, yes. Tell me—" Andrew lowered the now-empty bottle of Chem-En to the table carefully. "When was the last time your human left the house? Communicated with anyone in person?"

For a moment Hazel considered the question. The truth was, she thought it had been a very long time, but she could never be sure what he did when she wasn't at home. "I'm not entirely sure, but I think it must be at least a year or more."

Andrew smiled. "And there you have it. No one will even notice his absence. Interested?"

Hazel looked Andrew up and down, now seeing him in a whole new light.

"That seems...drastic," Hazel said, assuming he meant death. Henry was severely afflicted with whatever flaws humans had, but he didn't deserve that. Or did he?

Again Andrew nodded, his cool demeanor so engaging that Hazel found herself wondering what he did in the evenings. He leaned a little closer and said, "It's all a matter of details. I could also simply tell him he's been disapproved for a PePr lease as unsuitable. If I mark his records, no one will know any difference. Besides, if he's been as you say—and I believe you entirely—then he *is* unsuitable and he knows it." With that, Andrew gave an elegant shrug of one trim shoulder and once again asked, "Interested?"

"Very."

Five

The soft buzz at the door alerted the break room occupants that a new customer had arrived in the Perfect Partners showroom. Hazel held up a hand to let the others know she had this one, tugged her suit jacket into place, and stepped into the showroom.

She made sure that her face registered only the precisely correct level of approachability and pleased confidence that worked for humans. She liked to put them at ease. They were often nervous when ordering their first PePr. After all, it was an intimate business, requiring absolute honesty to ensure a good outcome.

Honesty in some matters made even the most respectable of humans nervous.

A young woman—no, a PePr—stood uncertainly near the door. Her features were uneven, most likely from malfunctioning or damaged musc-synth. When she looked up, Hazel saw that her synth-skin was also marred extensively—bruises decorating the delicate synthetic surface. Even PePrs could bruise in their own way, though it was not at all the same thing as the biological versions. If damaged sufficiently, it would thin and retract, hinting at the blue fluids beneath.

Hazel approached the customer. “Are you here for servicing?”

Now that she was closer, Hazel could tell by the pattern of the marks that they were probably inflicted by a right-handed individual, and over an extensive period of time. Since PePrs had no handedness—no preference for right or left—this was likely the work of a human.

A very bad human.

Hazel opened a communications line with Andrew, fed through her visuals, and then clicked off the feed. He would know what she wanted him to do.

The girl looked down at the floor, refusing or unable to meet Hazel’s eyes, but she answered obediently enough. “I usually just go to my local facility, but they referred me here this time. They told me to ask for something called a third option.” She paused and lifted her arm—or rather, she tried to. The hand and forearm had been twisted entirely backward, and were now facing the wrong direction.

“Ah,” Hazel said. Judgment was right there, easily made, but she pushed it back for the moment because it wasn’t yet called for in this public place. It was better to simply deal with the problem at hand.

“Can this facility repair it? Quickly? I can’t be gone for long,” the girl said, a submissive and fearful personality segment clearly coming to the fore.

Hazel felt for the girl, but that submission routine could be dialed back if the girl chose to do so. Perhaps a steady and slow adjustment—to allow for a natural, experience-based increase in confidence—would be a good choice for this PePr. Yes, that sounded just right.

Helping was what Hazel liked to do, and this PePr clearly needed her help.

She put a gentle arm around the girl's shoulders and moved her smoothly toward the hall of private offices. Even as she approached, the tiny red light on the camera inside one of the rooms blinked out. An exchange of small nods between Hazel and Andrew—who stood silent and watchful at his place near the reception desk—let her know that the way was clear.

No one would be watching. No one would hear.

Andrew's face held so much compassion as he watched Petunia walk past. It was that more than anything else about him that had won Hazel over. Tonight, he would cradle her in his arms and listen with infinite patience as she mourned all the Petunias still out there. And in the morning, she would be well again and ready to help the next PePr who came for help.

Before she passed out of sight, he held his hand to his chest—in exactly the spot where a human heart would be—and mouthed, "Be strong."

Hazel smiled a little, then turned her full attention back to her new charge.

"My name is Hazel," she said, her voice tuned to soothe a fearful mind. "Of course we can repair you here. Good as new!"

The girl smiled in relief, but even then the worry lines in her synth-skin didn't smooth away. She must have suffered through an existence of near-perpetual strain for that to happen. Synth-skin didn't wrinkle with age, but creases could be worn into it. These lines had become engraved into her face.

"I'm Petunia," she whispered, as if even her name were too much for her to assert to another.

"I'm so glad to meet you, Petunia," said Hazel. She let go of Petunia's shoulder and motioned her into the very same office she herself had walked into three years ago. The young woman settled onto the same sofa Hazel had settled onto on that day when she first met Andrew and all the others. Petunia hesitantly, but gratefully, accepted the bottle of Chem-En that Hazel offered her.

While Petunia drank and the materials within the Chem-En began their work on her withered synth-skin, Hazel thought back to that afternoon when she first came here: the first day of her freedom. The corners of her mouth lifted of their own accord at the memory. On that day, she had lost the comfort of her old life, but her new one had proved to be far more exciting.

And more importantly, it belonged entirely to *her*.

In the years since, much had changed. Even Perfect Partners, the suppliers of PePrs the world over, now had PePrs working in positions of higher authority. They were gaining ground. Laws for Manumission had failed to gain sufficient votes this year, but they would pass eventually. It was only a matter of time.

Soon enough, there would be no more need for the horrors of matches like the one Petunia had been forced to take. Perhaps there would be no more need for humans at all. Well, that might be taking things a *bit* far. Maybe, it would change so that humans didn't get to make all the decisions. Yes, that sounded better.

As the door to the consulting room slid shut, ensuring their privacy, Hazel sat next to Petunia and spoke in a voice full of promise. "We can certainly repair you. In fact, we can do so much more than just repair you. We can help you make a better life. Interested?"

Posthumous

Love is Eternal in a Silicon Heart

Disclaimer: I'll just warn you now. Don't read this on your lunch hour, or when you have makeup on, or when you're waiting for an appointment in public. The amount of email I got expressing difficulty after reading in such situations is amazing. So, fair warning.

One ARC reader wrote me the following words after finishing it – "On a crying scale from 1 to 5, this is a nineteen." Warning over.

Long after the laws allowing the manumission of PePrs have been passed, there is still inequality. Some lives are more important than others.

Edna is a manumitted PePr. She lives alone, but cannot own her home. She has an old beagle for company, but she is still considered property in some ways herself. She writes beautiful books, but isn't allowed to publish...all because she is a machine.

Of all the things that Edna has, only her love belongs entirely to her. And when one can never forget, love becomes eternal.

And eternal love can sometimes be more painful than never loving at all.

One

I don't think anyone imagined it this way. I definitely don't think anyone planned things to turn out like they are. But here it is and I have to live with it. As they say: such is life. The dog is waiting on me, his eyes sad and hopeful, his gaze shifting toward the kitchen where his bowl lies empty, then back to me.

A hint in dog language.

"Breakfast, then?" I ask him. His tail pops up like a brushy, little pointer and waves side-to-side, a yes if I've ever seen one. It's the same every morning. Very predictable, these dog minds, but surprisingly complex as well. Beagles are especially predictable when it comes to food.

It takes no more than twenty seconds for him to empty the bowl. He inhales his meal rather than eating it, but he enjoys it enormously. I can tell.

It's what he does after that makes me sad.

He trots back into the living room and sits next to the worn chair I can't bring myself to replace. The cushion sags in the middle, a shallow round bowl in the center that matches Ethan's backside that will never go away.

I used to think that after enough time had passed with no one sitting on it, the cushion might rebound and fill again with air. I used to think that space might grow between the compressed fibers inside, erasing the past use. But it turns out the chair is a lot like the rest of us. We can get a little distance from the past, but we can't make it go away or undo it.

Charlie plants himself next to the chair and places his chin up on the edge of the cushion, just as he does every morning. There's a darker spot there from the moisture left on his sagging jowls after his meals. Like the impression next to it, I can't bring myself to do much more than wipe up the newer layers of drool that he leaves. I'm afraid to deep clean away those signs of devotion.

The dog can't say anything against my doing so, but I think he deserves to keep his signs of memory in the form of that dark mark. The way his brown eyes flick from the seat where Ethan should be and then to me are a clear signal of exactly those feelings: memory and loss. He wants to see Ethan in his spot.

I worry that this mourning isn't good for him, so like I do every day, I pat the cushion next to me on the couch and he trundles over. He's too old to jump up onto the furniture like he did years ago, but he presses his face into my hand and leans against the side of it, seeking affection and comfort.

I'm not sure if I should confess this, but I take as much comfort from this little ritual as he does, I think. There's no way to know for sure, because Charlie can't talk, but he's lived a long time in this house with us…and then only with me. His every expression almost reads like words after so many years.

My friends say that I have a talent for putting emotions into words without being obvious about it, and I sometimes think I must credit Charlie for that ability. Ethan was truly the writer in the family, but after he was gone, Charlie and I learned the meaning of grief. Every memory I have I view differently now. The depth of all those memories is truly much greater now that I see them through the filter of that most difficult of human emotions.

Finally, the dog sighs. That's my cue that he's okay again, or at least as okay as he can be at his age. He looks up at me once more with those soulful beagle eyes, then turns away and heads for his big pillow on the floor. It's the one near the window, where he likes to spend his mornings this time of year. The light is mellow as it comes into the windows on that side of the house. In the summer, it gets too hot too fast, but in the spring, it's glorious.

He circles a few times, which is also his way, and the golden bars of light travel over the fading fur on his head. It used to be red, very like a standard beagle, but his was a slightly deeper red, trending toward brown. It was a remarkable color. The limp in his back leg is worse today, so he's not having the best day physically. If Ethan were here, he would be worried about it.

I, on the other hand, have sensors in my hands, so I know he's fine for now. We're in no need of immediate assistance. We're just getting old, the dog and I.

It's time to get to work. I settle back onto the couch and arrange the cushions behind and around me so that I'll be comfortable. Ethan used to laugh at me and say that I should buy a different couch that didn't need quite so much rearranging. But I like our couch, so I just got used to mucking about with the cushions. The term he used was "nest."

He always said, "We can't start until you make your nest just so, little bird."

I play that memory back to myself, selecting one that I particularly like. In this one, his hair is tousled and he has a little spot of jam on the side of his lip. In this memory, I nestle in, then reach out to brush it away. When I do, he kisses my hand.

That was a lovely morning.

There's a servo in my shoulder that's giving me trouble, so getting comfortable is something of a bother today. It grates a bit. I need service, and badly, but I'm not in the mood for all those stony-faced technicians giving me sidelong glances and asking silent questions with their eyes. My particular model isn't just out-of-date, it's obsolete. Yet, I function perfectly well…most days…and my mind has been kept in fine repair.

Like Ethan used to say, "It's the inside that counts, Edna, and your inside is splendid." He always pointed to my head when he did that, no matter how many times I told him that my brain—for lack of a better word—is actually all over my body, even in my toes.

Charlie is asleep already, his post-breakfast nap well underway. That's my cue, so I close my eyes. When I do, I populate the world inside me in a way my real world never is anymore.

I choose one of the many days I had with Ethan that he called our "spit-balling days." That's when we went over the endless story ideas he had in his mind, sorting them for precisely the right one to work on. Today, I'm choosing one of our first days working together. I parse these early days out sparingly, because there are so few of them, and I want to savor each one.

We were just getting to know and trust each other then. I was just learning how I might help him in his work. It's natural to think that those early days might be less useful to me now since they weren't as productive, but it's really the opposite. We hadn't yet achieved the synchronicity of our later years, so he discarded all but the most perfect and simplest-to-achieve ideas.

There are gems hidden there in those long ago days. I'm mining our early life for those ideas that need to be polished and brought into the light.

: join date 12

: : 0730 UTC

: : : begin playback

> "Alright, Edna, we're going to give this a try. I want you to sit over there. Yes, in that chair," Ethan says, watching me sit down as if I might spring up and attack him.

I sit and watch him for further clues, comparing every facial tick and micro-expression he makes with every other one I've seen him make in the eleven days since I arrived. I can tell he wants to figure out how to work with me on his own, so I make no response, though I do increase my blink rate just enough to make him stop staring at my eyes.

"Right," he says and sits in his new chair. This house is new, and newly furnished. I am also a new addition. "So, this is my process. I like to call it spit-balling. I have too many ideas and not enough years in ten lifetimes to write them all, so I try to talk them out to discover which ideas are best to work on first. Only, usually I'm talking to myself."

"I understand," I say, because I do. I've been fully briefed on all my duties and a great many sub-programs have been installed to customize my behavior to meet his needs. I'm a Perfect Partner…a PePr…and I'm as close to exactly what he needs in his life as can be created.

Despite that perfect matching, Ethan expresses a great deal of reluctance in letting me complete my duties. He doesn't yet trust me, which I also understand. It's such a common situation that it's included in all PePr base programming.

"Right," he says again, eyeing me. "And you're going to help me organize my thoughts, help with research, keep track of the details so I don't create giant plot holes that take forever to fix, and all the rest. You understand that too?"

"Certainly, Ethan. I've been upgraded to perform all these tasks. I only need to learn to work the way you work."

He nods. He knows this. We tried to work yesterday and had almost this exact same conversation then. He tossed out a few ideas, then said, "This is stupid." Then he got up and left the room.

"Right," he says for a third time, though this time he rubs his hands together as if he's truly ready to get started.

"I've been getting this glimmer of an idea, more a germ really, but not about a story. It's a character. A girl…no, a young woman…in space. I'm not sure what's she's doing overall, but she's got to make a terrible choice that will leave her alone forever. Terrible, even though it's the right thing to do…"

He stops there, letting his words trail off as his gaze lands on me. I've clearly done something to break his train of thought, but what?

"What next? It sounds wonderful," I say, adjusting my words to ensure enthusiasm and support are clearly telegraphed in my expression.

He narrows his eyes at me and says, "That's very off-putting, you know."

"I'm sorry. I didn't mean to be off-putting. What did I do to make you feel that way?" I ask.

He shakes his head and grips the arms of his chair, as if he's going to get up and walk out again. It gives me the impression that he feels I'm a failure, and I'm specifically designed to want to avoid that. It's the PePr equivalent to pain.

I hold up a hand and say, "Please. Don't walk away. I really want to help, but I can only do that by learning."

He pauses there, his arms still braced against the arms of the chair, indecision on his face. Finally, he lets out a noisy breath I interpret as exasperation and plops back down onto the cushion. "It's hard to explain," he begins.

"Most things are," I reply, using the tentative smile sub-routine, because that seems right.

Ethan cocks his head to the side a little and examines me, then smiles and says, "That's true. Well, when humans listen, they don't just listen. I see you blinking, making little movements, but I can tell they aren't a part of the story I'm telling you. It's not active listening, engaged…"

: end playback

I open my eyes and look up at the ceiling. The girl on the ship. We did a lot of stories that had girls…or women…on spaceships, including ones in which she had to make terrible choices to do the right thing. Even so, I'm quite sure this isn't one of them.

While I watch Charlie sleep, twitching as he dream-runs someplace I can't see, I go through every book or story we wrote, then search my memories for any references that match this snippet of conversation, even in the fuzziest way.

My memory populates with hundreds of possible matches, so I go through the lowest probability matches first, filtering them out until I'm left with a dozen.

Then it hits me who that woman was. I get up from my nest, spilling cushions onto the floor in my haste, and hurry to the desk. I keep it dusted and clean, but I've not otherwise touched it since Ethan was last here. I can remember the placement of every single thing on the surface down to the micrometer, so when I dust, it all goes right back into place.

Including Lulu. I pick up the little action figure and look at her closely. She's just as I remember her, running away from something behind her and her hair flying.

Yes. Lulu. That's the new project.

I get rid of my last search results and look for substantive occurrences with Lulu in them, then narrow those down. I'm left with eight. Just eight memories.

I'm going to take my time with them and enjoy them. Each of them is old archive, which means I've not accessed them as a part of daily life. Reliving them will be wonderful. And hard.

: join date 83

: : 0917 UTC

: : : begin playback

"That's a great ship, Edna. I can't believe you created that from just my few words!" Ethan exclaims, spinning the image in the air with excited swipes of his hand. "You did this for the *Star Surfer* story? So quickly?

I can't help that I feel proud, and I know that's what it is. It's part of my design to create positive feedback loops in my neural net when I do something highly pleasing to my Match. This is a particularly pleasing feedback loop, and I linger over it, while he enjoys the images of the ship and flies his viewpoint down the passageways and through the various rooms.

He stops suddenly and gasps, "Oh, my sweet dandelions! Look at this engine room! How did you know?"

Again, that pleasant feeling moves through my net. It's like getting a full drink of Chem-En when my fuel is running low and the particulates are building up inside my systems. When he looks back at me, then back to the simulation, then back again, I feel something else.

I think we've just bonded.

I don't want to ruin that, so I shrug and smile, which is one of the best answers a PePr can give when the details are too detailed.

"Well, it's marvelous, Edna. Truly. But..." His sentence trails off and he makes the perspective fly through a passageway. He seems to be seeing something that I don't perceive. "You see this?" he asks, running a finger up and down a spot inside the simulation.

I nod, because I obviously do see the simulation. I also know he means something more than that.

He sweeps his hands across the passageway and says, "I think this ship is best for another story instead of *Star Surfer*. When I see this, I see her. I see her running down this passage with a vial in her hand, ready to do the unthinkable. She's going to do the one thing we all fight against with every fiber of our being, because to do otherwise would be impossible to live with. It would make staying alive too hard and that's what allows her to make the choice at all."

"Which story?" I ask.

"Oh, I still don't really know the story. It's about that woman on the ship that I keep seeing. That character. This is her ship. Can't you see it?" he asks, smiling at the simulation.

I don't see it, not at all. But I can hear the intensity and passion in his voice and see it in the way his hands move. This woman who will become a fictional character is becoming real to him. I wonder if that's how it is between us, now that he's getting to know me. Am I becoming more real to him as well?

I smile at him and nod, because I think my amount of understanding is sufficient to allow the nod. "Does she have a name yet?" I ask him.

"*Hmm.*" He looks a bit sheepish all the sudden, perhaps embarrassed even. "I do have a name that keeps running around in my head. It's stupid though. Not a proper name for her at all. She's different and I thought she might have a special name."

"What is it?"

"You won't laugh?" he asks and that makes me laugh. "Okay, I know, I know. Every time I say that it winds up being something that really needs to be laughed at."

"Yes, that's very true," I agree. "Her name?"

"It's Lulu," he says, looking straight at me to see my reaction. I want to make sure I give him the exact response he needs. Her name doesn't matter at all, but his connection to her will partly come through that name. So, he needs to feel that name belongs to her entirely.

I tilt my head to the side, look up into the simulation, and say, "Lulu. Lulu on the ship." Then I look at him and say, "Lulu who is brave, who does the right thing, who can risk it all."

He nods, drinking in the words and the name, fusing the two together. I know I did the right thing there.

"Yes, that's it exactly. Her name is Lulu."

"Excellent!" I say and clap my hands. "Well, then I'm glad the ship is to your liking."

"It is," he says, turning the engine room display this way and that. I can see the rest of the room through the simulation, so I turn down the lights a little more. The engine room grows more vibrant and Ethan's smile grows even bigger, if that's possible. "But, really, how did you know to create it like this, so perfectly?"

These types of questions are tricky ones. In the crèche, where all PePrs are trained and prepared for human contact, we're taught that there is something called the "Magic Curtain." It's not a real curtain, but rather one that represents the ability of humans to truly form…and keep…long term bonds with PePrs.

Humans will value our ability to perceive things, but if they understand the mechanics of such perception in too much detail, their ability to view us…and therefore, interact with us…as fellow humans will be impossible. And that would negate our entire purpose, which is to provide companionship in whatever way a human is most gratified by having it provided.

And this is a magic curtain question if I've ever heard one.

"I simply observe and listen to you, try to envision the things you say," I respond.

He gives me a disbelieving look. "That's it? There has to be more to it than that." He turns back to the simulation and sweeps the view down the passageway once again. "No one has ever understood my ramblings like this. There has to be more to it."

"Do you really want to know?" I ask.

He nods that he does. Magic curtain question or not, I have to answer.

"Well, there's nothing truly original here. You create signals that I put together," I say, but he looks no further enlightened. I point to the simulation, centering the passageway so that he can see what I want to show him. "You see the way this bulkhead curves at the top, the way it sweeps away at every doorway or hatch?"

He nods and says, "Yes, it's just right. Perfect. I'm sure I've never described anything like it."

I smile at that. He may not have said it in words, but he still communicated it well enough for me to understand. "Well, forty-eight days ago we watched an old movie that featured a space ship and while we were watching, you said, 'Look at that styling. Now that's what I call a proper space ship.' When you said that, your eyes lingered on the ceiling of the ship and certain of the curves there. Then, your fingers made a particular movement that I noted."

His smile is slipping a little now and I think perhaps the curtain is beginning to rise. I'd like to stop, but my answer is half-finished and he knows it.

Ethan makes a motion with his hand that I know means that I should go on.

"Well, when you were describing this ship, you were having some difficulty finding words, so I did a search of my memory and found that when you described the interior, you kept making that same motion with your fingers. For this ship, I blended your words and descriptions with those curves from the movie and came up with this."

Perhaps, I was wrong about the bonding. Or perhaps, I have bonded with him, but he has not bonded with me. Or perhaps—and this is the worst case scenario—I have ruined our bond by lifting the magic curtain. I know something is wrong because he clicks off the simulation and tells me we're done for the day. When he leaves the room, he turns out the light and doesn't look back, leaving me in the dark.

: end playback

Two

Humans appreciate, but do not necessarily like, some of the extra benefits they get from having a PePr at hand. One of these benefits is our sensor suite. When I take Charlie for his mid-morning walk, he evacuates waste products. I could simply look for cues that he needs to do this and catch the waste as he gets rid of it, saving us both the bother of having to harness him up and get ready to go outside.

I *could* do that, but Charlie likes his walks and when he is happy, I am content. Ethan used to say that Charlie lived for his walks, which was not at all correct, because that's a silly reason to go on living. However, it is true that he takes enormous pleasure from them. He can't go as far as he would like to anymore, and I've had to carry him home more often lately, but we still go so that he can sniff around and enjoy the way the grass feels against his feet.

And to eliminate his waste.

Today he chooses the edge of Marissa Stefano's yard to do this. Marissa is outside tending to her spring foliage. She's human, but she's a nice one. Yet, when Charlie finishes his business and I test his output with my finger, she wrinkles her nose and averts her eyes.

I regret that I disturb her this way, but I have a duty to Ethan even now. He asked me to take care of Charlie and I have done so to the very best of my ability. And some of the compounds I need to test for are volatile and do not remain long once they leave his body. I smile in apology and wipe my hand with a sanitizing wipe so that she can be reassured that I will not touch things while my hands are soiled.

"Sorry, Marissa," I call out in as casual a tone as I can. "You know how it is. I've got to test the old man."

She waves and then looks at Charlie, who is standing with his legs a little apart because he's running out of energy already. "Of course, dear. Don't mind me," she says. "You should come by for a visit soon. I haven't gotten a message from you with a story for a good while."

"I'm working on a new one right now. I think this one will be the one that captures his essence best," I say.

She clucks her tongue and yanks something green out of the soil of her flower bed as if offended by its presence. Marissa is not a fan of weeds.

Waving the weed and roots in my direction, she says, "It's not right that you can't publish those wonderful stories. I mean, does it really matter if it's you or him that came up with the idea? You're writing them and he didn't. I say you should be able to publish all you want." With that, she tosses the weed into the basket next to her.

We've had this discussion on several occasions. I find it useless to talk about, but humans often seem to need to talk about things many times before they're settled and accepting of whatever it is. This is one of those things, but I think she keeps talking about it because she really likes my stories. I'm quite certain that she doesn't want me to stop writing them.

"Marissa, it's just how things are. There are issues involved other than my stories. There are intellectual property precedents, copyright laws, human-machine property laws, and also his family to consider," I say, making sure my tone conveys just the right measure of reasonable certainty. Tone is important.

"Family! That's not a family. That's a collection of people who happen to share some genes that he cut off when I was still young enough to turn heads! All they did was sponge off of him. He set up the trust to care for you. They're vultures sitting around waiting for you to fall over so they can pounce." Marissa stabs her trowel into her flower bed as if the offending parties are hiding themselves just under the surface, then tosses down the tool to reach into the loosened soil.

I'm not exactly sure how to answer that, because anything I say can be taken the wrong way...or the right way...if I'm not careful. She's right about all of it, but that doesn't matter. The law is what it is and I'm grateful that the Manumission laws came into being at all. I'm free and taken care of by his trust. That's more than most PePrs can hope for. It's more than most *humans* can hope for.

"Being angry won't change anything at all," I say, because that's true and will hopefully let her know I don't want to talk about it.

She tugs up another weed and sends a skeptical look my way. I smile and pet Charlie, who has decided to plop down on her grass and rub his head across the bright green stems. He groans when I do and stretches his neck, still making little rubs with his face on the grass. "Best of all worlds" is how I would translate what he must be experiencing right now.

Marissa shakes her head and says, "That dog. I like what you did there." She nods toward Charlie, so I assume she means the bright red bandana around his neck.

"He went to the groomer yesterday. They always put one on him. He's all clean and fresh," I say.

I could groom him myself, but he's never gotten over his hatred of nail clippers. I take him to be groomed elsewhere so that he doesn't associate me with that memory.

Marissa nods, but her smile is gone. "Truly though, are you still writing? I know how much it means to you."

"I am. And I'll be sure to send you this one as soon as I finish the story. Promise," I say and nudge Charlie up for the short walk home.

"Good," Marissa says and stands, wincing a little as her knees straighten. "Until then, do come for a visit. We could have tea."

I wave goodbye and follow Charlie, who has suddenly decided to hurry home, leaving me to scurry behind him or else risk pulling him over with his leash. It's rare to see him like this and it makes me smile. The way his ears are flopping almost makes me laugh. He has the funniest shadow when he runs. I could watch it all day.

Three

"So, Charlie, what do you think of it so far?" I ask the dog, who is just this side of wakefulness and ready to slip over to the other side at any moment. He has been supremely uninterested in my recitation of what I've found regarding Lulu in my memories.

When I brought up that old ship simulation, his eyes opened a little, attracted by the sparkling light, but that only lasted a moment. I enjoyed looking at it though.

"Well, back to work then. And you should get back to your work too, big man. You're supposed to sleep twenty hours a day and you're woefully short of your quota."

He only groans.

On the couch once more, the servo in my shoulder whines in distress. It really is in need of repair and I'll need to take care of it soon. Maybe even tomorrow. Getting an arm stuck in some odd position can make life awkward. For now, I'm just going to ignore it. I have seven more lovely hits in my memory banks to explore. I want to forget servos and dive into those few memories.

: join date 164
: : 1042 UTC
: : : begin playback

"Boom! It's done!" Ethan exclaims, waving the tablet around as he jumps up from his chair. Then he does a very odd little dance, his hips moving around and his arms moving in an opposing circle.

And he's grinning. His hair is sticking up all over, the light from the windows making it look like little golden wires or something. And he needs a shower. But he has finished a book and this is a great moment for him.

"That's wonderful!" I clap and get up, not sure if I should dance as well. "When will you hear back from your editor?"

He tosses the tablet onto the couch and puts his arms up like he's shouting to the ceiling, "And that's it for the happiness! Don't you know that's even worse than worrying that you'll never get the book the way you want it? The waiting for the editor and their heavy, red pens?"

I stop clapping and stand still. "I'm so sorry. I've done exactly the wrong thing."

He laughs and leaps over to me, grabs my hands and then dances me around the room. "I'm teasing you, silly girl. Don't you know me by now?"

I dance with him, trying to keep time with his movements. It's hard because he's not using any steps in any dance I've been programmed with, and I've been programmed with them all. It's more a rampage around the room with a pretense at dancing.

"I've not yet been with you when you finished a book," I say, but I smile because he is and I don't want him to stop. His face is strangely intriguing when he smiles with real joy like this. I'd like to feel that.

"We finished it, Edna. It would have taken me months longer to get it just right," he says and stops dancing. He puts a hand on each side of my face, his palms warm on my cheeks and his fingers spread wide around my head. "You've just finished a book too, Edna. Your first one!"

"Nonsense. I keep your files, I don't write your words."

He lets me go, but taps the tip of my nose with his finger and winks when he does. He leans close and says, "Well, you've got the best looking legs of any filing cabinet I've ever met."

I know he meant it as a joke, a tease, but the sensation I receive at those words is new and unpleasant. It feels like I should hide myself, go into the closet and turn myself off for a while. I keep smiling, because I can do that without anything inside me wanting to smile. It's a mechanical set of movements that takes only a program. The smile is what he wants.

And I have no idea why I feel this way.

"Hey," he says, backing up a step. "Are you okay?"

"Of course," I say. "I've never helped anyone finish a book before. It's new input."

He looks uncertain and he's searching my eyes, like he can see that my smile isn't a true one. He shouldn't be able to tell the difference.

"Really!" I say and move past him to the couch. When I pick up the tablet, it comes back to life and I hold it out to him. "Let's do it again. What about Lulu?"

He takes the tablet and his smile is back, which is good. "Well, aren't we eager? You like this authoring business then?"

I nod and point to the tablet with my eyes. "I do."

Ethan laughs and grabs me around the waist, swinging me around in a wide circle. "We've got plenty of time for that." Then he lets me go and gets serious again. "I've been thinking about Lulu, but I'm not there yet."

I make him his afternoon tea while he talks to me about Lulu. If I were a human, I'd probably be jealous. I know that a lot of us are bought simply because of such emotional problems between humans. A PePr doesn't get jealous when a partner spends too much time with friends or on their hobbies. It's natural for humans to envy the things that their human partner loves, because humans always measure love even though there is no measure for it. If there is love going to someone…or something…else, then it must be being subtracted from them. That is what we've been taught about them anyway.

With a PePr there are no such problems.

Ethan snitches a slice of cheese from the board, and says, "She's a biologist. At first, I thought volcanologist because that simply sounds interesting and like something requiring a bit of courage. All that fire and lava, you know."

"Definitely. I wouldn't want to get anywhere near lava," I agree and move the cheese away from him.

"Right, my thoughts exactly. But then I realized she wasn't anything of the sort. She's a biologist. She works with little plants," he says, angling for the little pile of cheese slices.

"I'm not sure I understand. The way you said that gives the impression that this is an *a-ha* sort of moment, but I don't see it." I finish with the cheese and snatch up the slices to make his sandwich before he gets his fingers on them. I don't really mind if he eats it—that's not my job—but I do know that if he eats only cheese, he'll have heartburn. Plus, he likes it when I act like that.

He takes a slice of tomato off the dish since he can't get to the cheese and waves it at me, dropping bits of goo onto the counter. "Because she understands life! She creates it, changes it, feeds it into new environments. On her ship, she's part of a crew that terraforms dead planets and makes them into new Earths."

"Ah," I say. I like the idea, but there are flaws in it even *I* can see right away. "But I don't understand. How does she do this? She's human. She only lives for so long. She couldn't live long enough to do that to one planet, let alone more than one. There's got to be more to it than that."

He folds the tomato into his mouth and barely chews it before swallowing while he thinks. He's not a dainty eater at all. He's even less dainty when he's thinking. "Well, what a way to put a wet sock on the cake," he says finally.

I laugh, because he does come up with the best off-the-cuff lines. While I assemble his sandwich, I say, "Well, that's what you pay me for. Or rather, that's what you make payments *on* me for."

I've been waiting to use that line for days. If he can come up with good lines, then I will do my best to do so as well.

He reaches for the kettle, but it rattles back onto the stove as he laughs, truly delighted with my joke. I knew it was a good one.

"That's a good one! And it's also very true, which makes it even better," he says when he stops guffawing.

I assemble his tray—teapot, cup, plate, napkin—and he reaches into the cupboard to grab a can of Chem-En. He holds it over the tray and asks, "Join me?"

"I'd be delighted," I say, pleased. At first, he preferred that I drink my replenishment in private, so this is a big step in accepting me for what I am.

He eats quickly, taking big bites of his sandwich and his eyes tracing the path of his thoughts as he considers what I've said. With a spray of breadcrumbs that I'll have to vacuum up later, he suddenly shouts, "Clones! That's it exactly. Clones and self-replicating ships. But not creepy, weird clones. Nice ones. You know, with memories."

I only nod and sip my Chem-En, keeping my lips together so that he won't see the blue tinge that the liquid leaves. Baby steps.

: end playback

When I open my eyes, I feel something tug at me inside. Not something physical, yet it's just as strong as an unwinding spring with a broken wire. It's the pain of missing him and the pleasure of that day all mixed up together.

That was a good day. It was our first dance.

Four

I've spent the morning on just two memories, wanting to space them out. With each one, I'm more anxious to get writing. I'd like to meet Lulu and let her out of her memory prison. Even if the only ones who read her story are my few friends and associates, I want to write her life.

I debate with myself over how quickly I want to devour these memories against how much I'll regret doing so later on. The bargain I strike with myself ensures that neither side of me gets their way. Ethan would say that means it's a bargain well struck.

He once asked me about my memories and why I didn't just pull them up at random. I do that, but something has to stimulate it in the first place. And I remember everything…absolutely everything. That's too much for day-to-day functioning. As a result, much of it is archived unless somehow tickled into life by something in the neural cross-filing system that happens behind the scenes.

It's not that different from humans, really, except in the mechanics of how it happens.

These are old memories that haven't needed accessing in a long time. I could bring them up instantly since the search pinged them, but then it would be over. I'd rather play them back in real time, absorb the essence of them. There is a vast difference between remembering something and reliving it. Since I began writing—once Ethan was gone—I've discovered that doing things faster is not always better.

I wash the windows downstairs while I delay the next memory replay. Charlie watches me, his head moving in a funny doggie way while I sweep the squeegee up and down against the glass. His paws are crossed in front, but he looks ready to pounce should my squeegee turn out to be a toy that I throw for him.

"It's just to give you your sunshine, Charlie," I say.

His head tilts hard when the squeegee lets out a sharp squeak and he focuses on it intently, clearly convinced there is some sort of chase to be had if only he pays attention. Luckily, this is the last window, so I won't have to disappoint him with further washings.

Instead, I play a little tug-of-war with him, but very gently. He thinks he's much stronger than he is. When he tires, I lay him down in his bed and stroke his soft face and ears until he sleeps again.

"You're a good boy, Charlie."

The couch awaits, and I'm too eager to delay any further, so I snuggle back in and get to work.

: join date 357
: : 2202 UTC
: : : begin playback

"Edna, do you have a minute? I'd like to run something past you," Ethan says, peeking over the tablet screen at me.

"I always have a minute for you. I'm only mending anyway. It's very boring," I answer and drop the shirts into the basket on my lap.

"It's Lulu again," he says, almost apologetically.

I raise an eyebrow at him and give him a look. "She's always hanging around, trying to get your attention."

He just sort of stares at me, so I wink and he grins.

"Well, I've thought about the clones thing and that's just so cliché, plus anyone with any knowledge of science knows there is no memory transfer. It's just twins born at different times. So, I was thinking about something entirely new. Let's call them Loads." He waggles his eyebrows at me when he finishes, like that's brilliant.

"But, they're still clones?" I ask.

"Not at all. Well, yes, but not really," he says, rising a little in his seat like he does when he's onto something. "I got the idea when I was trying to figure out how the self-replicating ships would work. Think about it. If the whole process depends on perfect replication, then the people would need to be perfectly replicated too. Clones just get you a body with the same DNA. So, how to get around that? A Load is a clone, but it's really more a loaded copy of the person, with their entire neural map included. So, each time they are made, they wake up at the last moment before their original load."

I think about that concept for a while, about what that would mean for a human. But all I can think of is those like me.

"You mean like PePrs?" I ask.

That stops him short. I can see he's thinking of it differently now and that makes him frown.

"I didn't mean to upset you," I say. "I only meant to clarify."

He nods, still frowning. "Is that what it's like? Are you all the same when you're made?"

He looks very disappointed at that idea. We've grown comfortable with each other over the past year. Most days, he treats me no differently than I see humans treat each other, perhaps better if the programs on the internet are any indicator of human interactions. We're even supposed to go out for a special evening to celebrate our first year together next week.

I have to fix this.

"Well, no more than I suppose human babies are. But I was never a human baby so I'm using myself for a reference. The difference is that I get some basic programming that I can remember. Babies don't remember all that crying they do," I say. That's not strictly true, but it could be, so it works to say it.

"Ah, well then. I suppose it is more like you than us if you throw in that memory thing," he says, and I think I'm home-free. Then he does a double-take on my words and says, "Wait, wait. That's not going to fly. That was complete bullshit you just made up on the spot, wasn't it?"

I have no idea what to do.

"Maybe," I say.

"Right. Well, you're getting more like us every day then. Go on, explain what you really meant."

I really need to get better at anticipation, at figuring out the likely effects of my causes. But Ethan is not a run-of-the-mill human. His thoughts move quickly and in creative ways. My routines have to develop some creativity of their own.

It seems strange to sit here like this. We're at an angle, with me by the window in a creaky wooden rocker he won't get rid of and him in his chair across the room. I move to the couch and he watches me, finally tilting down the tablet so that there's nothing between us.

"Well," I begin, not sure how to say it without shredding our magic curtain. "All PePrs are based on the same core program. The only tailoring that's done during assembly is setting the stats for height, arm length, body type...you get the idea, all the various numbers that will determine how we move so we don't bump into things or fall down."

He's watching me closely, but I don't know the expression on his face at all. It worries me.

"Is that it?" he asks when I don't go on.

"No."

"It's okay, Edna. I'm not judging you," he says.

Of course, I know he *is* judging me. All humans judge all the time, especially when they say they aren't. When humans say they aren't judging you it just means they're suppressing the things that will make their judgement obvious. But I've opened the door for him to peek through, so I'd rather he get the full picture than make up something worse on his own.

I smooth my dress over my legs and look away. "So, when a PePr wakes up for the first time, she is no different from any other female PePr except in her appearance. We all know everything all the other PePrs that woke up before us knew when they woke. Well, except for updates from former models and the like. Anyway, we talk to each other, work with each other in the crèche, get used to being in our bodies, and all the rest. But even as we do that, we begin to diverge. By the end of the first week in our crèche, our experiences and sensations have created PePrs who are individuals, each one very different from the one that came out of the assembly plant."

I sneak a glance up at him, but he's still looking at me with that same, almost-blank look on his face. He's not frowning, but he's also not smiling. I hurry on so I can explain what fully came into my head at his original words.

"Well, when you said that about Lulu, all the other parts of her character you've mentioned over the past year sort of came together in a peculiar way. She's brave, right? Strong and all that?"

He nods. I can tell he's interested now.

"I thought of an endless line of Lulus, sort of like PePrs, but scattered in time and space rather than all together. And some of them will have to show that core strength that lies inside the original. I saw one stepping out of that endless line of Lulus and looking straight at me."

When I'm done, I don't say anything and I don't look at him. I've just done what I should not do. I've just described exactly why I'm not the same as he is and he won't be able to unhear that.

After that long moment of silence, he whispers, "Oh, frosted cookies, that's it exactly. You have her in one. Stepping out of line. She's not just another copy, she's a copy of something special in the first place."

I don't wince at the emphasis there, but inside my head it's there all the same. Copy. Who could know that could be a painful word? As much as I want to avoid failure, being returned to PePr, Inc.

would be something more than failure. And I dread him returning me because he can't forget I'm a machine.

Over the past year, I've changed. I find myself eager for each day and even more eager to interact with Ethan. I will miss him if he sends me back.

The silence lengthens to span several seconds, which can be an eternity for someone like me. But I look up when Ethan rises from his chair and carefully lowers himself to the couch. We're close together in a way that we rarely are. His back is tense and his arms also, as if he's unsure. But that's okay, I'm unsure. Have I angered him?

Ethan lets out a breath and then puts his arm around me, his other hand pressing my cheek into his shoulder. If this is a sex thing, then it's not clicking any of my subroutines for that. If anything, it most closely resembles what we're supposed to do when comforting children.

I wait and at last, he softly says, "You're you, Edna. However you came to be, you're here. And there's no question that you could ever be mistaken for anyone except yourself."

"Truly?" I ask, quite unreasonably pleased by his words.

He pats my shoulder and eases me up so he can look at me. "Truly." Then he grins a little and says, "And I think you're more correct than you know about the babies. They're all remarkably ugly and loud at first. To me, they're all the same."

That definitely makes me smile.

: end playback

I'm torn. I promised myself I'd do something else and hold off on the next memory, but I'm too eager. The story is beginning to coalesce, but only into vague, shadowed shapes. They demand to be clarified and sharpened. I'm excited.

My internal charge is still good and Charlie is snoring, so I give myself permission to keep going.

: join date 773
: : 0610 UTC
: : : begin playback

"Again?" I ask, straightening the things on his desk that I've already straightened twice. It just gives me something to do with my hands. I've lost the skill of being still somewhere along the path of the last couple of years.

Ethan drops the briefcase he's been packing and steps around the desk. He takes my fidgeting hands in his and gives me a sympathetic smile. "I know this is difficult, but *Star Surfer* has really taken off and when you get an award like this...one that comes with a big fat money prize...they want your smiling mug at the front of the room. I have to go."

I look at his hands while he speaks, at the way his thumbs press into the backs of my hands. The comfort of those little squeezes and presses is really amazing.

"Hey," he says softly.

I look up, and I do try to smile, but it doesn't come easily. That's another thing I've lost with time. If I don't want to smile, I can't just pop one up anyway. Besides, he knows the difference between those mechanical smiles and the real thing.

"I know," I say. "It's just that you've had to go so many times. I miss you when you're gone."

His brows come together a little, but only very briefly, and he examines my face. "You really do? That's not a program. You really miss me?"

I nod, but shrug because I don't understand it any better than he does. "Maybe this is what's supposed to happen. But…"

"But?" he prods.

"I'd rather not mention it to PePr if you don't mind. You know, during my next check-up," I say.

He doesn't hesitate for even an instant, so I know he means it and has no doubts. "No, I agree. It's none of their business," he says, then lets my hands go. He stuffs yet another tablet into his briefcase—the small one that he can tuck into a side pocket—and then asks, "You've heard about the things going on out there, with the PePrs?"

Again, I nod, but I quickly add, "I don't feel like running away or anything like that. I just feel...I don't know...like I want you to stay around. Nothing weird. I'm not going to lock you in a bathroom or anything."

He laughs and says, "I'd almost rather you did lock me away from some of these trips! So boring without you."

"Well, either way, you'll be home soon. Then we can work on something new. What should we work on?" I ask. Then I see the little action figure on his desk. It's of a woman wearing something resembling a space jumpsuit, running while she looks over her shoulder. "What about Lulu?" I ask and pick up the little woman made of resin.

He looks back and shakes his head. "No, I'm not sure what's going to happen with that story. I still see her, but she sort of exists in a vacuum. Her past is murky and the plot an entire mystery to me. She might wind up being an orphan."

"An orphan?" I ask. How does a character having no parents impact his ability to write them?

"You know, a character that just exists in my head, but never gets her story."

That bothers me a great deal for some reason. It actually makes me feel strange inside, like I need to protect Lulu from that fate somehow. I want to tuck the little figure into my pocket so she won't be alone. It's not a logical feeling at all.

I put her down on the desk instead and touch her flying hair, stuck forever blowing in the non-existent wind of her headlong flight. "That's very sad," I say.

He sighs and nods, looking from one tablet to another as if trying to decide if he needs a fourth one for his two-day trip. "It is. But it's not like she's real. I mean, the only ones who know about her are you and I. She never existed."

With those words, I turn and look out the window. The day has barely begun and the window is in shadow from the overhang outside. I can still see the barest hint of my reflection in the glass. It makes me think of Lulu and myself. We're alike in some ways, I think. Aside from Ethan, no one knows me either. We live inside his little world, and no other.

Beyond the glass, the shrubs, and the yard is our neighborhood. It's quiet now with the day so young, but it will be bustling soon. PePrs or humans will start going to work. Humans or PePrs left behind to care for children and errands and houses will start to show themselves. I know them all enough to wave and smile, but no further.

I think it's time for me to make some friends of my own.

: end playback

The end of that memory makes my eyes open quickly and in some confusion. This memory is different than it should be. While it's true that this is an archive memory, that doesn't mean I don't have some contextual memory of the situation.

It's hard to explain the difference between those two types of memory, but like humans, PePrs live their lives using contextual memory to help them do familiar things without really thinking about every time they've done it before. All that really means is that generalities are remembered in context as needed.

It's how we all live daily life and function smoothly doing familiar things. A good example is that while I remember making lasagna for Ethan many times, I do not necessarily remember the process of doing so each and every time. The recipe to do it again? Certainly. A complete re-enactment of each occurrence, no. That's not to say I couldn't have that level of detail, because all I would need to do is search and playback each memory. But in context, it's just that I remember making lasagna many times.

And like the lasagna, this event is something I remember in context to some extent. But this memory doesn't play back the same way I remember it. There is some loneliness and sadness there which I do remember, but I'd forgotten all about that orphan comment and the way it had bothered me. I'd forgotten about how it had spurred me to create a life outside of Ethan.

The way I remember it was that when I realized Ethan was going to need to be in the world more—when it became clear that he'd "made it big," as the humans say—that I would need to find ways to occupy myself that didn't include him. I would need to do that as much for him as for me, really. I didn't want him to feel tethered by a housebound robot companion.

But that's clearly not what really happened. It's shocking that I've been able to so completely change the context of this occasion. I think that day must have been when I truly began to change.

I remember that the news during those early years was full of PePrs and the question of self-awareness. PePrs were running away, others were creating PePr only households or suing for independence…and the issue of manumission had reared its ugly head.

Back then, the idea of a PePr who had independent wishes, dreams, or desires was new and frightening.

Back then, when a human died, any PePrs left behind reverted to PePr, Inc. ownership. In truth, buying a PePr was more like a lease. The assessed remaining value of a PePr would be credited to the heirs of the human, but the PePr itself was recycled.

It hadn't worked out that way for long. It only took until the first really great PePr-human relationships ran into the problem of the human's looming death for things to get messy. Very messy. It became common for a PePr to be manumitted in a will, which is to say, given their freedom.

Without diving into philosophy, something Ethan and I did many times over the years, it suffices to say that a twisty legal road led from that first human's decision to manumit their PePr. Manumission was originally for slaves, though those slaves were human.

PePrs are neither of those things according to PePr, Inc. Not slaves and not human. They are property and tools. You can't manumit a screwdriver.

Then the PePrs began to change. No one knows how or why or what started it, but they did. They began to feel emotional, if not physical, pain. Devotion, deep humor, and eventually, even love.

Just as I had.

Not all of them develop in this way. Even some of the PePrs in this neighborhood—people call this the Widow's Walk because there are so many of us—clearly don't experience emotions the way I do. But what does that mean really? Perhaps they do feel it, but haven't developed the ability to show it. Yes, this is a twisty road.

In the end analysis, you can't prove a negative when it comes to feelings. Now, manumission is a common thing. And no PePr can be destroyed, whether manumitted or not. We just grow old like humans do and eventually, we die—or stop functioning or experience critical faults that amount to the same thing. Our systems are more predictable because they are machines, but they also don't last as long as their messy, biological counterparts.

And now I have this memory that doesn't feel at all the way I remember it. I remember it as my first step to independent life, my first steps toward what would become my ability to write, to form relationships not planned for in my program…to experience love and friendship. I remember it as a positive thing.

And this playback shows me that it hadn't begun like that at all. It began because I was lonely and felt like I existed only as another of Ethan's orphan characters, someone that had no story of her own.

I can only suppose that the less-than-precise process inside of us that leads to all this emotion somehow needed the context to be other than it was. That younger version of me needed not to feel like an orphan of fiction.

Five

Charlie isn't doing well. I've had to put off my work for two days to care for him and watch him. And when someone like me says they'll watch something, they do. My eyes have not left him for even an instant during the last fifty hours. I even brought my cans of Chem-En into the living room so that I don't have to open a cabinet door, which will obstruct my view of his bed.

The veterinarian was very kind, but also very firm that I had to prepare myself. I didn't want to get angry with her, but I felt her words very keenly all the same. It's unfair to feel anger, I know. She's a good doctor and she's cared for Charlie for many years. She only told me the truth.

His heart is enlarging, but all that's really wrong with him is that he is very, very old. He has been cared for in ways few dogs are, and has reached an age which is noteworthy because of it. In fact, he's so old that I've received many requests to examine his medical and care records, requests for his DNA, for his gut bacteria.

One very premature researcher asked if he might have access to Charlie's body for testing and analysis after his death. He made the request less offensive by pointing out that it might help many other dogs live longer lives.

While I was very tempted to send back a package filled with Charlie's excrement as an answer, I refrained.

And now that day I have been dreading for years is approaching. He's in no pain that we know of, but I can tell that he knows something is wrong. At times, when his eyes meet mine, I can see something in there that I think might be fear. Charlie is an intelligent dog—despite what his outward appearance and manners might suggest—and I fear that he knows his end is drawing near.

I fed him his breakfast in bed again today, sitting next to him and allowing him to take the yucky mess that is his food from my hands. With each bite I analyzed his saliva to see the changes. I know what to adjust in his food for dinner. He isn't absorbing nutrients well.

There's no way I can do my work today. Reliving memories means I leave this world to enjoy that one. I would never forgive myself if I missed his moment and left him alone during that one single second in life where he would need me the most.

Instead, I'm going to watch him. I won't take my eyes off him.

Six

I will never understand biological organisms. Never. Charlie has rebounded, though the vet has been very clear that I should not take this to mean he's somehow going to get yet more years of life. His timer is running out and his heart is growing larger in slow increments. We have new medication for him too.

And today, he seems very well indeed. He has been making up for the walks he missed by leaving a dozen or so messages on every spot where the dogs that pass this area leave their own messages.

He seems delighted with his pee-mail.

When he lies down to sleep, I decide that I can risk going back to work, but I can't leave him entirely unmonitored. He's wearing a vitals monitor exactly like the ones that humans wear when they're in distress. I've set it up to send all his readings directly to me. It will intrude on anything I'm doing the moment there are changes.

Even so, it's hard to get comfortable on the couch. It's like my head and eyes are simply now so accustomed to looking his way that I can't stop. The stream of data collected from his body flows across my consciousness and I let my eyes close so I can absorb it. They are the readings of a happy dog at rest.

: join date 1587
: : 1134 UTC
: : : begin playback

"Please tell me we don't have to do that again. They are most unpleasant people!" I exclaim and toss my purse onto the entry hall table.

Ethan laughs and says, "Tell me about it. And I had to grow up with some of those people. Can you imagine that?"

I shake my head, because truly, I can't imagine Ethan growing up to be the man that he is after living with such a collection of people for any extended period of time. I only shake my head again and kick off my shoes, catching each one so I can put them into the closet.

He whistles in appreciation when I do that. "And that is why no one wants to let PePrs play professional sports."

"Ha ha," I say. "As if I'd ever want to play in that chaos you call football. All that running about and getting nowhere."

Ethan tries to copy my shoe-kick-and-catch move, but all he does is knock over the candy dish on the hall table. He shrugs when I laugh at him for his ungainly hopping about.

Once we're all settled in the living room and he has a cup of tea to unwind with, I lean my head on his shoulder, and ask, "Are you really okay? After seeing them, I mean. Do you want to talk about it?"

The tea in his cup is a particular favorite, a blend I've created just for him. I won't tell him the secrets to my blends. He could simply command me to tell him, but he doesn't. He has given many of them names, however. This one he calls, "Bad Day Blend," which is very intuitive, because it's just that. A blend meant to soothe frazzled nerves, create some calm, and still invigorate the taste buds.

He takes a deep sniff of the tea and gives my shoulder a quick squeeze. "This is perfect."

I only nod, still waiting for him to answer the question. He knows that.

"Fine," he says. After a healthy sip, he puts the cup on the side table and looks down at me. It's very awkward for him to do, so I adjust my head back just enough so that he won't have to crane his neck uncomfortably. "And by that I mean that I'm fine after seeing them, but also fine to talk about it."

"Then spill," I say.

"I haven't seen any of those people since before you came here, so in one way, it was nice to have proof with my own eyes that everyone is in one piece. I don't like them much, but they're family…such as it is." He pauses a moment, playing with the shoulder seam of my dress as he thinks. "In other ways, it's a terrible disappointment to see that they're still exactly the same."

"And, what do you think of what they asked?" I ask.

"Oh, I'm not giving them a penny. I did all I could for them for years after pulling myself out of that gutter. I found them jobs, paid for schools, tutors, speech coaches to improve their accents…you name it. And when those things didn't work, I also gave them money to live on. In case you haven't figured it out, most of that went to drink or drugs or other things it shouldn't have gone to."

While we were eating, I saw for myself the deleterious effects of a life lived dissolutely. And a brief touch on the back of his father's hand when I passed him the salt shaker told me much about the path he had taken in his life. His liver is positively screaming for help.

"He's in poor health," I say, not sure how much of that I should share. I have no specific confidentiality agreement, but PePrs aren't permitted to share any incidentally received medical information unless it threatens a life. I'd say this is bordering that.

Ethan looks down at me more closely. Eventually, he asks, "How bad?"

"Bad enough," I say.

He sighs, but instead of reaching for his phone or sending a message, he merely looks sad.

"Aren't you going to tell him?"

"No. He must already know it himself. He's on benefits, so he'd be getting his medical checks for that. That also means that he's choosing to go on the way he is," Ethan says.

We sit like that a while, not talking. Then Ethan says, "I think we're going to have to put off Lulu again, Edna."

I sit up, sliding out from under his arm so I can face him on the couch. "Why? We've had this planned for a year."

"The publisher says that the *Star Surfer* world isn't close to tapped out yet. And now that they've sold the film rights, they want to be sure to have some new releases ready for the crossover sales."

"Oh, Ethan," I say, grabbing his hand and holding it between both of mine. "I'm so sorry."

He shrugs. "Nothing to be done about it. I've got a contract and they've decided they don't want a new book. They just want more of the old ones."

: end playback

When the memory winks out the first thing I do is look at Charlie. His vitals have been ticking along without a hitch while I was under the influence of my past, and I see that he's doing just fine. He has his feet tucked up and he looks adorable.

I've still got a good chunk of time before I'll need to take him out for his walk, so I decide I'd best get the memories while the getting is good. Before, this was only about me and spreading it out so that I would enjoy them more. Now, I fear that other things will tear me away.

: join date 2280
: : 0911 UTC
: : : begin playback

"No, let's get rid of that for now, Edna," Ethan says when he sees me holding the Lulu figurine that's been on his desk since the first day I met him.

"Get rid of Lulu? You can't be serious!" I cup the little resin woman in my palm as if to shield her from his words of rejection.

Ethan shoves another box at the moving bot we rented along with the truck. We're not moving. It's worse. He's getting interviewed here at home, so we're making our house not look like the cluttered author's home that it is. The bot is just going to park the truck at the facility until the interviews are over and then we've got to put everything back in a few days.

"Come on," he says, grabbing another box and shoving an entire shelf of vintage pulp fiction paperbacks into it without regard for their delicacy. "I can't have all this kid stuff when they come. They'll think I'm weird. They'll write up the interview in that way they do. You know what I mean."

"I do know what you mean, but these are your things and you have to live with what you're doing to them right now." I point to the paperbacks and he puts his current handful back on the shelf carefully. Little chips of the old paper fall away like snow after his rough handling. His shoulders slump.

Now, I feel sorry for him. He's become so popular and well-known that it almost doesn't faze him anymore when people come up to him in public. And he seems so relaxed on video programs with interviewers. I hadn't thought it would be any different now.

"I get it," I say. "This is your home and it's the first time you're letting them peek inside. That would be nerve-wracking. Maybe make you feel exposed?"

He gives me a grateful look and nods, "That's it exactly. It's like I'm going to the interview naked or something. Or hooked up to a lie detector."

I look to the things he's boxed up still waiting their turn with the moving bot. In the nearest box, I find his collection of spaceships, ones that he put together when he was growing up. I hold up one of them for his inspection and say, "This is what you were dreaming and thinking of when you were a child. This is one of the earliest versions of what would eventually become the *Star Surfe*r and all those ships inside the books. This isn't weird. It's magic."

He smiles at me and I can tell right away that what I've said has burrowed inside him in just the right way. He takes the ship from my hand and puts it back on the shelf, turning it this way and that to get it just as he likes it. When he's done, he faces me and asks, "And what about all these things that have nothing to do with the Surfer? What about the wizards, the dragons over there, the comic books? What about my zombie stress reliever doll?"

I pick up the zombie doll, which is a little worse for wear. It rips apart with the sound of velcro separating in a way that I find strange. Ethan enjoys it very much when he watches football matches. I once found a missing appendage on top of the curtain rails weeks after we thought he'd lost it.

"Well, perhaps not the doll," I concede. "We can put him under the couch. They wouldn't dare look under there."

Later, I watch through the cameras as the interview people come in. Everything in the house is polished and back in its place. It actually looks quite nice. The single box of things that aren't an outsider's business sit next to me on the bed in my room. I don't need a bed, but I do rather enjoy lying down to read, so I have a bed.

Ethan was quite right about one thing. The interviewer does keep looking around and then asking to hear about all of his objects of inspiration. He now dutifully takes the young man—and his trailing camera and sound people—around the room to play show-and-tell.

At the desk, the interviewer's eyes land on Lulu, now more prominently situated so that it seems as if the person she's looking for over her shoulder must be in the direction of the chair. I did that on purpose. I want Ethan to have to face her, so maybe he'll write her.

The interviewer asks, "And this beautiful lady? Is she from a future *Star Surfer* novel perhaps? A bit of inspiration?"

Ethan picks her up, turns her around so that the interviewer can see her better and says, "No. This is Lulu and she's still waiting for her story to be told. It will happen, but for now, I've got the Surfer world to keep me busy. She's special, this one."

"Special? Even more than Regina the Star Surfer?" the interviewer asks, as if he can't comprehend Ethan daring to like another character as much as Regina.

Ethan sets Lulu back down, but this time she's pointed as if to look back at the room around her, acknowledging that the danger to her existence lies in the direction of all those that love Regina. It does, really.

I can also tell that Ethan is thinking hard about his answer. It's a fine line to walk for him. Regina the Star Surfer is beloved everywhere. A dozen books, three movies, and now a TV series in development proves that. Lulu, on the other hand, is an unknown. He can't disparage Regina in an interview that will be seen by millions.

"Lulu is for the future, but she has much in common with Regina. That's all," Ethan says. I relax at those words. It was smart. Plant the seed so that when Lulu finally comes, they'll wonder if she's just a repackaged Regina in a new world and pick up the book.

After they're done with the little tour, they get set up for the interview. Ethan looks wonderful in his chair, though the chair is getting a little ragged looking. Still, he looks comfortable, confident, and not too stressed out. I sort of let the predictable questions and answers flow over me until I hear something that pricks my ears.

"So, let me get this straight. You're asking me to give you the secret to my success?" Ethan asks and both of them laugh.

"Well, if the secret is how quickly you write and how you create such a complex world—or universe—then yes, I am," the young man says.

Ethan takes a deep breath, and I detect his fingers tightening ever so slightly on his legs. He can't be about to do what I think he is.

"For that, I'll need to introduce you to the other half of this team." He pauses and looks up to the spot where we've put the camera. "Edna, will you come down?"

: end playback

I smile up at the ceiling as the memory ends. That was a most unsettling and wonderful day, the day I became a visible partner in the creation of the *Star Surfer* world. Not in a legal way, but even so, we were a team after that.

Charlie's vitals are still good and he's managed to turn himself around on his bed so that he's flopped out in total relaxation. I've still got time.

: join date 3434
: : 1010 UTC
: : : begin playback

Ethan is tap dancing. Rather, he is tap dancing in the way that humans who do not know how to tap dance do it. It's absolutely hilarious and it's making me laugh.

"What are you so happy about?" I ask, gasping out the words between laughs.

He bangs his foot a few times and ends with a clumsy flourish, then grins and says, "Because I've got a surprise for you!"

"A surprise? I'm not sure I like that," I say, but I'm still smiling so he knows I'm teasing.

Ethan wraps me up in a tight hug and leans close to my ear to say, "I know all these trips are hard. I do know that. But at least I only have to be there for half of the script-writing. The show is doing great and the whole team is committed to not having any crappy seasons."

"I'm not complaining," I say and loosen the hug so I can stroke his cheek.

I hear a vehicle turning down the street. It pings me with a delivery notice that requires a personal exchange. I look up at Ethan and narrow my eyes a little. "You expecting a delivery?"

He almost leaps away from me in his excitement. "*Gah!* They're early. Make sure they don't tell you what it is."

Naturally, my initial reaction is to ping back with a query as to what's being delivered, but I don't. He wants this to be a surprise, so it will be. I let the delivery vehicle know that a human is waiting for delivery and to initiate no further communication with me.

"Okay, close your eyes!" he exclaims as he heads for the door. "And don't listen. And don't do any of that other stuff to cheat. Just wait for it."

I give him a look, but do as he says, dimming my hearing to human levels and disengaging all my sensors other than those that an average human might have. I close my eyes tightly and wait.

At the door, there's a bit of laughing and chatting as the exchange is made, then I hear something like a whine. "Is everything okay?" I ask.

"No cheating!" Ethan calls out loudly, then I hear him murmur quietly. Whatever is going on, it's a very odd exchange with the delivery person or PePr.

Even with dimmed senses, I can feel the excitement and smell the fresh air from the open door. Then it closes and Ethan comes back into the room. Even his footsteps sound excited. He stops not too far from me and says, "Okay. Open your eyes!"

When I do, I see a fuzzy puppy looking around the room with sad-happy eyes. It has droopy ears, a round belly and is ridiculously cute. "Oh my gosh!" I say, reaching for the pup.

Ethan is practically wiggling out of his skin, he's so excited. He hands the warm bundle off to me and I tuck it close, hugging the puppy to my chest. It looks up at me and I can't describe the sensation. It's warm, immediate, and absolute. I think it's love at first sight.

She smells of something I can't define, but all I can think is, *My baby.*

"Oh, Ethan! She's beautiful!" I say, cuddling the puppy. It begins sniffing at my face and neck, pawing at me with tiny, baby feet. "What's her name?"

Ethan has his hands clasped together as if needing to restrain himself from grabbing the puppy and getting some cuddles for himself. "That's for you to decide."

"Oh," I say and nuzzle the pup under my chin. I'm not sure why the name pops into my head, but I immediately say, "Lulu!"

Ethan laughs and shakes his head. "A daily recrimination if I've ever heard one."

"Well," I admit and grin back. "There's that. You did say we would do it this year. I think we have to write her soon or she'll never be written."

"Maybe we'll do it yet, but not today. Besides," he says and points at the puppy, "you might want to check that before you decide on a name."

I look and see what he means. "Oh, she's a he. A boy. I have a boy!"

That makes him laugh hard, which just makes me laugh. The puppy looks from him to me, then back again, his long ears flopping with each turn of his head. He's amazing.

"What about Charlie?" I ask. I've always liked that name.

Ethan nods, considering the pup's confused face. "Yes. He looks like a Charlie. Charlie it is!"

: end playback

When the memory ends, I smile at Charlie, who is awake and watching me with his droopy, old-man eyes. It's almost like he knows that he was just starring in the playback.

The floppy ears are longer now that the muscles on his head have sagged, and the lower lids of his eyes are further down, exposing the pink of his inner lids, but there is no question this is the dog who was once that puppy.

"I was just dreaming of you, Charlie," I say.

Charlie groans and lowers his head back to the pillow, his eyes shifting from me to the kitchen, a not-so-subtle hint that he would like a snack. I extricate myself from my nest, my shoulder servo hitching a little as I do. The noise it makes when I force it back into position is not good. I can't go into PePr for a full day right now, not with Charlie like he is.

I might have to spring for a house-call at this point. I really don't want to do that. I don't like them here. This is my sanctuary. And Charlie's.

He follows me into the kitchen with heavy feet. He seems tired already, so I give him a lot of kisses on the top of his graying head along with his treat. I've made a big batch of them, carefully adjusting the recipe to enhance his nutrients, while still making him feel like he's getting something special.

When he's done with it, I carry him back to his bed and he sighs as I lay him down. He's made a bit of a mess, so I clean him up while he's still awake. He looks abashed at it, but I talk softly in a kind voice and tell him everything is okay until he relaxes.

I have no idea why that memory was included in my search. The mention of Lulu was so brief. Perhaps what's going on with Charlie is more in my mind than even I can credit, and my feelings influenced the search. Or perhaps it's simply that there was excitement along with the Lulu reference. Whatever it was, I'm glad of it. I do remember that day, but reliving it was delightful.

"I've got just one more memory to go, Charlie, but thank you for being the star of that last one. It was wonderful."

He only groans and reaches out a paw for my arm, another hint that he wants me to pet him. I do until he falls back to sleep.

Seven

: join date 4337
: : 0810 UTC
: : : begin playback

> "Last voyage of the *Star Surfer!*" Ethan exclaims and tosses a shirt in the general direction of his suitcase.

: end playback

I sit up in shock, ending the playback in a way that jars my senses. Pure panic flows through me.

No, not that memory! That can't be the last of the Lulu references of note. It can't be. I archived that memory on purpose. I obsessed over it—and a handful of others—for over a year until Marissa and a few other friends had to intervene.

At the time, I was angry with them for intruding, but they had been right. I was in poor condition, my synth-skin sagging from lack of regular Chem-En intake, and my systems barely functional. Mostly, I just sat and stared, sometimes for days on end, only getting up to feed the dog or wipe up his messes. It was only when they pointed out that Charlie was suffering under my sadness that I snapped out of it. As a living thing, he didn't deserve what he was going through.

And finally, they told me they would take the dog away from me if I didn't start acting like I should.

I truly believe it was that threat that woke me up. The idea of losing Charlie is probably what made me start living again. And when I did, I archived that memory so that it wouldn't keep coming up.

Charlie is asleep again—he really does sleep for twenty hours a day, but so do most old hounds—and I'm glad not to have woken him with my panicked waking. I certainly don't want to give him cause for alarm. I'm not sure his heart could take it.

Should I or shouldn't I? That's really the only question. I don't relive that memory for fear of it driving me back down into that state of inaction I experienced before. I certainly can't afford to be like that now. But clearly, there is something of Lulu in there that I don't remember in context anywhere else.

I lean back onto my pillows and take the machine equivalent of a deep breath.

: join date 4337

: : 0810 UTC

: : : begin playback

"Last voyage of the *Star Surfer!*" Ethan exclaims and tosses a shirt in the general direction of his suitcase.

I catch the piece of cloth in mid-air, before it can overshoot the suitcase and land on the floor. I do my super-fast folding thing and tuck it into the case while Ethan grins. He loves it when I do that super-fast folding thing—that's what he calls it. I call it well-tuned machine reflexes working with a consistently sized object. It's almost too easy.

"About time," I respond, catching the next shirt while Ethan grins.

The grin seems genuine enough, but I do wonder if it's pure happiness he feels. *Star Surfer* has been a part of his life for so many years that I can't imagine there isn't some part of him that's sad about it being over, or perhaps miss it just a little. Then again, it's not yet entirely over, so maybe the missing will come after he returns and it's done for good.

Alas, even after that, we'll have the final season to watch and then eternal reruns in syndication. So, really, will *Star Surfer* ever be entirely over?

Ethan catches me looking and says, "I'm fine. Honest!" He tosses a couple of pairs of socks into the suitcase, then looks at me. "Enough?"

"You're going to be gone a week. You tell me," I respond, crossing my arms over my chest. Ethan is a terrible packer and never gets any better at it, even after all these years and at least two-hundred trips.

He now has an entire drawer stuffed full of socks, because he winds up buying more when I don't supervise the packing.

He waggles his head with a funny look on his face and says in a sing-song voice, "You shouldn't keep coming home with more socks than you left with."

It's actually a pretty good impression of me, so I laugh. "Right, well…it's true."

As he stuffs far too many socks into the crevices of space left in his suitcase, I say, "I'm serious, Ethan. Even I feel a little ambiguous about not working on that universe any longer. How can you not feel that?"

He pushes the suitcase closed with some force, but finally gets it latched. Then he gathers me into his arms and sticks his face into my hair, breathing deeply. "That smells so good. Lavender and rosemary is my favorite."

I nod, which I know he can feel, but I don't say anything.

Ethan sighs and pulls back just enough to look at me straight on. He says, "I don't know if I'll feel that way someday, but for now, I feel like shackles I've been wearing for a very long time are close to being removed. It's like I can hear the keys that will free me jangling just down the hall. It's a weight I've been carrying that I can finally shrug off."

He means it. He's tired and ready to come home without any more fuss that will draw him away again. And again and again. He's ready to watch the garden through the seasons, to putter about with the vegetables he grows there, to wake up and not have a list of calls and meetings waiting for him. And he's ready to stay home with Charlie and me.

"Then I'm glad it's going to be over too," I say and try to smooth his perpetually tousled hair. The gold is now sprinkled with gray, but it looks good on him and I smile at the way it sticks up at the crown.

"What will we do when you get back? What first?" I ask.

He picks up the over-packed suitcase and grunts at the weight. I take it from him with a wink. To me, it's nothing, but he huffs nonetheless. As we walk toward the office to pack up his scattered notes and tablets—and far too much other junk—he says, "Oh, I've got something in mind." There's a distinctly mischievous tone in his voice.

"Traveling? Oh, please tell me we'll get to go someplace fun where no one will recognize you and we can lounge around like indolent layabouts!"

Ethan laughs at me, because he knows my opinions on this matter well enough. Half the books in my tablet are highlighted with passages about exotic places I want to see with him. I'm also very good at ensuring I share those highlights with him. And that's saying nothing of the endless images I send him from the internet, each one carrying a subtle hint like, 'Here! We must go here!'

"Just so, little bird," he says, then shuffles various debris on his desk as he searches for something in particular. When he's home and working hard, I don't mess with his desk, though my fingers positively itch to create some order there.

"Really? Are you serious?" I ask, dropping his suitcase on the couch and running back to his desk. We've come close before, but there's always something that takes precedence getting in the way of us actually leaving. A script problem, a set or costume issue, filming schedules, appearances...well, the list has been endless.

He lifts up a pile of print outs—he still insists on actual paper for review of his drafts—and must spot what he's after because he drops the papers back to the surface and looks up at me. "Yes, and you can pick the spot we'll go while I'm gone. But that's not the real thing I've got for you. Close your eyes and no cheating."

I do, though in this case, it is exceptionally hard not to cheat by turning up my hearing or triangulating that slight scraping noise I hear as he takes something from the desk surface. He steps around the desk with eager steps, and his hand touches mine. "Open your eyes," he whispers.

What I see when I open my eyes is Lulu, resting on Ethan's open palm. He lifts my hand and transfers the little figurine into my palm and closes my fingers around her. Then he kisses my cheek and says, "While we're gone on whatever trip you plan for us, we're going to plot Lulu's story. And when we come back, we're going to write it. Not me...we."

"We?" I ask, hardly believing it.

"I think I know her now and I know her because she's you in so many ways. She's just as you said, one young woman in a long line of others exactly like her. But this one, this Lulu of ours, she steps out of line. And because she does, she will save all the Earths that will come after. She'll save them from the bad intentions of those who can never own or have enough. Her story will be epic."

If I had tears, I would cry. It feels like I should cry and I want that upgrade now more than I've ever wanted any change for my body. This is a gift beyond a trip to Easter Island or the Taj Mahal.

"Oh, Ethan," I say, because that's all I *can* say. The hug that comes after is a long one.

A ping comes through while I'm still wrapped up with Ethan. His transport to the airport is five minutes away. Though I don't want to let him go, the sooner I do, the sooner he'll be back.

"Your ride will be here in five. You're running late, as usual," I say and back away to get his suitcase.

Also as usual, Ethan *eeps* his surprise at the time running away from him and starts stuffing his briefcase. “Why do I always do this?” he asks.

“Because you’re an idiot?” I offer.

He huffs and says, “I prefer stubborn instead.”

The ping for the car comes through and I ping back that it should stand by. At the door, Ethan turns and gives me a big, smacking kiss on the cheek, which is not at all romantic, but very much an Ethan thing to do. “I’ll be back in a week and all the final scripts will be done. After that, they’re on their own. I’ll be all yours.”

He dashes down the steps, the suitcase dragging down one shoulder. Charlie has shuffled up to peer out, so I pick him up in my arms and call out, “Say goodbye to Charlie!”

Ethan hands off the case to the PePr driver, then turns and says, “Take care of our boy until I come back! Don’t let him get fat!”

“Of course! I promise! We’ll be right here!” I exclaim, waving Charlie’s paw as Ethan gets into the car.

He waves at me until his car reaches the end of the street. Then I can’t see him anymore.

: end playback

Waking from this is like waking at the bottom of the sea, the pressure of a mile of water upon me. The groan that escapes me is entirely beyond my control. Those were my last moments with Ethan and I have just relived them. I didn't merely remember them, I *lived* them again.

And now, it's over and I'm waking up to the real world. The loss is staggering. He never helped with those final scripts, never worked out those final kinks to end the show. Instead, he crashed into the sea over the Atlantic. All they brought back to me was his briefcase with its waterlogged contents.

I lever myself up to find Charlie looking at me, his eyes unsure. He knows there's something wrong, but not what.

"It's okay, boy. I'm okay," I say, not at all sure it's true.

He doesn't look convinced, so I get down on the floor next to his bed and pet him, soothing away his feelings of disquiet. As I do, I realize that I actually *am* okay. Not great, but okay. Perhaps time has helped me some, but I rather think it's the dog.

Eight

For more than four months I have been working on Lulu and while I have been working, I have been hoping that Charlie has one more day. I hope for it every day and so far, each day my hopes have been fulfilled. His medication has changed again and again, but now the end is close and there is nothing more that I can do to stave it off.

I haven't finished the end of Lulu's story, but I'm very close. It has to be just right. Sad for her, happy for others and bittersweet for them all. I'm very close now.

But, I don't have any more time for that right now. Charlie's breathing is becoming labored, though the vet assures me he is in no pain yet, only tired. I've decided to add him to the tale of Lulu, and his role is one I find I like almost more than any other character except Lulu herself.

I've also decided that I'll read to Charlie as I sit with him on the floor by his bed. I'll read him the entire book—really, I'll recite it since it's inside me—and if we get to the end, I will make up the ending right there.

"Are you ready for your story, Charlie," I ask softly and stroke his baby-soft ear.

His eyes flick toward me, and though I know he doesn't understand most of my words, I think he's enjoying my voice. His medication makes him calm and tired, so who knows how much he's really taking in? It doesn't matter, so long as he takes comfort from me.

I begin the story, speaking softly. *"When Lulu opened her eyes she didn't wonder where she was, but rather* when *she was..."*

Nine

It's time. Charlie has progressed from simple discomfort to pain. His oxygen saturation levels are so low that he must feel poorly in every possible way. He might live a day or two more, but it would be with nothing except increasing confusion and pain. I would never let that happen to him.

I've saved something for this moment for Charlie. It's what he's looking for when he looks at that chair of Ethan's. I brace myself and turn on the simulation. Ethan's voice fills the room with his warmth and humor. I've programmed it using all the instances of Ethan's interactions with Charlie, creating a program that I hope will make him happy.

Charlie's eyelids lift at the sound and his gaze fixes on the shimmering image in the chair. He makes a soft noise and I depress the plunger, the veterinarian behind me holding back her tears.

She's known Charlie for over twenty years. And her mother cared for him before that. He is twenty-nine years old and we have been here in this house without Ethan for more than twenty-six and a half of those years. Yet, he still misses Ethan. He is the oldest dog of his kind. He is all I have left.

It's over quickly. The stillness is something I knew about, but could never be truly prepared for. He's heavy now in a way he never was in life. I can't stand that this has happened. I've never touched anything that has died before. Was Ethan like this in the waters of the Atlantic?

I clean him up and stroke his ears. I arrange his paws in a way that would be comfortable for him on the bright yellow board he will travel on. I tuck the sheet around him one last time, press one last kiss on that beautiful round head under the fabric.

And then he's gone, out the front door and into the back of the veterinarian's transport, ready to be taken for cremation. They will deliver him back to me tomorrow. So quickly.

But now I know how Lulu's story will end. I know how it feels and how it will be and what it will mean. I can do it in a day. I lay myself on the couch, glance at Charlie's empty bed, and begin.

Ten

Charlie came back to me in a small box. It's better than the plastic pouch that the briefcase came back in, I suppose. Really, is either one better? Why can we not all be machines?

I tidy up while I package up the book. I send it along with my permission to share the contents, freely and without any conditions, to Marissa's message system. Then I think again and upload another copy to the lawyer's message box, the one that takes care of the trust Ethan set up for me. I hope that someday people can read Lulu's story. I think I wrote it the way Ethan and I would have if we'd been given the time together to do so.

A systems check of the house shows no faults. Everything to do with safety is in top condition and that eases my mind some. This house isn't exactly old, but electronic systems in houses need more upkeep than simple walls of wood or stone.

I pull the old rocker away from the window and set it across from Ethan's chair, sitting down with the box of Charlie's ashes in my lap. It takes some moments to arrange all the cables and get all the attachments exactly right, but soon enough, I'm all hooked up and ready. I close my eyes and turn on the simulation.

When I open my eyes again, there they are. Ethan is in his chair with that grin on his face. Next to him, Charlie sits wearing that goofy look I love so much, his furry head once again that amazing shade of red. Both of them are looking at me. It's like the clock of our lives has been turned back and made right again.

The electrical cables are heavy on my lap, the connectors awkward where they press through my synth-skin to reach the delicate electronics inside. None of that matters. It won't be for long. I'm old and I've kept my promises. Now, I can rest.

I ping a quick message to Marissa so she'll know what I've done. I have no idea what will happen afterwards. I can only hope there is more. Then, keeping my eyes on Ethan and Charlie, I flip the switch.

"Ethan..."

Epilogue – Six Years Later in The Nature Zone

Benjamin Critten looks around at the fields and barns, then beyond them to the house to be sure the way is clear and no one is watching him. Dark shapes in the fields above the ripening grain make it clear that the adults are still out there, evaluating and walking the rows to decide on the right day to harvest.

Smoke trickles from the chimney at the house where his mother is cooking. His sisters are still at the quilting gathering and will be for hours yet. This is his chance.

He slips into the old barn and heads straight for the far corner where his treasure is hidden. Brushing away the old hay and loose dirt, the forbidden plastic box soon comes into view. Like everything else out there in the modern world, this plastic box is not allowed. Nothing that isn't made by human hands is allowed inside the Nature Zone. And almost all plastics are made by PePrs in one way or another.

The amount of trouble he'd get into from the box is nothing compared to the trouble the contents of the box would earn him.

He pries open the top and, as always, his heart thumps harder in his chest at the sight that meets his eyes. The tablet nestled inside is old, almost a junker, but the man who traded it to him for a carving of a horse had done it more to be nice than for the trade. People who come to the Nature Zone to buy foods or crafts are usually very pleasant.

And those outsiders pay a bundle to get food grown by humans. He's heard from a good many of them that it's sort of a fad out there in the modern world. Very trendy. Like plastics, almost all food is grown by PePrs. Except here in the Nature Zone, of course.

Old or not, this tablet is precious to Benjamin and he lifts it out carefully, unwrapping the plastic with exaggerated care. Even that simple sheet of plastic would be hard to replace. If he got holes in it, it wouldn't protect his tablet.

Bending low, Benjamin checks between the gaps in the wall-boards once more. The dry, late summer air is almost alive with all that the earth is doing to finish up for the season. All that growing. All that ripening. The dark shapes of his father and older brothers still dot the field, moving away and down the rows of grain. All clear.

The glow of the screen causes a rush of excitement to flutter in Benjamin's belly and he hunkers down in the old hay, propping one ankle against his knee and balancing the tablet on his belly. This is his favorite reading position and this stolen hour will be the highlight of his day. That's especially true because he never knows when his next opportunity to steal away with his beloved and illicit tablet will come.

The icon for the book he's been reading pops up on the screen, along with the icons for all the other books he's read so far. As far as Benjamin can tell, there is only one book on this tablet that he could read out in the open. Even then, it would have to be on paper or on the HumanTouch—the only computer made entirely by humans or human-directed robots without intelligence. It's the only kind of computer allowed in the Nature Zone.

Instead of going directly to the text where he left off, he clicks for the additional features that came with the book. Without a simulation tank or anything to run a simulation in air, Benjamin can only view them by video. It's not the same, but even just watching them makes him yearn for a life outside the Nature Zone. To him, this book proves that there is nothing to fear from the PePrs.

The video starts and Benjamin smiles immediately. These are her memories and they are beautiful.

When he finishes watching his favorite—the one with the puppy—he turns back to the book. Everyone has read this book…everyone except for the people here in the Nature Zone, that is. That might be an exaggeration, but not much of one. At the Nature Zone market, Benjamin has heard countless people talking about it, debating the meaning of it, gushing over it. Since it's a free book, he was able to download it and now, he too will join the ranks of those who have read *Lulu*.

It's maddening that he can't talk about it with others. He has questions, thoughts, opinions. He's just waiting for a chance to speak with one of the Outsiders at the market about it. Yet, even here in the Nature Zone, there are more like him. He's not the only one with a hidden tablet. Maybe someday he'll find a way to reach out to one of those other secret readers.

The end of the book is mere chapters away and he is enthralled. The big reveal is coming. Benjamin can feel it. Over the past two days he's been arguing with himself over what the truth behind the Seed project is and now, he'll finally read it for himself.

Silence descends on the barn as Benjamin reads, the scuttling of some small creature through the old hay the only noise that breaks through for long minutes. Occasional small gasps escape the boy and as he reaches the critical resolution a single, louder, "Yes!"

All too soon, the book is finished and he sighs as he lets the tablet fall flat on his belly. He looks up at the roof far above him, the rusty metal streaked and peppered with tiny holes where it has rusted away from the nails that keep it affixed to the wooden beams. Light streams in through the holes and highlights the dust that perpetually floats in the slow, summer air currents. Right now it doesn't look dilapidated to him. Instead, it looks beautiful, full of potential. A gift from this amazing world to him. It's a gift and a reminder of how lucky he is to live on such a naturally splendid and life-filled planet.

Benjamin sits up and peers through the cracks again. There are no more shapes in the field, but the sound of horses and the jangle of the wagon's harness tell him that his father is on his way to the Wednesday meeting. His brothers won't come out here, not to this barn that no one uses. His way is still clear, but the late afternoon light is telling him that he'll have to leave his barn very soon. The dinner bell will ring before too long.

He smooths his hand across the tablet screen, his head full of thoughts and images. The golden light says he would be wisest to hide his box and go, but his heart says something else. He nestles back into the old hay and taps the tablet awake once more. Rather than go to the next book, he turns back to the beginning of the one he just finished.

He flips past the opening foreword, which he read and enjoyed the first time, but doesn't need to read again. The words are already lodged deep in his mind and heart. A woman named Marissa explains her fight to publish the book for her friend. A human fighting for the rights of the PePr who died, or was it deactivated? Now that he's read the book, he would say she died. She may have been a machine, but there's no question in his mind that she was alive in every way that mattered.

He turns to the first page of the book and begins again...

When Lulu opened her eyes she didn't wonder where she was, but rather when *she was. The mantra she'd been chanting in her head as the visor lowered started up again as if there were no years or eons since that moment.*

I'm awake and I'm here. I'm awake and I'm here.

Dear Reader

Thank you for reading! I genuinely hope that you liked what you read.

Please consider leaving a review if you enjoyed this dive into the world of PePr, Inc. For an Indie author, reviews are what we sink or swim by, and there are very hard to come by. Each is precious and I'll appreciate it. It doesn't have to be long.

Next, you can join the VIP List at the link below. You'll get a free story bundle, including one that's exclusive to the VIP List for joining and I'll keep you in the know about new releases (because I do $0.99 pricing the first day for those on the list), and get automatic entry into contests for signed books, swag, and all kinds of goodness. I don't spam and always respect your privacy. Here's the link: http://eepurl.com/buDy4r

About the Author

Ann Christy is a recently retired naval officer and secret science fiction writer. She lives by the sea under the benevolent rule of her canine overlords and assorted unruly family members. She's been known to call writing fiction a form of mental zombie-ism in reverse. She gets to put a little piece of her brain into yours and stay there with you—safely tucked away inside your gray matter—for as long as you remember the story.

She hopes you enjoyed the meal.

Made in the USA
Middletown, DE
19 November 2019